The Candywine Development

Faced with mayhem and intrigue whose
origins were not local, but lay in international
finance and power politics, Commissioner
McKay of the Jamaican police decided to take
unorthodox counter-action. He set Jassy Vane
to follow up the slender trail of clues,
believing that Peter Blackmore, who had once
worked for him so effectively, would be unable
to resist her dark beauty and would be drawn
again into the half world of glamour and
deception, high life and sudden death. His
plan nearly came unstuck, but fortunately for
him the mysterious organisation which was
playing for such enormous stakes on the little
offshore island of Candywine took a life too
many. Small, unofficial and prone to human
weaknesses as Commissioner McKay's team is,
it soon proves itself capable of tackling men as
vicious as the Mafia and fanatical as only
political extremists can be.

By the same author

Fever Grass

John Morris

The Candywine
Development

The Citadel Press
New York

When in doubt, win the trick

EDMOND HOYLE

Twenty-four Rules for Learners

First American Edition, 1971
Copyright © 1970 by Morris Cargill and John Hearne
All rights reserved
Published by Citadel Press, Inc.
A subsidiary of Lyle Stuart, Inc.
222 Park Avenue South, New York, N. Y. 10003
Manufactured in the United States of America
ISBN 0-8065-0227-4

Prologue

2 c.c. Adrenalin

Hot water, three feet deep in a bath broad enough to spread one's arms; a woman expensive enough to wear panties that cost five dollars per square inch: these were what he had worked for since he was twelve. He was not really aware of it, but one evening at that age he had repudiated for ever the sour, residual odour of his grey vest when he had dried it over the hiccupping, felt-covered boiler in the basement, pulled it on, still faintly damp but warm, sniffed at the arm-pits of pink shirt, rubbed chalk on the black smears inside the collar and cuffs, sprinkled it with scent from the small, ugly bottle on his mother's dressing-table, and run out to the vacant lot behind the cinema. There in the back seat of an abandoned Buick straight eight, she had twisted petulantly in denial at first, then breathlessly giggling had surrendered as his busy, already expert little fingers crumbled the frail defences of priestly and parental negatives, the stronger walls of fear. When he had peeled the pink, lock-knit, knee hugging drawers down her thin legs, he could smell the harsh brown soap on them clean through the hot, pungent girl smell. It was cold in the car and the slashed upholstery of the back seat was mildewed and the rancid smell permeated clothing for days afterwards; seemed to cling to the skin no matter how often you scrubbed yourself at the sink in the little kitchen, using an end of coarse towelling as a wash rag and lathering thickly with the hoarded bar of lavender soap

5

your big sister kept wrapped in greaseproof paper in a drawer against her dates on Saturday nights.

Again, he was not aware of it, but his progress from then on had been marked by more and more hot water and girls whose underwear was increasingly expensive. As life became more and more what he made it, he would take long, nearly scalding baths the way other men went to the movies; and the women who serviced the needs of the men in his calling had learned that it was worth it to come to him in lingerie that cost them more than they had thought of paying. It did not have to be kinky, only as exquisite as fingers could stitch, and it always brought a bonus of many times what they had invested.

To get the baths and the underclothes, he had had to do things that sold the evening editions in millions and kept many patient men out of bed for forty-eight hours at a stretch while they followed obscure leads that ended in frustration. His name seldom figured in either the stories or the inquiries. Not directly at any rate. Sometimes it was suggested; and he had been questioned many times; but nobody had ever been able to connect him with even the seven dead men (and two dead women), the blind man with massive brain damage who dribbled as he tapped his way around the grounds of the county asylum, and the man in the wheelchair who had once cheerfully bet fifty thousand dollars on how long he could keep the ash on his cigar and who now husbanded his cigarette butts because the pain was sometimes very bad and drugs cost him everything he had except the rent.

Lying in the bath now, he could hear the telephone ringing in the bedroom. He closed his eyes and let himself go limp so that he floated; three feet separated his toes from the four gold taps and another three his thin, pale red hair from the

6

dark-whorled green marble at the other end; little smoke signals of pine-scented steam rose from the water. There would be somebody to answer the telephone; there always was; as there was always somebody, nowadays, to do the things that put men into coffins, asylums and wheel-chairs.

A voice said at the doorway, 'You're wanted on the phone, Max. You want I should bring it in here?'

'Who is it?'

He did not raise his nearly lashless lids; his plump, button-nosed pouty lipped face was glowing with heat, and rapt.

'You can guess who it is,' the young man said. 'You *know* who it's going to be until you say "yes".'

The man in the bath opened his eyes then and looked up at the young man with the flat yellow hair, flat white face and flat eyes the colour of water, who had crossed from the doorway to the edge of the sunken bath. The man in the bath had eyes like that too.

'Tell him to go to hell. I'm busy.'

'*You* tell him,' the young man said, and then anxiously, 'For Crissake, Max . . . You gotta speak to him.'

The man in the bath chuckled, the little sounds seeming to form and burst on his pouting lips like bubbles on a baby's mouth.

'O.K., O.K.,' he said. 'I guess you can't go giving him any message like that. He's too big for that kinda message from you. Bring the goddam phone in, but the answer is still going to be "no".'

The young man recrossed the yards of black and yellow malachite tiles, went into the bedroom and came back with one of the stand-up telephones that have the dial on the base. He plugged the flex into the socket on the wall near the floor and brought the telephone over to the bath. The man he had called Max was sitting up in the water, drying his hands in a fluffy white towel the size of a blanket that he

7

had taken from a pile on the floor beside the bath. When he had finished, he crumpled it into an untidy wad and flung it into a corner.

'Benny?' he said, taking the telephone. 'Yeah, this is Max . . . Fine, Benny. Fine, fine, fine. All the better for hearing your voice. It's been a long time . . . Well, maybe not so long at that, but it seems long . . . No, Benny, I ain't busy. At least I ain't busy right now. I expect to be a little later . . . Yeah, that's right. How'd you guess? *Benny!* You don't ought to say things like that on the phone.' He chuckled again, complacently. 'Well, you know how it is, Benny: a man's gotta have a little relaxation—an' with this meeting to-morrow, I want to have a clear head. Believe me, Benny boy, there's nothin' so good as a good broad knows what to do with it for clearing a man's head.' His white-lashed eyelid closed slowly in a wink at the young man. 'Yeah, Benny, I'm listening. I figured it was about the meeting.' He listened, playing his free hand in the water as the urgent susurrus of a soft, even voice floated from the earpiece. 'No, Benny.' He was friendly, almost fond, but unyielding. 'I can't agree to that, and that's the way I'm going to vote to-morrow . . . I already told you why. I don't like it. My nose tells me it ain't good, Benny . . . Yeah, that's all, but it's enough for me. This is our operation, Benny, and I feel we ought to keep it that way. I don't care how much they're prepared to put an' I don't care what they say they can do for us. I say we don't need 'em. We don't need 'em an' we don't want 'em—*an'* I carry enough votes that we don't have to deal them in. You know that, Benny . . . Yeah, Benny, that's my final word. Sorry.' He listened for a little, his plump face no longer amiable but frowning and tight. 'O.K., Benny, I guess we'll just have to argue it out, but I think the boys will go with me. That's how it stands on this deal . . . Yeah. Yeah . . . All right . . . An' Benny . . . No hard feelings, eh? . . . Good

8

... Good ... Great ... That's how it ought to be, Benny
... See you to-morrow ... 'Bye.'

He tossed the telephone to the young man and heaved himself out of the bath.

'That Vestucci,' he growled pleasantly. 'Goddam wop.
You'd think he'd know better.'

He climbed from the water and began to dry himself as
the young man went back to the bedroom with the telephone.
His chest, belly and even the backs of his shoulders were
pelted with coarse swirls of hair much redder than that on
his head. At one time he had been embarrassed by its
animality, its *uncleanness*—until he had discovered that many
women were excited by it.

When he was dry he went to the basin set in the marble
shelf that ran the whole length of the room under the mirror
fronted, built-in cabinets; the basin itself was only a little
smaller than the average bath tub.

He cleaned his teeth with an electric toothbrush; slid open
one of the mirror fronts and took out one bottle of *après-
bain* body lotion and one of after-shave; when he had
anointed himself thoroughly, he cleaned his teeth again, took
out a bottle of mouth-wash and gargled a solution of it for two
minutes; then he went into his bedroom.

From the stack of silk pyjamas in one of the built-in
closets, he selected a yellow pair edged with black, and its
match from the rows of silk dressing-gowns hanging in the
same closet. The closets were mirror fronted too, and there
was a huge circular mirror set into the ceiling immediately
above the huge circular bed.

He put on the pyjamas and dressing-gown, went over to
the rosewood dressing-table, and carefully combed and
brushed his thinning hair. Just before he left the room, he
inspected his nails—where they projected beyond his fingertips they were whiter than a surgeon's—and cleaned them

with the point of a little silver instrument. On his way out, he stopped, turned back and shook a breath-sweetening lozenge from a phial on the dressing-table into his hand and placed it on his tongue.

In the drawing-room across the passage from the bedroom, the young man with the flat yellow hair and the flat white face was watching colour TV from a white leather settee. There were a dozen bottles, ice in a gold bucket, a bottle of Dom Perignon in an ice-filled, bigger, silver bucket and glasses on a silver tray on the long, low table before the settee.

The man called Max said, 'O.K., Georgie, you can blow now. I won't be needing you any more to-night.'

'Thanks,' the young man said. 'They're running an old Bogie after this crap. *High Sierra.* I guess I'll watch that and then go to bed.'

'You do that, Georgie,' the man called Max told him, and blew a fat chuckle once more. 'I like Bogie myself but I don't think I'm going to find the time to watch him to-night.'

The young man got up and left the room. He went down the long passageway outside where the soft clarity of light from the crystal drops of the big chandelier bathed the prints that looked as if they had been bought because they were all of suit like a royal straight flush in poker. By a door at the end of the passage, he paused and listened, looking back towards the room he had left; then he opened the door.

The room he entered was neither as large nor as luxuriously appointed as the bedroom in which the man called Max had dressed, but it had not been furnished from a mail order catalogue either. The young man went over to the bed and sat on the edge and from the bedside table picked up the telephone, a single piece, stand-up telephone like the one he had brought to the man in the bath. He did not dial immediately, but held the receiver against his ear for perhaps half a minute before up-ending the instrument and putting his finger on the first digit. When he had finished dialling, he tucked the receiver against his ear again and lay back across the bed with his legs dangling over the edge; he swung his left arm in an arc above his upturned face until his watch cleared the cuff of his shirt.

'Mr. Harriman?' he asked suddenly and softly, then, 'Yes, this is Georgie . . . It's just like you expected . . . The jock is going to pull to-morrow . . . You're going to have to lay a little extra to even show . . . Yeah, I'll ring you back . . .'

In the drawing-room up the passage the man called Max poured himself a second, small Chivas Regal on the rocks, made a face at the TV screen before switching off and tucked himself full length into the settee with the sports section of the *New York Times*.

At a little after ten, the buzzer at the door sounded. The man called Max folded the sports section and laid it on the table, swallowed the remnants of his slowly sipped drink, rose and went to the door. On his way, he felt in the pocket of his dressing-gown just under the sash and took out the phial of lozenges for sweetening the breath. He put another on his tongue, and standing in the corner between the hinged edge of the door, said into the voice box, 'Yeah . . . Who is it?'

'Mr. Rilke,' a woman's voice said from the wall speaker above his head, 'I'm your Good Neighbour Welcome Wagon.'

He grinned.

'Come on up,' he said, 'an' don't stop to read a book on the way.'

'My, my,' the voice said throatily. 'We sound eager to-night. Maybe I should phone for reinforcements.'

'You need reinforcements,' Mr. Rilke said happily, 'like I need six fingers on each hand. Come on up, you bitch.'

When the chimes connected to the buzzer sounded, Mr. Rilke looked into the peephole of one-way, bullet-proof glass through which he could see up and down the passage outside as far as both corners. On the other side of the peephole looking back at him, although she could not see him, and pulling teasing faces, a girl waited. She was blonde, grey-eyed, five feet eight inches, one hundred and twenty pounds, and ran to type only as a custom-built Maserati runs to type. Wild swans coursed the grey heavens of her eyes and under pressure her full lips would yield wine.

Mr. Rilke unhooked the steel chain holding the door to the wall, slammed back the two top and bottom steel bolts and clicked two knobs on the lock. His chubby, very clean, very powerful fingers sank into what looked like an entire mink farm hanging from her shoulders as he pulled her into the room against him.

About three in the morning, she moved her right arm from under her head, shifted her wide-awake, steady gaze from the dark glimmer of the mirror on the ceiling and felt along the top of the elaborate, semi-circular unit which ran an arc nearly quarter of the way round the circular bed. Like the dressing-table, it was of rosewood and it was pigeon-holed and shelved, and had niches for a big F.M. radio and a small refrigerator.

Beside her, Mr. Rilke slept in the foetal position, his buttocks pressed against her hip and his plump fists tucked under his chin. When her walking fingers touched the cool, grained leather of her handbag, she opened the clasp and felt around inside until she found the tiny syringe she had tucked into the bottom left-hand corner, its needle wrapped loosely in a twist of cotton wool.

She took out the syringe and held it between her fore and middle fingers, thumb resting on the plunger, and slowly laid her right arm straight along her flank. With her left hand she twitched aside the sheet that covered them both and began to caress Mr. Rilke's limp penis.

At first, she only brushed it: her fingertips alighting and taking off again like butterflies in circuit. Then, as it began to swell and harden, her steady massage became more emphatic. Mr. Rilke began to twitch and murmur in his sleep. She nudged his back and when he came awake with a querulous grunt, she murmured against his ear, 'I can't sleep, Maxie darling.'

'Jesus,' he said, in a tone between half awake irascibility and gratification. 'Maybe I ought to get you a machine. One of them things they use in India.'

'Maxie,' she crooned reproachfully, and took his right hand and lifted it and put it between her legs. 'You shouldn't be so good. It's not fair to a girl when a man can ball it like you.'

He heaved himself round and his chuckle, as his left hand began to tickle the nipple of her right breast, was like the bubble breaking on the lips of the fattest, most self-satisfied baby on the block.

'Yes,' she said. 'Oh, God! Yes! *Max! Maxie*, darling! Yes. Like that. Like *that!* That's what I wanted . . . Slow, Max . . . Slow, darling . . . Yes . . . Pull it out . . . I want it . . . Make me want it . . . *Make* me want it, Maxie . . . Ye-e-e-s . . . Right out . . . *Oh!* . . . In . . . In, Max . . . Now pull it out . . . Oh, God, God, *God!* Oh, Max, you're wonderful . . .'

She straightened her legs, then, as Rilke withdrew his penis so that only the tip was gripped by the muscles of her *labia minora*. In that position and at that moment, it was no trouble at all to bring her right hand up from her side and plunge the thin needle of the tiny syringe into the underside of Mr. Rilke's tumescent penis near to the scrotum, and to depress the plunger, quickly and hard.

Above her, a sweetened breath carried a startled 'Ah!', as a man might cry suddenly stung by a wandering insect. Then, '*What the*——*?*' Mr. Rilke said, and rolled off her. She could see the blur of his arm in the darkened room as he groped for and found the switches on the control board set into the curving headboard of the circular bed. All the lights in the room came on as she said, '*Max!* Maxie darling. What's the matter?'

'I don't . . . I don't . . .' Mr. Rilke was fumbling at his genitals, taking shallow, rapid breaths, like a man at the end of a climb he has made too quickly. His pink face went very red and he said, 'I feel bad. *Jesus!* My head! My heart! It's going like it's crazy or something,' and clapped his half-clenched hand to the centre of his chest and seemed to fold over it. Then his face went very white and his firm, generously padded body stretched tautly and seemed to contract into a small knot and he fell over on his side in the foetal position, straightened, then contracted again, straightened, raised himself on his elbow and begged her with widely opened, terrified eyes, his mouth a pale O from which came the sounds, '*Wha*— *Wha*— *Wha*——' as if a small, pathetic animal were dying painfully at the back of a cave.

Then his eyes suddenly glazed and Mr. Rilke fell on to his back, his limbs flung wide and curiously twisted. His plump face was bluish and fallen in on itself and pulled out of shape. And the colourless, sightless eyes stared at his reflection in the circular mirror above the bed.

The girl began to cough, rackingly, and she swallowed several times against nausea until her breathing came under control. She swung her legs over the circumference of the bed, stood, walked round to where Mr. Rilke had dropped his dressing-gown earlier on, bent over, picked it up, put it on, and left the room.

Two doors down the corridor from Mr. Rilke's bedroom, she knocked. A voice inside said, 'Yes?'

'Janice.'

'Come in. It isn't locked.'

The young man with the flat yellow hair and flat white face, whom Mr. Rilke had called 'Georgie,' was sitting, in dressing-gown and pyjamas, in an arm-chair watching the Late Late Show on a transistorised, eight-inch Sony placed on the bedside table.

'He's dead,' the girl said. 'I've killed him.'

'You sure?' The young man did not look up from Bob Hope and Bing Crosby playing 'pat-a-cake, pat-a-cake, baker's man' as a setup for escaping from the villains.

'Go and see for yourself.'

She sat on the edge of the bed, slumped over her stomach; she looked grey and sick.

The young man said, 'Yeah . . . I better check. You gave him everything?'

'Yes,' the girl said dully. 'The whole needle. I gave him everything in it.'

The young man rose and left the room. The girl sat without moving on the edge of the bed, her hands resting palm upwards in her lap. When the young man came back, she looked up at him.

'He's dead all right, and you'd have to use a glass to see where you stuck him. There wasn't even a drop of blood, but I gave it a wipe with rubbing alcohol to make sure. You got the needle?' the young man asked.

She handed him the little syringe from which she had squirted two cubic centimetres of adrenalin into the swollen blood vessels of Mr. Rilke's stiff penis. The young man meticulously broke the syringe into four pieces and went through the doorway into the bathroom. She heard the toilet flush.

He came back and picked up the telephone on the bedside table beside the Sony and dialled. At the end of ten seconds, he said, 'Mr. Harriman . . . It's O.K.,' put the unit down, lifted it, and dialled again.

'Mr. Vestucci please . . . I know he's sleeping, but he'll want you to wake him. Tell him it's George.' He held the speaker against his chest and said to the girl, 'Try to keep looking like that. That's fine. That's just how you ought to be looking when the law gets here. A guy dies in your arms and even a tough hooker is supposed to be a little shook up.' A soft, even voice floated from the earpiece and the young man very quickly put it to his ear. 'Hallo, yes, Mr. Vestucci. This is George. I am sorry to have to disturb you at this hour, sir, but I knew you'd wish to be the first to know . . . It's—it's tragic news, sir. I—I don't know how to tell you . . . It's Mr. Rilke, sir. Max . . . He's dead . . . Yes, sir. I'm sure . . . Not more than ten minutes ago. It must have been his heart. I'm no doctor, but it sure looks like heart failure to me . . . Yes, sir, I remember your telling him to watch his diet. Many times . . . Yes, I know how you must be feeling, Mr. Vestucci. You and him were like brothers. Ever since . . . I feel like I'd lost my own father . . . Yes, sir, there is a witness. It's going to be a little embarrassing, I'm afraid, sir. You see, she's a—a lady. She was with him when he died . . . Yes, sir . . . Yes, sir . . . Yes, sir. Right away . . . Thank you, sir . . . Good night.'

He replaced the telephone on the receiver and grinned without showing his teeth.

'If the Feds have a tap on us let them make something of that,' he said to no one in particular, and then, briskly, to the girl, 'O.K. Haul your ass out an' start getting a little drunk. When the cops come, I want you looking a real mess. How're you at crying? See if you can get drunk enough to cry . . . And remember, baby doll, you don't know anything except he was trying for a world record or something an' didn't make it. Him being sixty-three years old and all. That's all you tell the cops. Not a goddam thing else. No matter how much they lean on you. Understand?'

'Yes,' the girl said. 'I understand.' There was an edge of dull hysteria in her voice and the young man nodded with satisfaction as he registered it. She said, 'I wish I believed in God. Really believed in Him, I mean. Like a Catholic or a Jehovah's Witness or one of those people who really *know*.'

'Why?' The young man's interest was momentarily diverted. 'Why should you want to believe in that?'

'Then I'd know you were going to be punished in hell.' There was a dead, deep hatred in her grey eyes as she looked at him and into him. 'Punished for ever and ever.'

'And what about you?' The young man was lightly but genuinely amused. 'It wasn't me put a needle of adrenalin into the Peter of an old man who's never given me anything but a lot of good times and presents.'

'Yes,' the girl agreed, as gravely as a child. 'I'd be punished too. But they'd punish you more. I only killed him. You betrayed him when he trusted you. That's worse than killing.'

'If you feel that way,' the young man said, 'maybe you won't feel like taking the ten grand you're getting from Harriman. Maybe you'd like for him to give it to the Salvation Army or for nigger relief up in Harlem or something. From an anonymous donor.'

'No,' the girl said, and stood and belted Mr. Rilke's yellow dressing-gown with the black edging more tightly around her. 'No. I want my money. I wouldn't have done it if it was only the money . . . It was that other thing about acid in my face if I didn't do it why I agreed . . . But now I've done it I want my money.'

'Ah, get outa here, you whore,' the young man told her,

'an' start liquoring up enough to make the cops think you're on the level.'

He was already dialling, and as she left the room she heard him say, 'Police? This is George Holtz. Yes, Holtz. I wish to report a death . . . No, no, an accidental death . . .'

Part One

Chapter One

Blind date at Corales

After five days, when nobody had yet tried to pick her up, she began to worry. Descending from the bus that evening into the *Calle de la Nacion Unida*, she decided to send a cable.

Walking down the baroque arcade, where every second shop-window framed like a brilliantly lit stage the enigmatic faces and squat bodies of Mayan statuary in crowd scene, she used the plate-glass, hopefully, as mirrors. But nobody followed her. The reflected figures—whether the dumpy, slope-shouldered Indians shuffling incuriously past the carefully arranged witnesses to their expropriation, or the lither, lighter descendants of the Conquistadores and their lust, or the rigorously clean North American visitors, pink and white as cheap china in the bleaching glare from the fluorescent tubes—seemed to be on business that did not concern her. She could not even catch, she noted with a not wholly light-hearted chagrin, any of those automatic, prurient appraisals of her body which should have been part of the amenities laid on for a still-young female tourist who knew the quality of her looks.

At the post office counter she said, in Spanish, 'I wish to send a night letter, please. To Jamaica.'

'Certainly, señorita. If you will describe your message on this form.'

The clerk pushed the yellow pad to her under the little

portcullis of his window, smiling. He was young and ivory-skinned, with just enough Indian in him to take the wave and blue out of his thick, liquorice black hair. She wondered what any Mexican male so handsome and so amiable was doing behind the counter of a provincial post office. Then, as she smiled back, she noticed his eyes: twin lakes of dark sherry, dumbly sweet as a Labrador's. He was probably too stupid, even, to be selling motor cars or insurance to the wives of the newly rich in the capital. He was offering her his pen, although she had already taken hers from the slash pocket of her skirt. Offering it with an innocent, pushing intimacy as if he were nuzzling her hand.

'*Obrigado, señor*,' she said, and gave him a slow, light burn upwards from under her big, impassive eyes, and put her pen back into her pocket and accepted his. He wriggled with pleasure as she took it, and writhed again, with a bouncing embarrassment, as it failed to make a mark on the top sheet of the pad.

'They never work when you want them to,' she assured him, and wrote her message in black capitals with her own pen: STUDY NEEDS FURTHER RESEARCH STOP WILL STAY ANOTHER WEEK STOP PLEASE INFORM PROFESSOR WALTERS. JASSY.

She frowned at the message for a few seconds, sucking the top of the pen, then added the words 'ARTPRISE JAMAICA' in the address box at the top right-hand corner of the form. She tore the form free of the lightly gummed binding and pushed it under the grille to the young man, scorching him gently again with an equivocal smile and a half-questioning, half-calculating examination.

He said mechanically, gazing at her with shy hope, 'Your pardon, señorita, but you have not put your address . . .'

'Yes, I have. See it there. It's a cable address.'

'No, señorita. Your address here—in Corales. It is necessary, you understand, for the regulations and for your reply?'

He laid the explanation before her as if it were a bird he had retrieved.

She said softly, 'Thank you. I always forget to do that,' and took back the form and filled in the name of her hotel. 'How much is that?'

'Twenty-three pesos, señorita.' The soulful and innocent eyes were still fixed on her. He did not glance at the notes she pushed across the speckled marble counter to his fingers behind the bars.

'There,' she said. 'I think you'll find that is correct. Good evening, señor, and many thanks for your courtesy.'

'It was a great pleasure for me, señorita,' he replied wistfully, and then with a sudden, gambolling resolution, 'You are visiting Corales?'

'Yes.'

'For long?'

'A couple of weeks.'

'Most tourists stay in Merida. There is more there for amusement.'

'I know. But I am not in Mexico for amusement. I am studying the ruins at Uxmal and Chichenitza. Corales is central. I am able to go out by bus each day.'

'You are a student, señorita?' He glanced down at the yellow form. 'In Jam-ay-ica?'

'I am a teacher. At the University.'

'A *doctor*? But you are too young to be a doctor.'

'Thank you. But I am a . . . not a doctor. I am what is called a . . . a,' she paused, squeezing lines between the heavy arcs of her brows, trying to remember the Spanish equivalent for 'lecturer,' and then decided to let it go. '*Si*,' she said, as if caught out in the innocent deceit of modesty, 'A doctor. Good night, señor.'

She turned and crossed the black and white chequerboard of marble floor, conscious of the beautiful, puppy eyes following the sway of her hips to the entrance. You had your chance, boy, she thought. I told you everything about me except my size in bras. And you could have found that out later. The way I'm feeling you could have had the whole works to-night. You only had to ask.

II

The short walk from the post office to her hotel seemed interminable. Quite suddenly, she seemed to be enclosed in a transparent bubble of weariness and something that was not quite fear, not quite anticipation, but an exhausting mixture of the two, forming a knot in her stomach. The short dusk of the flat Yucatan peninsula was over; above the muted blue glare of the street lamps, the enormous sky was dark grey with a few brown clouds being torn into wisps by the wind from the distant mountains inland; the façades of the houses were like draw-bridges raised decisively against an assault from the street. With the night, life had hatched suddenly in Corales. Energy pulsed in the high voices of the strolling figures who moved on the outside of her bubble—Mexicans did not waste strength in casual movement; everything was saved for talk, work, dancing and love. Everywhere there was the sound of children counterpointing without intrusion the adult voices. Behind the white walls of the houses, she knew, a whole warm world of intricately related domestic exchange also functioned; as separate from the world of the street as the life of the treetop dwellers in an equatorial jungle was from the existence of the denizens among the roots and undergrowth below. Yet each group shared the same ecology, a common home; understood the rules and limitations and possibilities that governed each level. She

24

was the only alien, the only intruder; unable to take part in the exchange behind the walls; passing through the life of the street in a cocoon of false identity and secret purpose.

When she reached her hotel, she was walking so fast that she had caused comment: speculative among the men, derisive among the women. The knot in her stomach had become curiously related to her breathing. Once in every two or three minutes all her concentration would seem to centre on what was happening to her just below the breast bone and she would forget to inhale. Oxygen starvation would hit her like a sledgehammer wrapped in felt and in a panic she would stop and take several deep breaths.

She was almost crying as, with bent head, she took the big key on its huge, numbered brass plate from the clerk behind the mahogany counter in the lobby of her hotel. She was crying when she opened the door of her room and hurried across to the dressing-table, in a drawer of which she kept whatever of the bottle of Scotch the hotel servants had left to her.

III

After two drinks poured straight, half-way up the tumbler taken from the rack above the washbasin, she said, aloud, 'Oh, shit. Oh, *shit*! Jassy, you're getting too old for this game,' and drank again. After another, she said, 'If you were ever old enough,' and giggled, and fell asleep with the empty tumbler resting on the counterpane beyond her right hand, near the pillow.

She slept only half an hour and came up slowly, but completely restored, into successive sensations of the ribbed counterpane pressing against her cheek, the high, white-walled room with its heavy, dark furniture, the muffled voices from the street punctuated by occasional riffs of juke-box music in the cafés. It was full night and the oblong of sky she could see framed in the top of the window was black between the crowded glitter of the huge stars. She rolled on to her back and rubbed her feet together until her sandals thudded softly on the rug beside the bed. When she switched on the bedside lamp, she saw there was enough whisky left for one more drink. This time she sipped slowly, leaning back among the pillows she had propped against the head-board of the bed, feeling the last of the knot in her stomach unravel, no, dissolve, in the heat of uncut liquor. With the anguish of tension gone, her senses and perceptions seemed to flourish suddenly, bright and crisp as grass after rain. With a childlike appreciation of shape, colour, scent and sound, she took in the glimmering stolidity of the deep Victorian furniture, the pink restfulness of the tasselled lampshade, the starch and hot iron smell of the pillows, the driftings from the noisy life in the street two floors below the opened window.

The telephone on the bedside table under the pink-shaded lamp rang once, with hoarse abruptness. It was an old-fashioned instrument: a slim black bar of iron joining the two bronze lilies of the speaker and earpiece; to make a connection from the lobby, the desk clerk had to twirl energetically a handle mounted on a squat little box. It was comfortingly part of the pattern in a room that had been new about the turn of the century. She waited for the man below to crank the handle again.

'Yes?'

'Señorita Vane?'

'*Si.*'

'A gentleman here would wish to speak with you.'

'A gentleman? For me? Are you sure? I know no one here. Who is it?'

'He is known to me, señorita. I can speak for him. He is

26

Señor Aurelio Arosemena. He tells me that you met this afternoon. At the post office.'

'Ah, yes,' Jassy Vane said. 'I will speak to him.'

IV

Aurelio Arosemena asked proudly, for the third time, 'The *Puerco pibil* is to your liking, Señorita Vane?'

'Oh, yes,' Jassy Vane said. 'It is wonderful.' She separated a small piece of the glazed, golden crackling from the creamy brown meat with her fork, picked it up in her fingers, crunched it with delicate gluttony and followed it with a fragment from the broken roll on her sideplate. She drank half a glass of the dry, fruity wine, passed the tip of her tongue across the film of grease and grape on her lips and winked at the young man. 'I have had *Puerco pibil* before, of course, but never as good as this. You must have special influence, señor.'

'The proprietor is my cousin,' Arosemena said. 'Everybody in Corales is my cousin,' he added sadly. 'I was born in Corales. I have lived here all my life. I will die in Corales.'

'It is a beautiful town,' Jassy Vane told him warmly and reached across the coarse linen of the tablecloth and rested her hand on his for a moment. 'Many people would envy you.'

His hand, as she gave it the smallest, encouraging squeeze, trembled slightly; with tender, almost protective amusement, she realised that he could not have had many women. In a town the size of Corales, the girls of respectable family would be too closely watched—it would not be like Mexico City where the young had begun to take infection from the examples of Europe and North America. And the whores, even if they were those not good enough for the houses in Merida, would be too expensive for a young postal clerk except on

27

occasion. She picked up her wine glass again and drank, looking at him over the far edge of it and put it down, still looking at him.

She said, 'You have given me a wonderful evening, Señor Arosemena—Aurelio,' and acknowledged to herself, with a wry guilt, that she was not entirely lying. No matter that she had accepted his eager, almost breathless, invitation to dine on the sudden intuition that she might use him towards achieving her real purpose in Corales. No matter that he was the dullest man with whom she had ever shared an intimate meal. He was good-looking, attentive and kind. An authentic benevolence shone from those clear, stupid eyes; sounded in the banal gallantries which he had humbly showered on her since she had stepped from the lift into the lobby of the hotel and he had come hurrying across from the reception counter where he had been chatting with the night clerk—who was doubtless another cousin.

In the profession she had adopted, kindness, the transparent stratagems of honest desire (like the dinner he was giving her and the compliments he had paid her on her appearance), the uncalculating need for another, which was in itself a sort of compliment, were all deliberately jettisoned dead weight. You performed a ruthless surgery on your emotions if you hoped to survive. Like an explorer about to plunge into unmapped, dangerous territory, you removed any non-essential attachments to your body—your appendix or your tonsils—or carefully examined tissue that might decay —like a doubtful molar—and had it filled with dead, indestructible metal.

She leaned back in the firmly-stuffed, black leather chair, making the most of her breasts, and smiling at him now with an invitation so candid that not even someone as inexperienced and uncertain as he could mistake her readiness. She was grateful, genuinely grateful to him for everything:

for his animal good looks; for his instinctive shy courtesy; for the little restaurant with its whitewashed walls, red tiled floor, glimmering bar of black mahogany and candles flaring steadily within the thick shades blown skilfully from the salvaged glass of broken beer bottles; for the simple yet delicious meal and the coarse, unpretending wine. Above all, she was grateful to him for the simple response he hoped to elicit from her. A gesture of love. A few moments' pleasurable torment in a bed. A few avowals exchanged.

In a surge of pity, as thick and sweet as desire, she silently promised him that he would have, at least, four or five days to remember without regret. After that, of course, he would have to help her discover what she was looking for in Corales. It should not be very difficult, she decided, looking at him as he began to whisper the proposition she had been working for ever since he had called her in her room at the hotel.

'Aurelio!' she said, with demure confusion. 'But we hardly know each other. What can you think of us in Jamaica if you . . .'

'Please,' he begged. 'I ask you in all honour. I have never met any woman like you, Jassy. You are not like our Mexican girls. All they want is a husband and money. And you are not like those—those creatures from the United States . . . You are so different. So beautiful. Please, please, my Jassy . . .'

'I am in your hands, Aurelio,' she murmured, and bent her head so as to conceal the glint of hard thought that might be showing in her eyes.

Chapter Two

A word to the wise

Below the window Kingston was turning slowly, like a huge scale model in a tilted plate, as the Mexicana airliner banked over the city and began the approach across the harbour to the airport.

Each time she came back to Jamaica now it seemed to Jassy Vane that the two extremes of the capital had grown, during her absence, with cancerous speed. On each return, a new rash of big white houses with foundations like castles had eaten across the green slopes of the Port Royal Mountains and the Red Hills that walled the Liguanea Plain in a wide arc on the north. On each return the slums that began on the shoreline of the western harbour had spread their dingy brown cells farther into the dividing territory of new housing developments, old residential districts and the random outcrops of stubby skyscrapers in which government and big business increasingly conducted their affairs. One day the proliferating cells would consume or surround all that lay between them and the bright, garden-moated fortresses fastened to the cool hillsides.

She shook her head briskly, like a swimmer surfacing after a dive. Too much reflection about what she could see through the window of the plane was dangerous because of its irrelevance. In the work that had been refashioning her over the last five years, she had learnt to reserve thought and commitment. Attention to problems outside, involving oneself except at certain precisely calculated levels, affected judgment and that appraisal of possible moves which were always open to those against whom you were fighting. And as the airliner shuddered against the drag of its brakes, she pulled her wide mouth into a small, disconsolate smile. No, not fighting. You never used that word. You spoke only of 'the competition,' or 'they,' or 'the opposition'; and what you did to them, or what you tried to stop them doing to you, was in the nature of a giant and fantastic game. You were all locked in a pitiless, sometimes lethal, encounter but 'they' were the only real people after a while: partners in a cold, exclusive intimacy that was sometimes very like incest.

II

The Customs Officer said, 'Are you bringing in any firearms, miss? Any jewellery, cameras? Literature of a subversive nature?'

'No,' Jassy said, 'Nothing like that—unless you count some silver. A bracelet for me, and a brooch and a pair of cuff-links as presents.'

'Will you open your case please, miss.'

She snapped the locks and raised the lid of the fibreglass suitcase, and watched him as he fingered primly through her clothes. He picked up one of the little boxes of silver she had brought, lifted the lid, nodded, and put it back. Just before he closed her case, he put his hand into a corner and a small, oblong trap-door set invisibly into the lining along the back half-opened and shut again on the very small but lethal 4.25mm. German 'Lilliput' automatic pistol and the flat, exquisite camera a ten-year-old girl could have worn on her wrist to go with her party dress.

As he was chalking his hieroglyph on the side of the case, Jassy said pleasantly, 'You're a very funny boy, aren't you? I think I'll have to tell your boss how full of tricks you are.'

31

She was smiling and her voice could not have been heard by anybody two feet from them, and her great, slanting eyes were stagnant with anger.

His lips twitched: a crooked line drawing of a placatory, conspiratorial grin. His face was suddenly untidy with alarm. He opened his mouth and Jassy, her head lowered as she turned the little key in the locks of the suitcase, added in the same slim whisper, 'Don't say anything, funny man. You know better than to do what you did.'

She turned and signalled one of the khaki-clad porters lounging at the end of the zinc-topped counter. A crumpled, tired looking Englishman was still trying to attract the attention of the Customs Officer as she followed the porter and her suitcase out through the swing doors to the reception hall.

In the hall, she raised her arms and embraced the plump, fiftyish blonde with the very bright, blue eyes who came out of the crowd like a small, bouncy pink pig. They touched cheeks closely and turned to the entrance through which the hard white glare of early afternoon was bouncing off the asphalt of the driveway.

'That one,' said the blonde to the porter, pointing to a yellow Rambler station wagon that had seen better days and which had been backed between two of the parking lines outside the entrance. The porter opened the passenger's door and swung the suitcase over the back of the front seat on to the floor behind. He held the door for Jassy as she put fifty cents into his hand and climbed in. She smiled at him distantly but without patronage as he closed the door. The blonde was already behind the wheel and they drove off as the door was pushed shut. Neither woman spoke until they were cruising at a steady fifty up the scrub and sand-bordered highway of the Palisadoes.

'Something's gone wrong,' the blonde said, not looking at

the big, black girl with the straightened hair cut like a bathing cap, who slouched in the corner between the door and the back of the seat.

'Yes,' Jassy said, 'Something's gone wrong.' She slammed a narrow, strong foot angrily on the floor and half turned, lifting her long legs on to the seat, so that she could look at the blonde, middle-aged woman in whose face the years had left the contours of a knowledgeable, disturbingly joyous sensuality. 'Something's gone bloody wrong and we're in a lot of bloody trouble.'

'We gathered that from your cables. You were right not to use the code. I don't like codes except in an emergency. Somebody always cracks them if you use them regularly . . .'

'Oh, for God's sake, Helen!' Jassy Vane said. She sounded like a needle jumping the grooves on a record. 'Do we have to have your favourite aphorisms on procedure? I've been hearing them for five years, remember? I know them by heart.'

'You poor dear,' said the blonde like an aunt absently soothing a temperamental niece, and patted the bent knee on the seat beside her. 'Was it very bad?'

'No,' Jassy said gloomily, 'I got frightened, but then I always do. Even on safe runs. It wasn't bad. It was frustrating, though, and I don't know if what I brought back is of any use.'

'No run is *ever* safe,' the woman called Helen said. 'That's another for you to remember. I'd like to have that one tattooed on the heart of every agent . . . Who exactly is this Aurelio?'

Jassy told her as they turned left on to the Rockfort Road at the head of the Palisadoes and joined the necklace of traffic that stretched between the low hills and the city. Helen nodded.

'He got you into the post office, then?'

'Yes,' Jassy said. 'With the trail as cold as it was, all I could think of was microfilming every cable out or in for the past month. Christ! Do you realise how many that is—even in a place the size of Corales. Bodden is going to have kittens just classifying them, let alone finding those that might give us a lead.'

'How secure is Aurelio?'

'He's O.K. He's too frightened of what might happen to him if he ever talked. Besides, he thinks he's in love with me. Besides, I paid him very well.' She chuckled maliciously. 'Robin is going to blow his cool when he hears how much . . . Sex and money,' she continued, as if communing with herself. 'Soft cunt and hard cash. They're still an agent's best friends, you know, Helen? They're the only constants. No matter what gimmicks we invent, a good lay and a stack of the long green will get you a ride on any subway you want. They're old-fashioned models, maybe, but they were built to last and . . .'

'Shut up,' Helen said.

'Why?' Jassy asked in a voice that seemed to be steadying itself on a thin wire over a long drop and no net. 'I thought you always wanted impressions when we come back from a run. Isn't that another of your aphorisms: "Talk it out." The way you felt when a chambermaid knocked at your door with fresh sheets may save another agent's life. I haven't got it exactly. Not your style. Not pithy enough, but . . .'

'Jassy, my sweet,' Helen said, braking the Rambler to a crawl as a huge, diesel-fuming truck swung arrogantly out of the cement factory gate ahead of them, 'If you don't shut up, I'm going to pull over and slap your face before all these beautiful people.'

'Oh, fuck you, Helen McKay,' Jassy said. 'Fuck all of you,' and began to cry, the tears coursing suddenly from the dulled eyes and glinting on the high oval shields of her cheekbones until she put her face into her hands.

'That's better,' Helen McKay said. 'That's much better.'

III

The Doberman leaned into the choke collar without a sound: only a faint rippling along a body, lean as a bullet and taut as a watch-spring, suggested the gathered, ferocious power held back by the young East Indian in the waiter's tunic who stood at the head of the steps with the dog. As the small grey man with the thinning curly hair, pouchy eyes and flat, poker player's face came up the steps from the darkness of the garden on to the veranda of Jassy Vane's bungalow, the beast turned its narrow head: pointed whiteness showed briefly in the black frame of its drawn back lips and the East Indian's arm straightened slowly as a new surge of silent power strained the short lead he was holding. There was a measured scrabbling of claws on the tiles and a faint rumble, like the distant mutter of big guns, reverberated in the deep, narrow chest.

The little man edged his way on to the veranda like an anxious crab, not taking his eyes from the mask of grinning savagery that followed his every movement.

'You're sure you can hold that thing?' he asked. His accent had been formed in the America of Groton, Harvard and the sort of brown houses to which Lowells came for tea.

'Oh, yes, sir,' the East Indian said. 'We call him Ulysses. He's a Doberman Pinscher,' he added proudly.

'You could have fooled me,' the little man said. 'I would have said he was a Pekinese.'

'We have a bitch too,' the East Indian told him. 'She's in the run in the backyard.'

'I'm very glad to hear that,' the little man said. 'Believe me,

35

Joseph, that's encouraging news. I hope you intend to keep her there.'

'Of course, sir. We only let them into the house after Miss Vane has gone to bed. The others are inside, sir. You are expected.'

'And I'm glad to hear that also,' the little man said fervently. '*That*,' he began to gesture at the dog and stopped himself quickly, 'is for anybody who wasn't expected, eh?'

'Yes, sir.' The East Indian bent over and gently massaged the brown gloss of the animal's throat. 'We have to be careful nowadays. It's not like it used to be. That's why we got Ulysses and Penny.'

'Penny?'

'The bitch, sir. Her name is really Penelope, but Miss Vane calls her Penny. You have to keep a bitch, you see, sir, or the dog tends to stray.'

'Penny,' the little man muttered. '*Penny*. My God.' He turned and scuttled into the cheerful light of the living-room.

It was a spacious, high-ceilinged room with many books between low shelves built up on green glass bricks around three of the cream-painted walls; there were seven good West Indian paintings and no reproductions; bright cushions on deep, gaily-patterned furniture, the dark, pooly glimmers of careful polish and white Dominican straw mats, which looked as if they had been crocheted; a big stereo player, two S.R.3 speakers and an open-fronted cabinet full of records and cartridges of tape were set against the fourth wall. It had the stainless, colour-plate sparkle and order of a room which no male used regularly.

Beyond the living-room, through a doorless archway, Jassy Vane, the blonde who had met her at the airport and a middle-aged, stocky man with closely trimmed grey-flecked hair, a bony face hachured like a map, and huge, furry-backed hands, were seated in a close arc at the circular dining-table. Unlike the rest of the furniture, the table was old—a generous diameter of finely-turned rosewood which might have been a gaming-table in another age—and the low chairs with their coverings of shot silk had been carefully imitated by somebody very good to match the period from which the table had survived.

The stocky man said, 'Hallo, David. Sorry we had to bring you here, but things aren't looking very happy. Your tip didn't pay much at the tote.'

'I gave you what I knew,' the little man said. 'As soon as I was sure about the Mafia connection I laid it all in your lap, Robin. I stand to lose too much if those lads move in. You know that.'

'Yes, we know that,' the stocky man replied. He watched as the American went to the tray of drinks on the sideboard and made himself a mixture of a little vodka, nearly a bottle of tonic and four ice-cubes in a tall glass. 'But it didn't work out. Jassy spent two weeks in Mexico making herself into bait. She was right there on the hook, David. Just waiting for somebody to take her off it and ask questions. The only thing is that there wasn't anybody there to bite by the time she went in. They'd come and gone.'

'They had been there, all right,' Jassy Vane told the little man, as he came back to the table and stood looking down at them with a faint, questioning squint. 'They have a *finca* on an old sisal plantation outside of Corales. It's still in the owner's name, of course, but he's living pretty well in Mexico City for somebody with only a beat-up old sisal farm and his blue blood between him and charity.'

'I didn't promise you contact,' the small American said mildly. He pulled a chair out from the edge of the table directly opposite the three Jamaicans and sat. 'All I knew was that there was going to be a meeting, some time in the last month, in Corales. I didn't even know about that *finca*, Jassy, although it figures. They weren't going to hold a board meeting in a café. How are you so sure they have held it? Maybe you left too soon.'

'We're sure.' The blonde spoke for the first time. Even the flattery of the soft dining-room lights could not camouflage the hard set to her face. She no longer looked like a cuddlesome, jolly pig with a relish for sex: her blue eyes glinted dully, like fool's diamonds turned in white clay, and all her years showed.

The little man gestured irritably, passing his hand through his fine, spiky curls. He took a drink of his vodka-flavoured tonic water and said, 'I wish you people wouldn't do that.'

'Do what?' Jassy Vane asked him.

'You see,' the little man said, and scolded her with a pointing forefinger. '*That's* exactly what I mean. The cross-talk business. The Gallagher and Shean act. Every time I meet you three I never know who I'm supposed to be reporting to. It may be great vaudeville, but it's hell on the nerves.'

He grinned suddenly: a tight, sardonic glimmer of yellow breaking the flat, patrician face. Perched neatly at the beautiful old table, he looked like a gnome of high lineage.

'All right,' he said. 'I'll play it your way. You're the boss ... the bosses. Why are you so sure, Helen?' He addressed the blonde as he reached for one of the porcelain rimmed, cork coasters from the little rack at the centre of the table and put his sweating glass on it.

'These,' Helen McKay said. She slid a quarto size, manila envelope from under her forearm and across the quiet lustre of the table-top towards him. He picked up the envelope, opened the flap and took out a sheaf of 5×3 blow-ups. 'They're some of the cables,' Helen McKay told him, 'that Jassy microfilmed in Corales from the post office duplicates.

Not all of them, of course. Only the ones that check out with our business.'

The little man grinned again; the same carefully measured and sardonic stretching of his lips. He looked at Jassy with an amused yet unqualified respect.

'You're playing in the big league, aren't you?' he said. 'Fooling with the post office will get you twenty years any place—even in Latin America.'

'If you get caught,' Jassy said. She smiled under his admiration with the discreet triumph of a girl being asked to go out into the moonlight. 'Did you ever do a post office job, David?'

'No.' The little man shook his head. 'Blowing bridges and hijacking Wehrmacht payrolls was as high as I aspired to. They knew my limitations. All I ever did in a post office was to collect my mail. I don't suppose you'd like to tell me how you pulled it off.'

'No,' Jassy said, but the little man was already reading the prints.

He read in the old-fashioned, efficient manner of one who can no more remember when he learned words than he can remember his first steps: a quick, effortless comprehension of the contents of each print. When he had read them all— there were over thirty of them—he gathered them, fanned them and extracted three, with certainty, from various places in the spray. These he kept on his side of the table, and pushed the others with the envelope back across to Helen McKay.

'O.K.' he said. 'You're right. They did have a meeting between April ten and fourteen. Jassy was a week too late. It's all there: the Mafia and their front men. I recognise all the addresses. But what I don't recognise are these . . .' He tapped the three prints he had kept. 'These aren't in the pattern at all. Who the hell is Mayhew?'

'We were hoping you'd know,' the stocky man said. 'Doesn't it mean anything?'

'No.' The little man shook his head ruefully. 'Not a thing.'

'It couldn't be a new front man buying in?'

'I don't think so. I'm almost dead sure not so. The cables don't fit. Look at the rest . . . An accountant or a company lawyer could build a structure from them. They're straight business, Robin . . . Percentages. Voting powers. Capitalisation . . . Candywine is going to be a big development, you know. Mafia money maybe, for the most part, but no different from any other joint stock venture. They can't afford to be nowadays with the Internal Revenue boys counting each time they flush the toilet. The procedures for skimming will have been agreed upon already. Everything in those cables is the standard horse-trading between the Mafia families and a couple of convenient outsiders. Everything but this damned Mayhew. If he's a front man then I've been in the hotel business for twenty-five years for nothing.'

'What's he then?'

'I don't know. I'm not sure I want to know. Look, Robin, I've always co-operated with you, gladly. So long as it was anything you needed to know as a policeman. And I have a good reason for doing that. Everything I'm going to need for the sort of old age I was brought up to think of as being natural is tied up in the two hotels I own and the other two I have shares in. I want the North Coast kept clean of any rackets except conning tourists into believing that limbo dancing and fire-eaters are old Jamaican folk art. No big gambling. No syndicate stuff. When those boys move in my type either moves out or ends up shining shoes for some armour-plated blackguard whose name sounds as if it should be on a packet of *pasta*. I've seen it happen in Miami, and I knew it was going to happen in the Bahamas. That's why I came to Jamaica. And that's why I tipped you off about the

Candywine Development. But Mafia is one thing, Robin, and what I'm beginning to feel about Mayhew is another. You didn't bring me all the way over from Montego Bay at this time in the season just because you wanted to find out if I knew Mayhew . . . And my answer is "No." I'm not built for what you have in mind. I never was, even in my O.S.S. days. But I was twenty-five years younger then and there was a war on and all. You don't *know* who or what Mayhew is, but you *feel* something. So do I. I learnt that much in O.S.S. But count me out. I'll always have a piece of my time for Robin McKay, Commissioner of Police, but it will be strictly for information. What he does with it, or who does it for him, is his business.'

Jassy Vane had risen while he was talking and gone to the sideboard and mixed herself four fingers of Scotch, barely diluting it with a parsimonious splash from the water jug. She had stood there while he finished, with one elbow resting on the sideboard, listening hard and sipping her drink frequently. Now she came up to the table again: her powerful legs were just long and slim enough to carry off the yellow and black banded skirt that stopped at the top of her thighs.

She said, 'All right, David, we just thought we'd try. We're so short of good material that we *had* to try.'

'I'd be no good to you,' the little man said sombrely. To the stocky man he added, 'I suppose you think I'm just a shit? A frightened old O.S.S. dropout who wants to keep his nose clean and his pension warm?'

'No, David.' The stocky man smiled briefly and nicely. 'We don't think that. You've done all you can.' He leaned forward, stretching his thick arm, and took the three blow-ups. In his hand, they looked like playing cards in a gorilla's paw. 'Thanks for confirming what we felt about Mayhew.'

'David,' the middle-ageing blonde said. Her face was no longer hard and remote, and her eyes held splinters of warm

41

light. She winked at the little man. 'You're all right, David. You don't have to feel bad about anything. You've earned your pension. I mean it.'

'Thanks,' the little man muttered. 'If I could help you, I would.' He pushed his chair back and rose. Half his drink remained in the glass. 'I don't have the nerve for it, though . . . Well, I guess you'll want me to be going, eh?'

'See you around, David,' Jassy said. She bent and kissed the top of his head, putting her free arm around his shoulders. The glass she still held was nearly empty. 'You can give me lunch when I'm next over in Montego.'

'Sure,' the little man said. 'Sure.' He lifted his hand to the others. 'Well, good night, all,' and turned to walk through the archway, and turned suddenly back. 'Hey! What about that—that thing you have out there, Jassy? I thought the Baskerville breed died out when Sherlock Holmes shot that one on the moors.'

'Ulysses,' Jassy laughed. 'Not to worry, David. Joseph will have put him in the run.'

'With Penny?'

'Yes. Why?'

'How in God's name can you call anything looking remotely like Ulysses "*Penny*"? It's like calling a leopard "Kitty." You sure Joseph has those brutes locked up?'

'Quite sure.'

They watched him as he crossed the pale green tiles and white Dominican matting of the living-room. Half-way into the room, he stopped and came back towards them: a slight, stoop-shouldered figure with bags under his pale eyes and untidy, faded hair, whose full-page picture in the right magazines would have sold good shirts, expensive pipes, old whisky or the sort of wristwatch for which only a plain black leather band will do. He stood in the archway with his hands in his pockets and said, 'I'm not telling you how to manage your business, but I like you three. I like you enough to tell you that you're too damned vulnerable. A commissioner of police shouldn't be running the sort of side-show you're running, Robin. Somebody who can get you called in occasionally by the right politicians, to help him out, should be doing what you're trying to do. You're a police-man—and policemen don't like what Jassy had to do in Corales. They're supposed to be against that sort of thing. One day Interpol or somebody else legitimate and above board is going to rumble you and there's going to be a lot of embarrassment, and you're going to lose a lot of people.'

'I know,' Robin McKay said. 'But we're a developing country, David. We've got to build our bridges while we're crossing them. Besides, I don't have that many people to lose. On the budget I'm able to squeeze out of the secret vote, how could I?'

The little man remained still for a moment after Robin McKay had answered. Then he shrugged and smiled with a gentle and understanding commiseration.

'I only hope you make it,' he said. 'Jamaica wouldn't seem the same without you three.'

This time he went through the living-room, on to the veranda and down the steps into the garden without looking back. The others waited in silence until they heard his Mercedes clear its throat politely and hum like an electric sewing-machine as it was reversed up the drive. Jassy Vane went to the sideboard again and made herself the sort of potent mixture she had drunk like a glass of lemonade.

'Well,' she said. 'How do you like hearing the truth?'

'From that source,' Helen McKay said, 'I don't like it at all. He didn't tell us anything we haven't realised already, but it doesn't make it any more comforting coming from him. I don't know what that little bastard did in O.S.S. during the war, but I'm damn' sure it was something more

43

than just blowing bridges and spoiling pay-day for the
Wehrmacht. You saw how he cottoned on to the Mayhew
cables?'

'Yes,' the stocky man who had been called Robin McKay
said, and took another, smaller manila envelope from one of
the twin pockets on the skirt of his Guayabera shirt. 'That's
why I didn't show him this.' He extracted from the envelope
a single print and placed it on the table beside the three he
had taken from the little man. 'Come on, girls. We're in
trouble. Big, big trouble. Mayhew is bad enough, but this
one to Anyo means something more than I like to think about.
What are the Chinese doing in this business? Why Anyo?'

'It seems to me,' Jassy Vane said from her place at the
sideboard, 'that Anyo is the best man to tell us that. After all,
he has to, doesn't he? We can blow him higher than a sputnik
if he starts being coy. Why don't you just send for him and
ask?'

'I already have,' Robin McKay said. 'He should be here by
Saturday.'

'Three cheers,' Jassy Vane said. 'Or at least two cheers
and a tiger ... Well, I don't know about you people, but I
have a business to run to-morrow. Did I ever tell you that
advertising is a cut-throat game? If you get up too late, you
wake up with your head in your hands ... Good night,
sweeties. Joseph will lock up.'

She walked not very steadily across the room, carrying her
glass, and into the passage. They heard a door slam.

IV

Helen McKay half reclined on top of the sheet, leaning back
on the pillow she had propped against the headboard of the
oversize double bed. She was wearing the top piece of a
turquoise shortie pyjama suit. Her husband was seated at

44

her dressing-table, gloomily staring into the mirror and massaging his seamed face with astringent lotion.

She said, 'That stuff costs me thirty shillings a bottle, you know. You aren't suppose to bathe in it. A few drops will do.'

'How long has Jassy been drinking?'

'For quite a while.'

'Why didn't you tell me?'

'I should have. I hoped it was only a temporary thing.'

'You ought to have told me. A drinking agent can be worse than a defector.'

'Lots of agents drink. Look at Kim Philby.'

'Philby is a man. Men can get away with drink. A woman drinker is a grenade with the pin drawn. If she goes on like this she's going to be useless and dangerous in a couple of months.'

'Yes. She's frightened. She's frightened all the time now. Except for that boy in Mexico, she hasn't slept with a man for over a year. That's how frightened she is.'

'Oh, hell,' McKay said. 'Oh, bloody hell. What are we going to do?'

'I'm going to get Peter Blackmore back into the game. It may not work, but it's the only thing I can think of. She's still burning a big fire for that puritanical son of a bitch. If he comes back in, it might just stop the rot. We'll have to get him in again, anyway. We're going to need him for Candywine.'

He swung round on the low stool and faced her.

'You really think you can get Blackmore back in?' he asked. 'I've tried, you know. He doesn't like us and he has the conscience of a Boy Scout.'

'He *thinks* he doesn't like us, but we fascinate him. *That's* what he doesn't like: the fact that he got so involved with the one job he did for us. I can get him back . . . Will you please

45

put the top back on the bottle. That stuff evaporates quicker than chloroform. Why are you using it anyway? You'll smell like a whorehouse all night.'

He stood and picked up the elegant little bottle and the cap which was shaped like a hussar's busby. She watched him as he slowly and thoughtfully screwed on the cap.

'All right,' she said. 'That's enough. If you screw it any tighter I'll have to get it off with a monkey wrench when I next want to use it.'

'We don't have a monkey wrench.'

'Exactly.' She giggled suddenly.

'What's so funny?'

'You,' she said softly. 'Even in pyjamas you look as if you're wearing a uniform. Put your cap on, and that swagger stick.'

'Don't be ridiculous.'

'Go on,' she urged. 'Just for me. I just want to prove something.'

'Well you're not going to prove it on me. Prove it on some other policeman.'

'I don't know any other policemen well enough to ask.'

'You're a fool, you know, Helen. You're as crazy as a cuckoo.'

He walked over to the bed and she lifted her arms and hugged him tightly as he bent down to her.

'You do smell like a whorehouse,' she said.

'You've been reading cheap novels,' he told her. 'This is not how whorehouses smell,' and then, as they rolled together into the middle of the big bed with the effortless rhythm of long practice, he said, 'You get Peter Blackmore back in and I'll buy you that monkey wrench.'

'God,' she murmured, and began to unbutton the top of his pyjamas, 'What woman could resist an offer like that? He's as good as yours.'

46

They were not a couple that had ever read any of the marriage manuals. Somehow, in the thirty-odd years they had been together, they had never seemed to find the time to.

Chapter Three

Old acquaintance unforgot

It was not the time of the day when there were many casual strollers along the road. And she had selected a stretch of the highway up from the coast where there was no settlement because the hills were too steep and rocky. A woman, any woman, and particularly any white woman, whose car broke down on a country road in Jamaica, was likely to be offered such an abundance of immediate, gratuitous and chivalrous help that it could be an embarrassment. So she had chosen carefully where she was going to press the end of a matchstick into the valve and let the air out of the left rear tyre of her Rambler.

Once, a little boy in ragged trousers, carrying a damp wicker basket of crayfish and looking like a Donatello cherub in blackface, came up the path from the shallow, bronze river and said, 'De cy-ar puncture, ma'am?'

'Yes,' Helen McKay said. 'But it's O.K. Somebody has gone to get help.'

'I can fix bicycle puncture, ma'am, but car tyre too heavy for me.' He gravely considered the situation for a moment and added, 'You want buy some *jonga*, ma'am?'

'Are they fresh?'

'I jus' tek dem out of de river, Ma'am.'

'All right,' Helen McKay said. 'I'll take some off you. How much you selling them for?'

He took about half a pound of the small brown crustaceans from the basket, scooping them up in his cupped hands.

'Twenty cents, ma'am?' he suggested.

'Yes,' Helen McKay told him. 'That sounds very fair.'

She gave him twenty-five cents.

'Thank you, ma'am.'

He emptied the *jongas* into the plastic bag she took from the rack under the dashboard by the steering wheel.

'Thank *you*,' Helen McKay said. 'Walk good.'

She twisted and knotted the neck of the plastic bag, put it back into the rack, and watched the little boy go on up the road.

A few minutes later, a big white Fairlane with power steering came down the empty road, going very fast. It was stopped against the opposite bank and a man with a broad, prosperous brown face above a beautiful white collar and resplendent tie asked, 'Anything I can do?'

'No, thanks,' Helen McKay replied, and waved deprecatingly. 'We got a flat and the spare was too soft. My husband got a lift down to the gas station. He'll be back in a minute.'

'Sure there's nothing I can do?'

'Quite sure, thanks. Don't let me keep you. You look as if you're in a hurry.'

'I am a bit,' the man said. 'I've got a lunch meeting in Ocho Rios for one o'clock and left Kingston too late. You're sure you're all right?'

'Hungry,' Helen Mckay smiled. 'And cursing that husband of mine, but otherwise I'm fine.'

'It always happens at times like these,' the man said. 'Hope you get it fixed soon.'

The Fairlane pulled away down the road as if it were gathering take-off speed on a runway.

Helen McKay waited, leaning against the back of the

station wagon: a plump, trim but forlorn middle-aged house-wife of the middle classes, with a floppy straw hat pulled down over her dark glasses. A big yoke tree, growing strongly out of the nearly vertical limestone hillside, shaded the spot on the road where she had stopped; a barely perceptible but steady breath of cool air drifted up from the river. Two or perhaps three woodpeckers were drilling like lunatic road-menders into other yoke trees farther up the hill, and once the sudden, exasperated bray of a tethered jackass shattered the stillness of noon.

When she saw the red Ferrari come decorously round the corner, quarter of a mile down the road, she gave a relieved sigh and smiled faintly. He still drives that thing as if it was a Model T and he was eighty years old, she said to herself. She stepped out into the road and waved.

The Ferrari began to slow for stopping, before the man driving it recognised her. When he was close enough to see who she was there was a falter in the engine, as though he had done something confused with gear shift and brake; then the car stopped a few yards from her.

The man who opened the door and swung himself out of the bucket seat was tall with long, heavy bones—like a horse which would always be too solid for the flat and which would lead the field over the jumps but would always be pulled back on the level of the finishing stretch. His hair was thick and glinting, like slightly waved copper wire, and his face would have made a good figurehead for a ship if figure-heads had not been, by tradition, feminine.

He said, without pleasure, 'Hallo, Helen. Having trouble?'

'Hallo, Peter,' she said. 'Long time no see and all that.' She gestured irritably to her flat tyre.

He walked past her to the tyre and performed the obli-gatory masculine ritual of kicking it.

'O.K.' he said. 'Where d'you keep your jack and the spare?'

She said with the half-defiant sulkiness of a woman whose day has been inconvenienced by the unreasonable world of machinery, 'I don't have a spare, dammit. It was going soft, so I left it at Constant Spring to be fixed. I only went over to Highgate for the morning,' she added, as if inviting him to witness the injustice of it all, 'to visit a friend. I was going to be back in Kingston in time for lunch.'

'They give you spare tyres,' he told her with the heavy, unctuous patience of his sex when it is offered the opportunity of chiding hers for not being sensible about machinery, 'because you can get a flat between your garage and the gate . . .'

'I was waiting for a lift,' she told him. 'I'll get a lift into town and Robin will have one of the patrol cars come out with the spare and drive it back.'

'You'd better come with me,' he said. 'At this time of the day you're not likely to get much going to Kingston except a truck or two.'

'Oh, thank you, Peter,' she said brightly. 'I'll just get my handbag and keys. Roll up the windows on that side for me, will you? In case it rains. What a stroke of luck for me, eh? Your coming along like this, I mean.'

'Yes,' Peter Blackmore said dryly. 'What a stroke of luck, indeed.'

II

Twenty minutes later, when they were driving up the opened hairpin of steep road before Stony Hill village, Helen McKay said, 'This *is* a beautiful car, Peter. Just sitting in it makes me feel about thirty years younger.'

'It's a good car,' Peter Blackmore said, looking straight

over the sleek curve of the bonnet, 'but if you press a matchstick into a tyre valve you'll let the air out just like with any
other car.'

'So you spotted that, did you?'

'Didn't you intend me to?'

'I hoped you would, but I really didn't bank on it. I
didn't think you'd notice an old match lying in the dust.'

'It wasn't an *old* match. It still had the head on. And it was
clean. The wood was still white. And it was lying in the dust
beside *your* flat tyre.'

'Why did you play along then? You had me fooled and I
don't fool easy.'

'For the fun of it,' Peter Blackmore told her. 'Just so that
I could have the pleasure of telling you and that ape you're
married to and Jassy to—to go ... Oh, for God's sake,
Helen! Why don't you people leave me alone? I don't know
why you pulled this little stunt. I couldn't care less what dirty
business you're mixed up in now. All I'm telling you is that
you're not getting me into anything like it again.'

She said, 'Can I talk to you for a little ... No, not here;
not like this. At your place.'

'I've got business to attend to. You know that. You know
I come up to town every Thursday.'

'Please, Peter. I'm not asking for anything more than to
talk to you. No strings, except I may ask you to give me a
sandwich. I'm hungry.'

Something in her voice made him look at her quickly. He
had seen her face, in the past, set in lines of a pitiless and impersonal calculation, or bright with humour, intelligence
and that honest carnality of a woman who has lovingly
matured her passions in a good marriage. But he had never
seen it sad and worried as it was now. It disturbed his sense of
security, as if he had come suddenly across the fault line on
a mountain slope that augured a landslide.

He said, 'I guess I can run to a sandwich. You're not my favourite person, but I wouldn't want you to starve to death.'

'Thank you, Peter.' She smiled at him. He wished she was not wearing dark glasses so that he could see her eyes.

III

'How's Coniston?' Helen McKay asked Peter Blackmore. 'Have you had a good year?'

'Apart from two strikes, a week of rain just when I didn't need it and nine months of drought, I've had a great year,' he said.

'That's what you sugar boys always say,' she laughed. 'To hear you talk the only thing between you and poverty is the fact that bank managers have such soft hearts.'

They were seated at the Formica-topped, aluminium-legged table in the kitchen of the house Peter Blackmore maintained on a side road off Stony Hill village overlooking Kingston. It was not the residence he regarded as his home —home was the white, pillar-fronted great house another Blackmore had built two centuries before and which stood on a rise surrounded by six hundred acres of sugar cane between the mountains and the sea—but it was a place to camp in comfortably when he came up to the capital. And indeed, set as it was on steel stilts driven into the steep hill, with its huge unceilinged living-room roofed with plain cedar, its two vestigial bedrooms and its large kitchen, it did resemble the headquarters tent of a commanding officer in the field.

Helen McKay was eating the three-egg omelette Peter Blackmore had insisted she have instead of a sandwich and which he had cooked at the six-burner Moffat stove set against the wall beside the Imperial Frigidaire in which one could have garaged a Mini-Minor; against the opposite wall

53

there was a deep-freeze on which one could have safely landed a small plane.

'Sorry I couldn't offer you anything more enterprising,' Peter Blackmore said. 'I keep most of the stuff in the deep-freeze and it takes time to thaw.' He reached forward and re-filled her glass from the half-bottle of Beaune that stood before her. 'Would you like me to open you a tin of something? Fruit salad? Guavas?'

'Peter!' she protested. 'Don't you realise I'm a forty-nine-year old woman with a weight problem? I've eaten about twice as much as I should have already.'

'You're a fifty-three-year-old liar,' he said, 'and eggs don't put weight on you. Go on. Eat up. You look beat.'

When she laughed, it came from deep down in her belly. She flung herself back, and her face, for the first time since he had picked her up, lost its look of tense sadness.

'You know something?' she said.

'No. But I'm sure you're going to tell me. What?'

'You're a very feminine man. You look as if you could knock a hole in a brick wall with your head and from what I've heard you get your hands up more skirts than a gynaecologist; but inside you, really inside you, there's a lot of woman crying to be let out.'

'How did Freud manage without you to help him? You should be writing a book.'

'Seriously, Peter. I meant it as a compliment.' She put out a small plump white hand that would have attracted the respectful recognition of a sculptor or a concert pianist or a karate instructor. She touched his forearm briefly. 'Come on, man. You're too bright not to know I was telling you something nice about yourself.'

'I'm too bright not to know that you're leading up to something else. Would you like some coffee, or shall I take you home now?'

She said with a flat, chilling sadness, 'Jassy is going to get herself killed. We're on to something very big, Peter. Much bigger than anything we've had to tackle before, and Jassy is going to get herself killed in it.'

Peter Blackmore looked at her steadily for a minute, with contempt and a sort of weary anger. Then he rose.

'O.K., Helen,' he said. 'Let's go. My God! You people never learn, do you? Although I must admit that line about Jassy is pretty good. What was it supposed to do? Bring out the white knight in me?'

She drank slowly from what was left of the wine in her glass, not looking at him.

'No line, Peter,' she said slowly. 'I'd have tried anything to bring you back in with us, but what I said about Jassy is true. She's running scared. As scared as she can be, and what she's about to get into is going to kill her if she doesn't get her nerve back.'

Peter Blackmore came round the table to where she sat and gripped her shoulder, pushing her against the back of the chair. He studied her face. Her eyes met his without blinking. When he let go of her shoulder, she massaged it gingerly.

'I told you I'd never work with you people again,' he said. 'You're the scum of the earth. All of you. And you dirty everything you touch. So if Jassy has suddenly found enough sense to be scared, tell her to get out.'

'She won't. I said she's frightened. I didn't say she was a coward.'

'*You* pull her out then. She's not going to be much use to you dead.'

'We can't pull her out. There are not enough of us and she's too good. She'll be very good right up to the time she makes a mistake because she's frightened. Have you seen her at all in the past year?'

'Once. At some damn' reception. King's House, I think. We didn't speak.'

'She's drinking. She's half-drunk all the time now.'

Peter Blackmore said furiously, 'What the hell are you telling me all this for, Helen? So Jassy has become a lush . . . because she's frightened. Well, that's your fault. Your's and Robin's. *You* got her into this filthy murderous business. You conned her into becoming an agent or whatever it is you call it. You get her out of it.'

He sat suddenly, like a man boneless with fatigue.

He said sullenly, 'Give her my love. Tell her I hope she doesn't get killed.'

'You tell her. You owe her something. Just tell her something nice.'

'I don't owe her anything. I don't owe any one of you maniacs anything, except that you nearly got me killed once. What do I owe her?'

'Some of the best loving you ever had in your life. Not just a good screw, Peter, but the real thing . . . That and the job you did with her. You know what you owe her.'

'God damn you,' Peter Blackmore said. 'God damn you, you clever bitch.'

He rose and crossed the floor to the swing door between the kitchen and the drawing-room. Helen McKay sat and smiled like someone whom a doctor has just told good news when she was preparing herself for bad.

'Her number is 24———,' she began to call after his back as he pushed open the door.

'I know her number,' he said.

She smiled again as she heard the click of the lifted telephone in the drawing-room.

IV

'I want you to undress me,' Jassy Vane told him. 'I'm just going to lie here and not do a damn' thing until you take all my clothes off.'

'That won't take long,' Peter Blackmore said, and smiled down at her with great gentleness and kissed her forehead and her eyes softly as he might have kissed a child. 'The clothes you girls wear nowadays! They make me feel like an old man. I've heard of mini-skirts, but that thing you have on is an incitement to riot. D'you realise,' he added as he stroked her cheek and tugged lightly at the big brass ring at the top of the broad zip which closed her dress up the front, 'D'you realise I could see your pants when you were sitting down earlier on?'

'You're supposed to,' she said. Her austerely handsome face was soft and luminous with confidence and abandon. 'And you *are* getting old if you still call them mini-skirts. That's what they called them last year.'

'What do they call them this year?'

'Pussy pelmets.'

When he peeled the dress back from her stretched-out body and put his hand on the mound at the bottom of her stomach, she uttered a sudden, half-choked cry, not of passion but of relief, and flung herself against him, holding him with an astonishing, desperate strength, burying her face in the hollow between his neck and shoulder.

'Peter,' she said. 'Peter . . . Peter . . . God, when I heard your voice on the phone this afternoon I . . .'

He lifted her face and kissed her on the mouth, but not as he would have kissed a child. When her shivering began to turn into the rapid, deep undulations of desire, he raised his lips from hers for a moment.

'You always did talk too damn' much,' he said softly.

Two hours later, hugging his back and lightly passing her hand up and down his chest as they prepared for sleep, she said, 'I'm glad you brought me back to my place. Any place would have been all right, but I'm glad you asked to come back here.'

'Why?'

'I don't know. You don't have to have a reason for everything. I'm just glad it was here.' She propped herself up suddenly on one elbow and pressed him hard against her. 'Peter,' she said urgently into the darkness. 'Peter . . . listen! Even if you don't come back in with us it's all right, you hear? I don't care what Helen told you, but you don't have to come back in because of me.'

'Relax.' She felt his big body heave briefly with silent laughter. 'I'm back in. Boy, am I back in.'

Chapter Four

Who the hell is Mayhew?

At about nine o'clock the next morning, Jassy Vane rolled over on to her stomach, lifted the telephone on her bedside table and dialled a number that began with a '2' and a '4.' It connected her with one of the two secretaries at Art Enterprises Inc., the advertising firm which she had begun seven years before in one room above the old Press Club and which she now had to keep carefully reined in against too much success.

'Daphne?' she said when she heard the telephone lifted at the other end.

'Yes, dear,' the girl replied.

'I won't be in to-day.'

'I didn't think you would be.'

'Is that any way to talk to your employer?'

'I wouldn't know. You're the only employer I ever had!'

'Anything new come up?'

'Helvetics were on to us again. About five minutes ago. I don't think we're going to be able to dodge them much longer, Jassy. They sell a lot of watches in this town and they think a Jassy Vane promotion will sell more.'

'Oh, Christ! That's just what we needed at this time. Stall them, Daphne. I'll think of something over the week-end.'

'You'll have to. We're turning down too much new business lately. I mean, how exclusive can you get? You're too good, Jassy.'

'I know,' Jassy Vane replied. 'It's always been my curse.'

'Jassy?'

'Yes.'

'Is he back in?'

'Yes,' Jassy Vane said after a short pause, looking back over her shoulder at the sleeping man. 'Yes, I guess so.'

'That sound you heard,' Daphne said, 'was me heaving a sigh of relief. There aren't that many good men around.'

'Yes. It's a pity we can't use them better than we do.'

'Ain't that the truth, though,' Daphne said.

Jassy Vane replaced the telephone softly, eased herself off the bed and padded over to the full-length mirror set into one of the sliding panels of her clothes closet. For a minute she stood frowning at the reflection of her naked body with the unpitying self-criticism of the woman just past thirty. She touched briefly the sides of high, firm breasts and half-turned to examine the long smooth black slopes of her back and shoulder. She thought, Bless you, Africa; they just don't make them like that anywhere else. Then she went into the bathroom, splashed water on her face, tugged a stiff brush through her hair, put on a short, white housecoat and went out past the bed where Peter Blackmore was still sleeping, and through the dining-room to the kitchen.

'Good morning, Joseph,' she said to the young East Indian who was taking inventory of the tinned food in a cupboard above the draining board.

'Good morning, Miss Vane.'

'Set for two, will you.'

'I have, ma'am. On the back porch.'

'Good. Mrs. McKay should be here shortly. She'll probably want coffee too.'

'Yes, ma'am. Grapefruit or orange juice, ma'am?'

'Grapefruit. And scramble me two eggs. On toast. But don't tempt me with an extra slice.'

'Yes, ma'am. It's the first time in nearly a year I hear you ask for two eggs.'

'It's the first time in a year I've been hungry in the morning.'

She went from the kitchen on to the tiles of the adjacent back porch. A close grille of ironwork enclosed the porch on three sides, stretching from the tiles to the ceiling; clumps of euphorbia and hibiscus bushes—red, double pinks and double yellows—grew in the backyard beyond the porch. She sat at one of the places laid opposite each other on the glass-topped breakfast table with its wrought-iron frame and legs, and unfolded the morning's newspaper.

When Joseph brought out half a grapefruit dusted with brown sugar she said, 'You'd better go and wake Mr. Blackmore. Ask him what he'd like.'

'Yes, ma'am,' Joseph said and turned to go inside. He paused in the doorway between the porch and the dining-room. 'Is Mr. Blackmore joining us?'

She nodded.

'Has he worked for us before?'

She nodded again. 'Once,' she said. 'About eighteen months ago. Before you came in. No more questions, Joseph.'

'Sorry, Miss Vane. I can never remember that.'

'That's O.K., Joseph. I've been in for over five years and I can't always remember it myself.'

She was pouring her second cup of coffee when Peter Blackmore came out. He was dressed, and his face had the burnished look of a man who renews a lot of himself in nerveless sleep.

He sat opposite her and said, 'I see you still have the razor I left.'

'Yes.'

'With the same blade in it. The whole thing was so rusty

I had to scrub it with the nail brush and use one of your blades.'

'Well, you left in a hurry, you know.'

'Surely somebody else must have needed a razor.'

'There were a few, but I didn't let them stay till shaving time.'

'Why? You should have.'

'Sometimes I thought I was going to, but I always changed my mind about five in the morning.'

'Stupid cow.'

'That's the nicest thing I've heard this time of the morning for over a year.'

'Well, if it's any consolation, I haven't been too happy either . . . Who's Joseph?'

'We recruited him about a year ago. We're still a small outfit, but we've grown a bit since you knew us. Too many people are beginning to realise there must be something like us around. Joseph is a—a sort of security measure.'

'And what am I supposed to be? What d'you people want from me this time?'

'Shall we leave that to Helen to tell? She's coming round shortly.'

Joseph came from the kitchen as she spoke, carrying a tray on which there was a glass of orange juice and a plate of bacon and eggs. He served these to Peter Blackmore and went back to the kitchen. Peter Blackmore drank the juice and began to eat. Jassy Vane sat sideways with one arm resting on the back of her chair and watched the man opposite her, fondly and a little sadly.

She said, 'I meant what I said last night. You don't have to come back in because of me. If you want out, now's the time to go.'

He raised his face and said, 'Be quiet a minute, will you. I'm thinking,' and looking into his light, unblinking eyes she realised that his dismissal of her was not a gesture. He was already preparing himself for what might need his attention, like a big and sensitive predator testing the scents and noises of a new territory.

II

The photocopy of the first cable was dated 9th March. It read:

CANDYWINE DEEPWATER CONCESSION STILL OPEN STOP HAVE OFFERED RECIPROCALS AS PER LETTER MARCH 19 STOP ALL AGREE EXCEPT RILKE STOP PLEASE ADVISE MAYHEW

It was addressed to Lode Invest, New York.

The second cable, dated 11th March, was from Lode Invest, New York:

RILKE HAS HEARD THE ANGELIC VOICES STOP RECIPROCALS NOW ACCEPTABLE LODE INVEST

It was addressed to Mayhew, Finca Rivera, Corales, Yucatan, Mexico.

The third message was from Mayhew to Lode Invest and was dated 13th March:

CANDYWINE DEEPWATER CONCESSION SECURED STOP WILL NOW OFFER VENEZUELAN HOLDERS FIRST PURCHASE SELL OUT RIGHTS MAYHEW

And on the same date Mayhew cabled to Saul, at a poste-restante number, 73946, in Caracas. It was in Spanish:

CANDYWINE DEEPWATER OPTION NOW MINE STOP SUGGEST LIMITED LIABILITY HOLDING YOUR PRINCIPALS MAYHEW

'Is this all you have?' Peter Blackmore asked Helen McKay.

'That's all. Except for the Mafia stuff which you can read later.'

'And you don't like Mayhew?'

'I don't like him at all.'

'Have you checked out this Lode Invest? What is it? A company, or just a cable address?'

'They're Logan, Orr, Dalkeith and Everett. An investment advisory partnership who specialise in developing territories. We've checked them out, all right, and they're solid gold. They have a Dunn and Bradstreet rating so high you have to track it by radar, and our people in New York say you can't even become an office cleaner unless you went to the Harvard Business School. Mr. Logan, Mr. Orr and Mr. Everett are dead. They think Mr. Dalkeith might be dead too, but nobody can summon enough nerve to ask him when he comes up from Westchester on Wednesdays and Thursdays. There are eleven partners who do the actual work.'

'Well, what's worrying you? Their business is to advise on investment and Candywine is going to be a good investment for this Mayhew and his associates.'

'And for the Mafia.'

'Mafia nothing. You mean money. I'm not saying the Mafia haven't bought in, but so what? If people kept out of everything the Mafia have bought into nowadays they'd keep their money under the mattress ... The only thing I don't get,' Peter Blackmore added as he frowned over the photocopied cables, 'is this business about deep water concessions. I didn't know there were going to be deep water facilities at Candywine.'

'There are not going to be.'

'Then it must be a code name or something for part of the development.'

'That's what we hoped.' Helen McKay poured what was left in the coffee pot and shook her head as Jassy moved to take away the quarter of a cup of sticky, cold fluid. 'We don't like the idea of Mafia money developing Candywine.

But that's the politicians' business. Robin begged them, warned them, even hinted he might resign. When he saw that they might accept his offer, he dropped that. So we were left with the promise of bigger and brighter casinos and all that those mean—until Mayhew stepped in. Before him, we just anticipated the usual problems that come with the Mafia. You know: a few politicians bought, prostitution, narcotics, an extra couple of murders, tax evasion. All clean and above board. Until Mayhew bids for a piece of the action and gets it.'

'Who,' Peter Blackmore asked, 'the hell is Mayhew?'

'We don't know. But we do know who his Venezuelan associates are . . . that's when we began to get really worried.'

'Who are they?'

'They're Anyo, Peter. . They're Chinese Intelligence.'

'*Anyo!* You don't mean that little . . .?'

'Yes, the same gentleman. Our Mr. Anyo.'

'But I thought he worked for you.'

'He works for us as much as it pays him for us not to sell him to the Russians. Running a double agent is always like carrying a snake in your pocket to guard your money. We never suspected Anyo, of course, until we put a watch on that poste-restante number in Caracas. It's not the pick-up number we use when we want to contact him. He collected three more cables from the new number after our friends in Caracas began to watch it.'

'Cables from Mayhew?'

'No, from his old granny in Sze-chuan . . . We don't know who from, Peter. Our friends were only told to watch who collected. They didn't read the messages over his shoulder. But he'll tell us what we want to know when he gets here. We've sent for him.'

'Supposing he decides not to come? Or suppose he doesn't tell you if he does come? Maybe he has made a deal with the

Russians, too. Or the Americans. Or everybody. Perhaps he doesn't need you to keep quiet about him any more.'

Helen McKay smiled thinly. 'I doubt any of those possibilities,' she said. 'He has been doing some funny work in Venezuela recently. None of it is really our concern, but we do know for a certainty that he sold thirteen Fedelista guerrillas to the Venezuelan Army the other day. Seven of them were shot dead and the others captured, in an ambush where no troops had any right to be. I don't think he'd like it if we told the Cubans about that. The men he fingered were not simply Che Guevara enthusiasts. They were straight down from Castro himself.'

Peter Blackmore was looking at her steadily; leaning back in his chair with his legs straight, and sitting on the end of his spine; his hands clasped at the back of his neck. The cool of the morning had given way, imperceptibly, to the first still heat of forenoon. The light outside had begun to dazzle and the colours of the hibiscus had become suddenly very hard.

He said with a sort of weary amusement, 'I had forgotten. You know, I'd really forgotten how you people operate. Seven men dead and all that means to you is a piece of information you can use for blackmail. Helen, are you sure you aren't making a mistake? I'm not the sort you need, you know.'

'You're the best we can think of,' Helen McKay told him. They sounded curiously intimate; more so than he and Jassy had sounded after their night of making love. A sort of family resemblance—like that of an orphaned nephew and the aunt who had brought him up—seemed to knit their exchange, excluding Jassy. 'We're short of men,' Helen McKay said flatly. 'It's the great Jamaican problem, or haven't you heard?'

'O.K.,' Peter Blackmore said. 'You can take the pressure

66

off. I told Jassy I'm in . . . although what I can do for you I can't imagine.'

'It may be necessary to give you a little training,' Helen McKay said. 'You'd have to leave the island for about six weeks. Would you agree to that?'

'Training? What sort of training? Now hold it, Helen. I've given you the horse. Don't expect me to throw in the saddle too. A piece of rope is all you're entitled to when you buy a beast in Jamaica.'

'Would you go if we asked you to? There are a few things you might need to be taught, and we don't have the facilities here.'

'Where would you want me to go?'

'Somewhere. It's a small place, like us, and it doesn't have any ambitions except to stay alive. That's why its intelligence is so good. Other people around them have ambitions, extended organisations . . . You can always find somebody who is willing to talk for a consideration when you're dealing with the big, ambitious boys.'

'Is that why you know so damn' much?'

'Yes, I suppose it is . . . Well, how about it? Would you go if we asked you?'

'Ask me when the time comes. I'll have to think it over . . . whether I want to remain as I am or become like one of Jassy's trained dogs out there.'

He rose and strolled across the patio, opened the heavy gate set into the grille-work and went down the steps and across the yard between the hibiscus to the run of stout chicken wire where the Dobermans lay beside their kennel under the deep shade of a mango tree, like two figments from a dark folk tale. When he lifted the catch of the gate to the run and the dog rose and came bounding forward, Jassy called out sharply, *'Peter!'*

He did not answer or look back. The dog began to snarl and

dropped to a crouching rush as it neared him. He stood still and the dog's progress became less purposeful. It stopped, began to circle him, until he squatted on his heels and extended his hand. After a long minute, it came forward, almost shyly, and he scratched the narrow, cruel head between the ears until it began to whine ecstatically. He stood up again and, with its tail thumping on the narrow drum of its body, twisting in mid-air, the dog followed him to where the bitch sat like the cocked trigger of a shotgun. Slowly and carefully, he fondled her head and throat, the dog nuzzling his hand; the bitch's tongue rolled out and licked the salt from his fingers; he turned and walked back across the run and through the gate, shooing the two animals back before he closed it.

'The bastard,' Helen McKay said. 'The arrogant bastard.'

'Yes,' Jassy said. 'Isn't it nice?'

II

By lunch-time they were all a little drunk.

'Will I ever like you?' Peter Blackmore asked Helen McKay as he turned the knob on the Ostermix. White rum, lime juice, instant Daquiri additive and ice-cubes frothed and rattled against the walls of the container as the little propeller whined into high revolution. 'That's why I'm back in. To see if close association makes the heart grow fonder. Oh, I admire your great qualities,' he added, as though the woman tucked into a corner of the settee beside him had begun to interrupt, 'but whether I'll ever believe they shouldn't be confined on the right side of an electrified fence is another matter.'

'I'm like rape,' Helen McKay told him comfortably. 'Nobody likes me, but when I become inevitable you might as well relax and enjoy me.'

68

'Here,' Peter Blackmore said, grinning. 'Take this. I can't think of a come-back to that one. You've been practising much longer than me.' He poured her a champagne glass of the Daquiri mix; it was so stiff with crushed ice that it flowed out like honey. Jassy Vane was lying full-length on the other settee with her hands behind her head, smiling absently. From the two stereo speakers, Big Bill Broonzey was pushing the sort of sound that only he could find among the chords in a twelve-string guitar. A small midday breeze had risen and was playing a gentle game of tag with the curtains.

Peter Blackmore was reaching across Jassy to refill the glass she had put on the window sill above the settee when the telephone extension sounded in the dining-room. They waited while Joseph came from the kitchen and picked up the receiver.

He said, 'Yes, this is Miss Vane's house . . . Oh, yes, sir, I'm sure she would like to speak to you.' He put his hand over the mouthpiece and added, 'Mr. Patterson. He's calling you from Montego Bay.'

'David!' Helen McKay sat up straight, swinging her feet off the settee and looking at Jassy. The euphoric relaxation of two women enjoying the attentive company of a worthwhile male had given way to a sudden alertness. 'Now why would David be calling us now?'

'Hallo, David,' Jassy said. 'Yes, I'm in the pink. In the black, rather. You've got to keep your ethnic integrity these days . . .' She listened and said, 'Well, yes if you'd like that . . . Yes, I'll come over to you . . . Quite understand . . . Either this afternoon, or to-morrow morning . . . Good . . . I'll call you back . . . See you.'

She came back into the drawing-room slowly, and stood before Helen McKay. The older woman sat as she had after

69

the telephone first rang, and asked the question without speaking.

'David wants me to take over his advertising,' Jassy told her. 'He says his image needs a new look and all that.'

'He couldn't be serious.'

'Oh, he was being serious, but not about advertising,' Jassy said.

'I see,' Helen McKay said. 'D'you think it's something new about our funny friend?'

'Maybe. Maybe about something we know already. Whatever it is he wants to see me.'

'Why couldn't he come over to us? He always does.'

'He said he couldn't leave. That he has a new lot coming in this evening. Special people who will be useful for boosting him among their friends.'

'I see,' Helen McKay said again. 'You think he doesn't want to come over?'

'He didn't sound like he wanted to go anywhere.'

'In that case you had better go to him.'

'That's what I thought,' Jassy said, 'but I couldn't agree until you gave the O.K.'

'Did he sound worried or frightened?'

Jassy shook her head—reflectively rather than in denial.

'It's hard to say how he sounded. Not frightened certainly. And not worried. He sounded sort of pleased. You know. Excited—like a woman wanting to hint a bit of gossip on a party line.'

'Yes,' Helen McKay said, 'I know exactly what you mean. All sub-agents get like that when they have something juicy they think you'd love to hear. Even the old pros like David. Only he *is* a pro, or he was once. You get over there, Jassy. This afternoon. Don't fly over. Go by car with Peter.'

'Peter hasn't said he'll go,' Peter Blackmore said to her from the record changer where he was slipping Big Bill

Broonzy and his guitar into their sleeve. 'Peter might have his own business to look after. I'm a volunteer, remember?'

'Don't be cute, Peter,' Helen McKay said with the casual asperity of a governess. 'Now listen, Jassy . . . Be careful on this. If David feels you ought to go over to him then he's probably on to something that could blow up in his face. It may be no more than a feeling, but anybody who lasted through his sort of war did so because they learnt how to feel when the situation wasn't right.'

'I once read somewhere,' Peter Blackmore said, 'that the really high-class criminals acquire that sort of feeling too.'

'That's quite true,' Helen McKay replied. 'Any police-man will tell you. So do the best chess champions, by the way. A computer could do all that thinking they go through between moves. They're only thinking out *what* makes them feel the way they do about the pieces on the board.'

Chapter Five

Mayhew is as Mayhew does

The little man with pouches under his eyes lay on the raft and watched Jassy Vane and Peter Blackmore playing like one black otter and one white in the watered milk of the swimming area. A slim twelve-footer, driven by a twin-propellered, 16 h.p. Iver-Johnson outboard, rode by on its stern just outside the rope buoyed by little canisters of bright red polystyrene; sixty feet of nylon cable behind the boat, a mahogany blonde in a baby-pink bikini tried to do something clever on her single ski and went head-first into the deep water. She surfaced and waved to the man in the yachting-cap at the wheel of the boat, and retrieved her ski as the boat straightened, shifted into a high-pitched snarl and headed for the pier on the west side of the rope. Pushing the ski with her left hand, dog-paddling with her right, the blonde swam under the rope and to the raft. She asked, panting, 'How d'you do that damn, reverse, David? It looks like flying the way you do it, and every time I try it I end up with my lungs full of water.' She coughed prettily, bobbing with her right hand on the raft's edge.

'Just keep on keeping on, dear,' the little man said. 'Unless your father had syphilis your balance ought to be O.K. at your age. You just need a little more practice.'

'How about him?' The girl gestured with her chin across the hundred yards of water to where the very black man in the very white yachting-cap was snubbing the boat against the pier with a double bowline around a bollard.

'Ask and it shall be given you, dear,' the little man said. 'I am told he's very good, and he's free this season.'

'Thanks, David. You're sweet.'

The blonde, sodden head disappeared, a taut pink rump surfaced briefly and purposeful ripples began to close the distance between the raft and the pier. The little man lifted the abandoned ski out of the water on to the raft and smiled indulgently. 'I didn't expect you until to-morrow,' he said as Jassy began climbing the ladder on to the raft.

'Helen thought I ought to come over right away,' Jassy said as she pushed the bathing cap from her head and sprawled beside him.

'And you?'

'Me too. But she's the boss.'

'She is indeed. Who's your friend?' He pointed casually at Peter Blackmore.

'He's with me. You can tell me whatever you want to . . . Peter, this is David Patterson . . . Peter Blackmore . . . O.K., David, what's happened?'

'I was up in the States for two days after I left you the other night.'

'Why?'

'Oh, call it instinct,' the little man said. 'Or conditioned reflex. Or whatever you like. I went to a few people I know . . . Mayhew is serious business, Jassy. I don't know if you people can handle it.'

'How serious?' Jassy asked him.

'Just about as serious as you can imagine. Nobody knows about him but everybody has heard of him. They're worried, Jassy. Everybody is worried. This is all the way from up.'

'How high,' Peter Blackmore asked as he floated in the water with his forearm on the raft's edge and his head near to theirs, 'is up?'

'Just what I was going to ask,' Jassy Vane said softly.

73

'Pretty high,' the little man said. 'High enough for you people to take notice.'

'Shit,' Jassy said, and sat up and put her bathing cap on again. 'You could never get that high, David. Not any more. All the people you knew are dead or retired.'

'I didn't say that I had got that high. I simply said that high was where the news came from.'

'What's your source?'

'Oh, come on, Jassy. You couldn't ever trust me again if I told you. It's authentic, though. You'd better believe that. And you'd better believe the flap that's on. The agencies are hardly speaking to each other. Military is sure that the C.I.A. have formed a splinter. The C.I.A. is looking under Navy's bed. Navy feels that everybody is after *them*, but then the admirals have become a little paranoid since nuclear submarines . . . Mayhew has them all running to the john just thinking about him—or it.'

'What d'you think?' Jassy asked.

'Me?' The little man sighed comfortably, sprawled flatter as if he were being massaged by the gentle rays of the afternoon sun. 'I don't have to think any more, Jassy. My most serious problem is whether Tod there will service Miss Porter so well that she'll want to come back next season.' He waved a priestly hand in benediction to the jetty where the pink bikini top was very close to the black chest of the man who had steered the boat.

'Ha bloody ha,' Jassy said. 'All right, I'll play along. I'll beg. Please, dear darling David, what d'you think?'

The little man grinned at Peter Blackmore: a small, quirky smile that was more an acknowledgment of their shared caste than anything to do with amusement.

'Tell Robin and Helen,' he said, almost murmuring into the space between the two younger people, 'that whatever Mayhew is, it's homegrown. American homegrown, I mean. They may have the Russians or the Limeys or the Krauts in with them for all anybody knows, but they're as American as an Ohio hog or the Lincoln Memorial.'

'My, my,' Jassy told him affectionately and ruffled his damp grey spikes, 'you have been a busy little David since we saw you last. Thanks. We won't forget this. If you want something done soon, call us.'

'How about a work permit for a fellow I know in San Francisco? He can do things with sea-food that would make Vatel run himself through with his sword all over again. I want him as a chef.'

'You *are* asking for the moon with a fence around it,' Jassy said. 'Work permits yet . . . O.K., David, I'll see what Robin can do . . . Come on, Peter. We'd better be getting back.'

'You're not staying the night?' the little man asked her disappointedly. He half raised himself on his folded forearms.

'Can't, David. We were thinking of it coming over, but after your good word on Mayhew we'll have to report back to Robin and Helen.'

'I've got some baked lobster,' the little man pleaded seductively. 'A new recipe, known only to me and the readers of *Good Housekeeping*. And a bottle of some really superlative Chablis. We'll eat early . . . Blackmore, why don't you persuade this dutiful creature to stay?'

Jassy shook her head again. 'Bless your sweet old Bostonian heart, darling,' she said, 'but it's still "No." Robin would nail my hide to a door if we didn't check in now. Another time, eh?'

'Another time,' the little man echoed dolefully. He watched her with fondness as she stood up, patting and tugging at her cap, and at the two canary-coloured fragments that made up her costume. To Peter Blackmore he added, 'This would

75

be a great profession if women were not eligible. They bring an ugly note of seriousness into it that I have always deplored.'

'Into everything,' Peter Blackmore agreed. 'See you again, Patterson.'

'Surely,' the little man said. Jassy suddenly dived, in a low underslung arc that landed her five yards away in the cooling water. She began to swim to the small crescent of beautifully tended white beach. Peter Blackmore waved farewell to the little man and swam after her.

II

The little man, David Patterson, stayed on the raft for half an hour after Jassy Vane and Peter Blackmore had left him. Then he glanced at the heavy, knobbed diver's watch he wore and slipped into the water himself.

He swam ashore leisurely and walked up the fine grit of the beach, through the sawn-off dwarf coconut trees crowned with thatched mushroom tops that shaded the tables. He stopped for a word with the man in charge of the beach bar, and went on to the kitchen to inspect the evening's menu. Then he climbed the service stairs to the owner's suite.

He showered and put on a dressing-gown before sitting at his desk to make up the pay sheet for Saturday.

At about seven o'clock, one of the waiters brought him an early supper of stuffed avocado, the lobster he had spoken of so highly, strawberries and cream and a half-bottle of Taitinger. He ate this at his desk before changing into a white dinner jacket.

Between seven forty-five and midnight, he did an excellent job of convincing the seventy-odd guests in his hotel that this was their home from home.

At midnight, he went back to his suite, undressed, put on

his pyjamas, brushed his teeth, and looked briefly down from the balcony outside his bedroom at the couples dancing around the swimming-pool to the music of the band he had bribed away from a fellow hotelier sixty miles down the coast at Ocho Rios.

He was awakened after one by the first cramps of dysenteric pain. At two o'clock he just made it to the service telephone, and the porter two floors below who answered could barely understand his whispers of agony as he called for a doctor.

Neural paralysis set in at five. And at six-thirty, his ageing heart suddenly surrendered.

Chapter Six

Our Mr. Anyo

'Poor little beggar,' Robin McKay said. 'He didn't have to go that far out on the limb for us . . . Dammit, why didn't he tell us he was going to go sniffing around on his own? Poor stupid little beggar.'

'Maybe he wouldn't have if you'd shown him that cable from Mayhew to Anyo,' Peter Blackmore said. 'You should have levelled with him. As far as I can gather he always levelled with you.'

McKay looked at him across the table with a bleak anger that was somehow dispassionate and general . . . 'Botulism!' McKay flung out the word like an obscenity. 'Why didn't they gun him down in the street and leave a calling card? D'you realise that genuine cases of botulism are so rare the medics in Montego Bay didn't even recognise the symptoms until he was nearly dead? And they've got some good people over there. Between the locals and what the tourists bring in, they've seen about every disease there is to see.'

It was ten o'clock at night of the day on which David Patterson had died, and they were waiting at Jassy Vane's house for the taxi that would bring Anyo in from the airport. McKay and Peter Blackmore sat on opposite sides of the table in the dining-room, and the two women were together, through the archway, on one of the settees, talking in low voices. It had rained earlier in the evening and the house held the scents of damp green and flowers like a church during a funeral. Nobody was drinking, but there was a

double-decker tray set on coasters before Jassy and Helen
McKay with two Noretaki cups and saucers and a slender
coffee pot in Danish steel that looked like the casing of an
elegant shell; two more of the cups and saucers had been
pushed to the centre of the table by the two men.

Helen McKay said, 'The thing we must decide now is
whether Peter and Jassy are blown. Whoever got David must
have been watching him all day.'

'If they're going to start getting anxious about everybody
who spoke to David yesterday, they'll have a lot to choose
from,' McKay said. 'No, I don't think we have to worry
about that. Whoever fingered him didn't like what he'd been
up to in the States. One of those old pals of his, perhaps, or
somebody who heard that he had been asking questions.'

'If he was as good as you say,' Peter Blackmore suggested,
'it must have been one of his old pals. He would have known
how to ask discreetly. *And* if it was one of his old pals, then
you'd better start thinking that Mayhew is as big and efficient
as Patterson said it was. Big enough to have someone who
used to work with him turn him over. Big enough to get hold
of botulinus toxin . . . You can't just buy that stuff in any
drug-store, you know . . . Efficient enough to have him followed and poisoned within forty-eight hours. *And* if they're
that serious, how come the other agencies don't seem to
know more about them than they do?'

'Because the other agencies didn't have the right girl at the
right time in the right town who let a post office clerk make
love to her,' Jassy told him. She looked as if her cheeks had
fallen in on themselves, and there were smudges under her
eyes, rough against the smooth matt of her skin. When she
plucked at one of the cushions against which she was leaning,
they could see the faint trembling in her fingers. 'It's the
only bright spot in this whole bloody business so far—that we
know things about Mayhew nobody else does.'

Without taking his gaze from the woman's twitching hand, Peter Blackmore asked softly, 'Why the hell don't you just pass what you know over to one of the big chaps, Robin? Who do we keep fooling ourselves we're fooling? A little shitty-arse country like this . . . Tell one of the big bad wolves what you know and let them take it from there. They want Mayhew. From what Patterson said, they want him badly . . .'

'You don't understand, Peter,' McKay said, as softly. 'But I think you should if you're going to stay with us . . . Information is the one thing you don't *give* in this business, unless you get something in return. You sell it . . . Sometimes you *look* as if you're giving it, but there's always a conditional clause about equal payment in the future . . . The only thing that counts is having hard news to bargain with . . . We're not telling anybody anything about Mayhew—except what we want them to know . . . Don't ask me why. That's the way it is.'

'Then pull her out of it,' Peter Blackmore said. 'Now.' He leaned forward and stabbed his forefinger harshly at Jassy. 'Look at her, McKay. She's been shivering like a wet cat since we got the news about Patterson this morning. She's not going to be much use the deeper in we get. Pull her out now—or *I'm* out . . . Don't ask me why. That's the way it is.'

Helen McKay stood up suddenly: a taut, dense little sausage with vibrations of cold wrath. She came through the archway and put her hands on the table and leaned forward, putting her face close to Peter Blackmore's.

She said, 'Now listen to me, Peter . . . It's the last time I'm going to say this . . . You're nothing special. You're a volunteer like everybody else who works for us. If you stick with us you could become very good because you're very bright, but at the moment you're just somebody we need who has agreed to help—on our terms . . . We'll decide who to tell what and who to pull out. If you're not going to be worse than useless you'll have to accept that . . . Jassy offered you one chance to opt out. Now we're offering you another. If you think we don't know what we're doing, you can drive out of here . . . But if you mean to stay, we're not going to give you a third chance. You may be king of the castle in your canefields, but with us you'll just have to learn a few of our ground rules.'

Peter Blackmore met the gaze of inquiry in her hard little blue eyes calmly. McKay and Jassy were intent and still.

'These rules of yours,' Peter Blackmore said finally, 'are stinking rules. You know that?'

'Yes,' Helen McKay replied without heat. 'But if you try to play by any others you end up dead. Or a lot of people who depend on you end up dead. We didn't make the rules, Peter —they were wished on us.'

'When d'you begin to like the rules?'

'Never.'

'That's not true. *You* like them, Helen. Robin doesn't, and Jassy hates them. But *you* find them fun, don't you?'

'In a way . . . Don't you too, Peter? Isn't that the reason you try to bitch me whenever you can? Because you find the rules are the ones you have always wanted to play by?'

Peter Blackmore shrugged. He glanced at McKay, who managed to examine him and the file he was holding at the same time, without appearing to look at him. Jassy had stopped plucking at the cushion and was half reclined on the settee with the edge of her skirt up around her waist, staring at the ceiling. Only her stillness showed how hard she was listening.

'Yes,' Peter Blackmore said finally, and it was characteristic of him that there was no false or sentimental tone of regret in his confession. 'I wish I didn't get such a nice big kick in the guts when I think of your rules, but I do. It's been a part of me I've never liked, and I'd have kept it quiet, too, if you bastards hadn't come along and let it off the chain. Why didn't you leave me alone to grow sugar and look after my people? I was getting pretty good at that, and I'd have got better.'

Helen McKay smiled—a curiously comforting and understanding smile—and reached forward, patted his cheek and gently pulled his ear. Again, it was as though the two of them shared a family resemblance: a closeness of blood and a shorthand of past intimacies that excluded the others.

She said, 'Whatever you do, Peter, never lose that conscience of yours. We need it as much as we need everything else you can bring in. It's not a commodity that lasts long in this business.'

'What you mean,' Peter Blackmore said sourly, 'is that Puritans make the best soldiers. That's it, isn't it?'

Helen McKay smiled again.

'Something like that,' she said. 'Give the man a drink,' she added over her shoulder to Jassy, 'and give yourself one too.'

'Should I?' Jassy asked, beginning to rise. 'You know what it's been like these past few months. Aren't you afraid I might get started on another jag?'

'Go on,' Helen McKay said. 'You need it. I don't want Anyo to see you like that. Besides, we have our resident conscience around now.' She grinned at Peter Blackmore.

McKay's huge black pelted hands beat a triumphal tattoo on the table, like two bears dancing a jig. His chipped, deeply scored face, in which there was always far too much humour for a policeman, creased deeper with a lopsided smile.

'In the Middle Ages,' he told his wife, 'you'd have been the Abbess of one of those big convents—so long as there was a fat lusty Abbot in the neighbourhood to come visiting. In the Renaissance, Machiavelli would probably have consulted you about that book of his. Nowadays . . . well, I'm glad you're on my side . . . You and your protégé there.' He gestured to Peter Blackmore.

'*My* protégé!' Helen McKay said. 'I seem to remember it was you who recruited him originally.'

'And I seem to remember it was you who spotted him,' McKay replied. 'I thought it was a rotten idea at first.'

They were both looking very pleased—with themselves and with each other.

'You two,' Jassy said, her back to them as she mixed drinks at the sideboard. 'You two old frauds. You could sell ham sandwiches in a synagogue.'

II

The taxi-driver who was somehow always waiting for a reserved fare when anybody at the airport wanted him said, 'He's outside, sir,' to Robin McKay.

'Did he come alone?'

'Hard to say, sir. I think so, but Anyo plays it close to the chest. We weren't followed, that's for sure.'

'I know. But you wouldn't have to be. Anyo knew where you were bringing him. Get a trace on everybody who was on his flight. I don't think it will turn up anything. If he was bringing in anybody, they'd have come before this, and not from Venezuela either. But we might as well keep the chaps in Collation on their toes . . . What's so funny?'

The taxi-driver's face had begun to swell slightly at the cheeks and to glow with the suffused blood of a man who is trying not to laugh. He was tall, with the long, hosepipe arms of a fast bowler or an opening pitcher, and he had the pen-sharp face and wide thin mouth of a chocolate-coloured Voltaire.

'Sorry, sir,' he said, 'but that Anyo is a comedian. On the

way in he was telling me about a ghost agent they once planted in the French files: Count E. Bitertitzov. A White Russian who the K.G.B. had recruited. The Deuxième Bureau had a dozen men trying to find him for a year.'

'And he got away with *that*?' Peter Blackmore asked incredulously. 'But man, that's one which little boys tell each other in kindergarten: *The Czar's Revenge* by E. Bitertitzov.'

'Evidently they don't tell it in France,' McKay said. 'I'm glad you mentioned this, Sparkie,' he added to the taxi-driver. 'Our Mr. Anyo is a very cute fellow. Already he has you sharing a joke with him. That means if you ever have to clobber him you're going to be that fraction slower and you just might not make it . . . O.K., Sparkie, bring him in, then get down to Collation. We'll telephone for you when we want you to pick him up.'

III

It had always seemed to Peter Blackmore that white people who said all Chinese looked alike to them were either racially prejudiced or myopic. He felt the same way about those who made similar statements about Negroes, Hindus, Eskimos, Polynesians or any of the coloured races. In his honest moments, he would admit that this feeling was probably based on a subtle racial prejudice in himself. Like so many of his Creole kind—Europe's descendants who were the end products of three hundred tropical years—he found most foreign white faces bland and boring until he got to know their owners better. It disturbed and irritated him, when he was abroad, to be taken for an Englishman, and he would glance apprehensively, as soon as he could after someone had made such an observation, into the nearest wall-mirror or plate window to see if indeed his skin had taken on the pallid pink transparency of the temperate denizen.

But not even the most obtuse white could have claimed that Anyo looked like any other Chinese. At a rickshaw stand in Hong Kong, bent over a hoe in a line of peasants in some paddy field, or seated in a group photograph of staff officers, he would emanate the tooled and exquisite distinction of a hand-made doll carved by some master craftsman for a royal client, never to be repeated for common consumption. Yet anybody who made the mistake of thinking that there was anything fragile and toy-like about the tiny hands and feet, the neatness of the nose, lips and chin on the brown, weather-cured face and the delicately fashioned symmetry of the impeccably suited body would hardly have time to realise the seriousness of his mistake. No toymaker could have created the small, deeply set and shiny eyes that surveyed the four Jamaicans who had risen as he came in. One had the impression that people always stood whenever Anyo came into a room for the first time.

'Anyo,' McKay said genially. 'You're a welsher. You agreed to stay out of my territory. What d'you think you're doing playing around with Mayhew?'

' "Welsher"?' Anyo's perfect forehead wrinkled decoratively. 'I don't think I understand that term, Commissioner. Is it a Jamaican idiom?'

McKay grinned and uttered a single syllable in Cantonese which none of the others except Anyo understood. Anyo smiled: his teeth were porcelain white: replacements from a time when conditions had destroyed his own, and when nobody of his value to a cause could afford to have toothache. 'That's what "welsher" means,' McKay told him. 'I learnt that when I was a young inspector breaking up peaka-pow* combines in West Kingston.'

* Peaka pow is a South Chinese gambling game based on number series which are changed every week. It is so complicated that only a Chinese can manage to keep track of its weekly permutations and

85

'Cantonese,' Anyo said. 'A barbarous dialect. You can hardly call it a language. Confucius or Li Po would have gone mad if they had ever tried to think in it.'

'You Sze-chuanese,' McKay said. 'You really dislike the Cantonese, don't you? They always bring an untidy element into your plans.'

' "Dislike," ' Anyo said thoughtfully. 'Not dislike, Commissioner. *Loathe*. As a Sze-chuanese, I sometimes feel closer to even the Russians than I do to my comrades from the Pearl River.'

'What will you drink?' Peter Blackmore asked. 'Brandy?'

He had not seen Anyo for eighteen months; and then only briefly in circumstances he did not like to remember; but he could recall the small, lethal Chinese taking brandy then as most men would have sipped coffee from a demi-tasse.

'Mr. Blackmore,' Anyo said and smiled and inclined his head slightly. 'I thought he had left your organisation,' he added to Robin McKay.

'You must have been misinformed,' Robin McKay said without expression.

'No,' Anyo said. 'No, I don't think I was misinformed . . . You're very lucky to have got him back in. If you hadn't, somebody else would have recruited him sooner or later.'

On a telephone, one could not have told where Anyo's English had been formed. It might have been fashioned from the conversations overheard at the tables of a very good restaurant in London by a young waiter; it might have been learnt in a Berlitz School in Zürich where his tutor had been a penniless Anglo-Irish novelist; it might have been moulded in the news-room of the B.B.C. Home Service. Or perhaps he had been once stationed in mid-Atlantic on a raft, with two

---

combinations. For this reason, it has been declared illegal by the largely non-Chinese authorities in Jamaica.

receivers and had made his own mixture of whatever came over from England and America.

He took the tulip-shaped glass of brandy which Peter Blackmore offered him and asked, with another slight inclination of his head, for permission to sit. Helen McKay waved to the seat on the far side of the circular rosewood table, where he would have to face them all. He bowed, sat and with the delicacy of a humming-bird sipping from a flower, drained his brandy. Peter Blackmore brought the decanter from the sideboard, filled the glass again, and left the decanter beside him.

Helen McKay said nicely, 'I'm glad you came when we called you, Anyo. Whether we ever call you again—whether anybody ever calls you again—depends on what you tell us about Mayhew. You realise that, don't you?'

Anyo carefully filled his glass to the brim from the decanter. He took a packet of Gauloise Disque Bleu from somewhere in his jacket, where it must have been magically flattened like a calling card since his suit fitted him like the creaseless hide of clothing in a fashion plate.

'Of course,' he said, and looked at the four faces across the table, without fear or dislike or nervousness or hate—or anything but a deeply interested appreciation. 'That's why I came.' Somehow he managed to appear to be addressing only the two men, not so much dismissing the two women as making them an insignificant part of the furniture. 'How did you find out that I was in with Mayhew? Or is that a stupid question?'

'It could have been,' Helen McKay said. 'It could have been until Mayhew killed one of our operatives yesterday over in Montego Bay.'

'*What!*' Anyo lit another Disque Blue from the half-smoked tube he was holding, and looked irritably around until Jassy rose and brought him an ugly, impractical ash-

87

tray in Jamaican ceramic from the sideboard. 'Helen . . . Robin . . . They assured me there'd be no killing. I was most emphatic on that point . . . No killing. You'd never have known anything about the operation. It was all between my people and them. Nothing to do with you . . . I swear, there was to be no killing. They assured me of that. I wouldn't have gone in with them otherwise.'

'How about Rilke and his angelic voices?' Peter Blackmore asked from the wall next to the sideboard, against which he was leaning with his hands in his pockets. 'Is he really among the angels? Or did you and Mayhew just lean on him hard enough for him to hear the echoes of the heavenly choir?'

Anyo looked across at him and gave a smile that was half a salute.

'You know Rilke, Mr. Blackmore?' he asked. 'I wouldn't have thought . . .'

'I know enough Rilke to recognise the first lines from the "Duino Elegies," ' Peter Blackmore interrupted him evenly. 'We think you killed whoever was coded as Rilke, Anyo. We have that on one of the cables to you from Mayhew.'

'*Rilke.*' Anyo filled his glass again, put the stopper into the decanter with a gesture of contemptuous finality. 'Yes, we had to kill Rilke . . . But he was nothing . . . A squalid little gangster. Not even a Sicilian, but a mongrel from the South Tyrol. Greedy as only a German can be. Stupid. With no more sense of compromise than a pig. We had to kill him . . . but not here. He was killed in New York . . . Believe me, I did not know that anybody had been killed here until you told me . . . Believe me.'

He gestured at all of them with the cigarette he had lit, but barely puffed. His newly filled glass had not been touched. The exquisite, toy face had taken on disturbing planes and lines of bewilderment: a doll's face should never crumple

88

before any challenge if we are to continue to believe in it. 'Who was killed here?' he added. 'Why?'

'Anyo,' Helen McKay said, and it would have been more comfortable if her smile had not been, again, so pleasant. 'You have a lot of talking to do . . . And believe me, Anyo, it had better be convincing or we're going to set Jassy's dogs loose on you in the garden . . . That way nearly everybody will be happy: your people will believe you got careless; our police will just have to fill in a report about a foreign commercial gentleman who came calling on a nice Jamaican girl; and we will come to your rescue just too late to save you from being bitten to death. The only mourner will be Mayhew . . . You'd better start talking, Anyo, and we had better believe what you say.'

'Yes,' Anyo said, and took a very small swallow of his brandy, and lit another cigarette. 'Yes. I see what you mean. You don't have any Chinese blood in you, do you? Somewhere far back? Perhaps an adventurous ancestor in the tea trade?'

'No,' Helen McKay said, 'but thanks for the compliment.'

Chapter Seven

Candywine

The six-seater, twin-tailed, push-pull Cessna 180 taxied up the little airstrip which was veneered with the lemon and rose of dawn. High scrub, wild almond trees and dense cactus surrounded the strip on three sides, concealing it from the dirt road off which it was built; on the fourth side, at the end of its eastern approach, a grey, flat morning sea heaved as sluggishly as oil over banks of coral.

As the propellers stopped idling, a bouncy little Mini-Cooper came on to the runway and was driven up to the aeroplane. The door to the passenger's seat was opened and Anyo stepped on to the tarmac. He was wearing a green cotton sports shirt, green cotton slacks, sandals, dark glasses and a white plastic golfing cap. The outfit looked, as his clothes always did, as though he were modelling them for a very hard sell in *Playboy* or *Esquire*; but he managed to give the impression that he considered it unforgivably frivolous.

'My,' Jassy said as he stepped into the cabin from the footrest on the fuselage, 'You look really with it. Anyo, you're gear!'

Peter Blackmore in the second pilot's seat, had tilted it forward, leaning against the instrument panel, to give Anyo enough rooom to enter. Now he pushed the seat into position leaned back and turned round to watch Anyo as the little Chinese tightened the safety belt across his thighs and snapped the lock.

'Don't tease the gentleman, Jassy,' he said. 'He's old enough to be your father . . . You *do* look good in that outfit, Anyo,' he added. 'Rich . . . but confidently so, if you understand me.' He smiled.

'Can I roll this bloody bus now?' the pilot asked. 'Or are you all waitin' for somebody else?'

He was a chunky, middle-aged Virginian with red hair and a cheerful, utterly disillusioned face. Every year, fifteen thousand dollars were put into a numbered account in a stolid grey building on the Bahnhofstrasse in Zürich for him, and he was one of the very few foreigners in Jamaica with a permanent work permit to continue his real occupation which was crop spraying. He could have taken a light aircraft in through the front door of a small bungalow and out through the back. His only loyalties were to the mint-condition, First World War Fokker triplane he kept at the Flying Club on the Palisadoes and to the numbered bank account in Switzerland that accumulated yearly because he did for Robin McKay the sort of occasional job which meant no more to him than brushing his teeth.

II

The Arawak Indians called it Kandaywena. So did the Spaniards who had roasted the last Arawak chief of Jamaica on a griddle at the water's edge of the cay's most beautiful beach. The English who took Jamaica from the Spaniards had, with their unfailing instinct of practical poetry, gradually corrupted the name to Candywine.

It lay north-west of Montego Bay, just over the horizon if one was at sea level: a fat question mark of scrub-covered limestone, about seven miles long and three miles wide. The Indians, the Spaniards and the first English had used it as a hunting ground for the great green turtles that came to its

beaches to lay their eggs. Then as the Caribbean began to
fill up and the white and black men began to do what the red
had not—lift the eggs because they were supposed to in-
crease potency—the turtles had disappeared. During the
great wars between the French and the British in the
eighteenth and early nineteenth centuries, a fort and a
careenage had been maintained in the sheltered hook of the
question mark. Both had been abandoned before Napoleon
died on St. Helena, and Candywine ceased to be of much
value. Fishermen used it as a refuge in bad weather if they
were too far out when storm or hurricane struck. With the
coming of the motor-boat, picnic parties went out to it from
Montego Bay. An American millionaire of powerful but
eccentric mind had once tried unsuccessfully to restock the
beaches with turtle. During the Second World War, an
energetic commander of naval intelligence with more time
than occupation on his hands had insisted that the fort and
careenage be occupied again by a small detachment of
Jamaican volunteers and a submarine chaser. The local
soldiers and the British sailors had spent a halcyon war, with
just sufficient duties to flavour the monotony of frolicking
on the beaches by day and sailing the eight miles to Montego
Bay by night, and back again at dawn, in the liberty launch.

After the war, it returned to its uses as a fisherman's
occasional haven and as a picnic spot. The beaches along the
north coast of the main island were too good, too numerous,
and as yet too undeveloped, for the booming tourist industry
to bother with Candywine. It made a pleasant day's excursion for those staying at the big hotels in Montego, the
name looked romantic in the brochures, and there was even
some genuine architectural value to the solidly graceful fort,
the old naval hospital and the eighteenth-century reservoirs
which had all been constructed in a time when anything not
planned to last five hundred years at least made men feel

uneasy. The sands drifted into the barracks and rooms of the fortifications; plump iguana lizards waddled across the rocks under the tough, austere scrub; picnic parties and fishermen left small middens of emptied tins, broken beer bottles and used toilet paper.

The coming of the cheap jet fare and popular travel began to affect Jamaica, as they have affected every other place that sells immovable assets of climate, scenery or culture. The basic instinct of the rich—to put as much distance as is practical and possible between themselves and the merely prosperous—began to assert itself. Candywine, suddenly, was an ideal territory for an exclusive development. Close enough to the mountain drives, to the duty-free shops, to the polo fields, to the insulated hotels of the old money that had got in first along Jamaica's north coast to make commuting by hydrofoil, hovercraft, light aeroplane and helicopter an easy matter, it was yet far enough away from all amenities and public services to need heavy initial investment before it could become profitable. Inquiries began to be made. Four and five figure cheques began to be lodged in banks far away from Jamaica. Forgotten title deeds were found in government offices and removed. More four and five figure cheques were lodged. Candywine became hot property over a fire of dollars before the first bulldozer cleared the first site for the first terrace leading down from the first casino to the first hundred yards of private beach rights.

III

They approached Candywine from the north-east, as though they were coming in from the Bahamas or Miami. Five miles from it, the Virginian pilot pushed the nose of the Cessna down and levelled when they were a hundred feet above the sea. By the time they reached the curve at the top of the

question mark, they were down to thirty feet with the flaps
hanging vertically and the two throttles at maximum boost.

The pilot shouted cheerfully as they crossed the band of
white foam along the reef, 'If one of these engines even clears
its throat, this ol' bus is going in like a stone. I could land
her faster'n we're making now.'

'Can't you bring us in any lower?' Jassy asked. Her face
was pressed against the perspex of her window as the bush
and rock of the islet rushed under the fuselage. Anyo and
Peter Blackmore were looking down from their windows too
and once Peter Blackmore made a hurried note on a scratch
pad he held, without glancing at the paper. Almost before
Jassy had finished her question, they had cleared the tail of
the question mark and were climbing in a steep wide bank
over the open sea. Under the starboard wing they could see
the buildings of Montego Bay hugging the coast and strag-
gling in clusters up the green hillls.

'Next time over,' the pilot said, 'you can lean out and pick
yourself a lizard right off the ground. Hang on, folks, we're
going to get an arseful of cactus, but if that's what the lady
wants . . .'

The little cabin quivered with the beat of the straining
engines, and gravity was like one passenger too many as the
lowered flaps pushed aside the air beneath them.

They could distinguish the features of the workmen looking up from the roofs, scaffolding and foundation areas of the
sprawling, multi-patioed bungalows which were being built
all along the white beach inside the hook of the question
mark leading from the old fort and hospital. Bulldozers had
already landscaped over two hundred acres of the sloping
ground that rose to the knobbly spine running the length of
the cay. Barges full of topsoil had come and gone from
Montego Bay, and already the first patches of the moss-like
zoysia grass were beginning to sprout between the tastefully

positioned flower beds. Fully grown trees—almonds like opened green umbrellas, palms, lignum-vitae, cedars—had been brought out from Montego Bay too, and cast nicely calculated patches of shade across the development. By the time the winter season started, the fort which was being fitted out as the casino and the old hospital which was being converted into the service area would be ready. Only the huge reservoirs which had been meant to contain enough water for two thousand men during what might have been a six months' siege were being left as they were. Built by slaves working in Candywine's limestone and a mortar of a forgotten formula, they still held water better, after two hundred years, than the most modern of the main island's concrete tanks and catchments.

Along the eastern flank of the cay's spine, two miles from the tranquil, lucid bay around which the bungalows were being built, the beginnings of an airstrip had been gashed and stamped across the scrub and rock—long enough and wide enough to permit the landing or take-off of the largest executive jet. Its outer edge skirted the stony beach on which the sea broke in cloudy green surf. From the Cessna, they could see the abrupt transition of colour as the deep water pushed by the north-east winds was checked at the edge of the shallow shelf running down from the beach to the Candywine Trench quarter of a mile off-shore. Three slate-grey nurse sharks patrolled the deep in open formation like submarines, waiting for the schools of fish to come in to feed on the small marine life that lived at the lip between the shelf and the trench.

Jassy leaned forward and put her face between the shoulders of the two men in the front seats.

'Don't make another pass,' she told the pilot. 'There's some joker down there in the fort with field glasses. Big ones, judging by the lenses' reflections.'

'Yes, ma'am,' the pilot said. 'I saw them too. Once is happenstance, twice is coincidence, but after three times a smart man starts askin' himself questions.'

The little plane suddenly became lively and more manageable as the pilot began to take it up and around in a wide arc over Montego Bay and the backdrop of hills. He flew southeast for five minutes until they were above the sugar valleys then turned east by north and brought them out over the coast forty miles down from Candywine, above the little airstrip from which they had taken off an hour and a half before. When the rear wheels touched they made no more sound than the palms of two hands pushed across a table top, and the bump of the front wheel on the tarmac would not have spilt a glass of water balanced on the fuselage. At the side of the runway there was a small, aluminium shack, used sometimes as a hangar when a hurricane or a big blow suddenly threatened and one of the Flying Club members had to secure his aircraft and go back to Kingston by road.

The Virginian swung the little Cessna across the tarmac and taxied it into the doll's house hangar and cut the engines. Except for the noises of a switched off, finely tuned engine settling to rest, it was suddenly quiet. Quiet and cool and restfully shadowed under the double roof of the little hut with their backs to the first glare of the day on the asphalt strip outside.

'You lying little bastard,' Jassy said to Anyo. 'I ought to have shot you over Candywine and dumped you out where the sharks could have made a business breakfast of you.'

The Virginian pilot said in the anxious and conciliatory tones of a man caught between two belligerent drunks in a bar, 'I'm sure you got good reasons for wantin' this gen'l-man dead, Miss Jassy, but please don't go lettin' off no side-arms inside this lil ol' bus. It bruises easy. If you got to shoot him, take him outside, Mister Blackmore an' me will help you gladly . . . An' I'll drop him clear out over the China Sea afterwards if you want me to.'

Peter Blackmore had unfastened his safety belt. He was half turned in his seat, looking over the back and down at the inch of blue-black tube bridging the space between Jassy Vane's hand and Anyo's stomach.

'It's all right,' he said to the pilot, without looking at him, 'she's not going to blow any holes in your aeroplane. She's not even going to blow any holes in our friend . . . All the same,' he added to Anyo, 'I'm surprised at you. Taking a risk like that. You can see she's edgy. Why the hell didn't you tell us the truth the other night?'

Anyo shrugged. Under the peak of the golfing cap and behind the visor of the sunglasses, much of his face was hidden, but there were marks of age around the corners of his nose and mouth, which Peter Blackmore could not remember seeing before.

'What made you suspect that I had told you less than the truth?' Anyo asked them. His voice was even but very tired.

'Less than the truth!' Jassy whispered savagely. 'You've got a nerve, Anyo, if you call that fancy packet you handed us less than the truth. You didn't expect to get away with it, did you?'

'Anyo,' Peter Blackmore's voice was carefully casual and he had not taken his eyes from Jassy's face. 'Don't press your luck any further. You're as near dead now as you ever have been, and if she decides to go ahead with it I can't stop her. She'll be sorry afterwards, but you'll still be dead.'

Anyo said to Jassy like an adult in the doorway of a kitchen watching a baby reach up for the pan of water boiling on the stove, 'Put your gun away. You still need me and I'll tell you the truth this time. When do you want to see me?'

'To-night,' Jassy said. Neither of the two men watching her saw the pistol she had been pressing against Anyo's side

97

disappear from sight: they only saw her fingers snapping shut the clasp of her handbag. 'Eleven at my place. Robin and Helen have a government reception to attend and they won't be able to leave it before then. Be there, Anyo. Don't try to pull any funnies like flying out from Montego Bay this afternoon.'

'Don't be silly,' Anyo scolded her, almost paternally. 'You know I have to be there.'

They all got out then, and the three men pushed the little aircraft from the hangar and turned its nose into the wind. Jassy Vane stayed inside, leaning against one of the aluminium walls. In the time that it took to manœuvre the Cessna, she had smoked a quarter of a king-sized Pall Mall and was lighting another from it.

The pilot said, 'Mr. Blackmore, my business is takin' you all wherever you all want to go, but I have to tell you, sir, that you got a crazy woman on your hands. D'you realise what might have happened if she'd evah pulled the trigger on that lil toy of hers inside there? The cabin of a prop job like this is so full of high octane vapour just after a switch off that a gun flash could send it up like a bomb.'

'She'll be all right,' Peter Blackmore told him, with more hope than conviction. 'She was getting something out of her system.'

Anyo said dispassionately, 'You'll have to be careful with her, Mr. Blackmore. As she is now, she's dangerous to your organisation.'

'She won't do yours any good either.'

'Exactly. I don't think you should continue using her.'

'She'll be all right,' Peter Blackmore repeated. 'She was paying you back for Patterson. Your friends shouldn't have done that to him.'

'I told you that I had nothing to do with Patterson's death. Even if I had known of him, I would never have agreed to it.'

'You lied about Candywine. You might be lying about Patterson.'

'You know I am not. Patterson dead is an embarrassment to me.'

'Then you ought to choose friends who don't embarrass you. I think Mayhew is out to fuck you fifty-seven ways, Anyo. If I were you, I'd be worrying.'

'I am. That's why you can be sure I'll tell you the truth.'

'You could have saved time by telling us the truth the other night,' Peter Blackmore said, and sniffed derisively. 'Submarine pens! Christ, Anyo, you must be simple-minded if you thought we'd swallow that. One submarine, maybe, to land somebody or pick him up, but you could do that just as easily anywhere along the coast here. You wouldn't need Candywine. But not submarine pens . . . A regular shuttle . . . The Americans would be on to you before you could say "Chairman Mao".'

Anyo had taken off the extravagant sun goggles. Now he put them on again hurriedly, as if to hide the symptoms of a painful embarrassment.

'It was not one of my better inventions, Mr. Blackmore,' he said. 'But your news about Patterson was . . . disturbing. I was committed to the preposterous fiction as I uttered it . . . But why did you join the comedy? I could not believe, at first, that my fairy tale could be convincing . . . To you, perhaps, or even to her,' he gestured with a slight lift of his chin to Jassy Vane inside the hanger, 'but not to McKay or the wife. Then I began to hope—foolishly. Especially when this tourist flight over Candywine was suggested.'

'We had to be sure,' Peter Blackmore interrupted him. 'Also we wanted to see what you might be trying not to look for when we went over. And then, of course, there *is* a submarine in it somewhere. It *must* have been on your mind for an old pro like you to try selling such a gold brick. But we'll find that out to-night, won't we? When you talk to the big brass. Here's your car,' he added, as the Mini-Cooper in which Anyo had arrived at dawn appeared over the rise at the end of the runway.

They watched as it was driven down the tarmac and swung to a halt twenty yards from the Cessna. The driver was trim and off-brown and young, with crisp, butter-coloured curls scoured into white glints by sun and salt water. He wore dark glasses as big as the mask of a welder's helmet and a trim sweat shirt with the words SCUBA DUBA in big black letters across the chest, top and bottom of an imprinted red badge. The Mini-Cooper seemed to fit around him like a saddle.

Peter Blackmore and Anyo walked over to the car. The young man opened the passenger door from inside, stretching his arm across the seat, without looking at them.

'He's all yours,' Peter Blackmore said, closing the door as Anyo settled himself in the car, 'until to-night at eleven. Jassy's place. Don't let him out of your sight.'

'I could take him out after marlin,' the young man suggested. 'Dicky Hernandez has a new engine he wants run in before the tournament.'

'Splendid,' Peter Blackmore agreed. 'That is, if you like fishing?' he inquired of Anyo. 'You'll have a good day with him.' He pointed at the young man. 'He's part marlin himself.'

'Why not?' Anyo said. 'A man in my profession should never miss the opportunity of learning something new.'

'Good,' Peter Blackmore said, stepping back a pace from the car. 'Have fun.'

'I will,' Anyo promised him politely, as if Peter Blackmore's last words had been a piece of unfamiliar slang, the meaning of which could only be derived from its context.

Part Two

Chapter Eight

Manhattan to Westchester

A gust of wind balled itself tight between the buildings on the corner of Fifth Avenue, rolled furiously down the street pushing rain before it and sprayed them with hard drops as they ducked from the taxi into the shelter of the canopy. The long slickers worn by the doorman and the porters shone with wet and flapped soddenly around their ankles.

In the lobby, the smells of tweed, leather and silk steaming dry in the central heating overlay the expensive fragrance of a good hotel.

Peter Blackmore and Jassy Vane went up to the reception counter. Like the counters in all of this class of hotel, it looked as if it had been fashioned from one solid block of mahogany. And the carpet did not have to reach knee-high to proclaim what it had cost: it was the dress uniform of the buttressed floor beneath.

'Peter Broome, please,' Peter Blackmore said. 'I believe you have a reservation for my wife and me.'

The clerk said, 'Mr. Broome . . . From Jamaica is it not, sir? Yes, indeed. It was a pleasure to get your cable . . . We were able to give you a suite overlooking the Park. Sixth floor if that is all right, sir.'

'Splendid,' Peter Blackmore said. 'Have our things taken up, will you, after I sign in . . . It's been a damned wet drive in from Kennedy and I need a damned wet drink.'

'Certainly, sir,' the clerk said, and opened before him a ledger which looked as if it might have been the visitors' book in a very good, very old house. The clerk added unhappily, 'If you don't mind, sir, we have to ask our guests to fill in this form . . .' as if explaining a sordid but necessary requirement of hygiene to a mixed audience.

'Quite understand,' Peter Blackmore said as he wrote on the heavy, slightly dimpled paper of the ledger. 'It's the same everywhere nowadays. Hardly worth travelling unless you have to. By the time you've finished filling in all the damn' forms, it's time to start thinking about going back home.' He wrote *Mr. & Mrs. Peter Broome, C/o Halberd & Silverman, 326 Duke Street, Kingston, Jca.* 'My lawyers,' he explained to the clerk, Now, where's the bar?'

'The Park Room is over there, sir. Or if you and Mrs. Broome would prefer something a little cosier and more informal, may I suggest the Retreat . . . Front!' The clerk tapped the knob of a large silver dome and a discreetly penetrating *ping* counterpointed the hum of voices in the lobby. A small figure in a blue pillbox cap, a blue shell jacket and several winking buttons appeared as if a lamp had been rubbed. He had the face and body of a very old child or a very young octogenarian.

'How about it, my dear?' Peter Blackmore asked Jassy Vane. 'Shall we be cosy and informal in the Retreat?'

Jassy Vane shrugged a shoulder on which green cashmere was laid like a second, thicker skin, and smiled the absent, assured smile of the wife for whom every oyster will yield a pearl.

The décor of the Retreat was faded rose and mellowed gilt,

with a small, horseshoe bar of almost black teak. The bottles ranked behind the bar looked as if each had been custom made. Each alcove seemed set behind a screen of opaque, yet invisible glass.

'A Manhattan for me, please,' Jassy said to Peter Blackmore, 'and I recommend you have one too. They're New York's greatest contribution to Western civilisation, and only a New York bartender can make them properly. Everywhere else they taste like a mixture of meth and brown sugar.'

'All right, Mrs. Broome,' Peter Blackmore said. 'I'll take your word for it. You know this city.' He raised his hand and a waiter shimmered and materialised on the other side of the low table before the banquette on which they sat. It was one of those hotels where a guest is incognito until the moment attention is required. 'Two Manhattans, please,' Peter Blackmore ordered. 'My wife tells me they can cause the dead to walk. What are you giggling about?' he added as the man dematerialised.

'I'm not giggling. That was a chuckle.'

'O.K. Let's compromise. Let's call it a chiggle. What are you chiggling about?'

'You . . . The way you're playing the husband. When you were checking in I *felt* like your wife. I'm sure you even fooled the clerk. And those boys learn to spot Mr. and Mrs. John Smith the way a policeman can read fingerprints. You must have had a lot of practice.'

'You aren't doing too badly yourself.'

'Oh, it comes naturally to women. Especially when they can act it out in a place like this. There's nothing like a little luxury to bring out the Sarah Bernhardt in a girl.' She looked around at the other alcoves where couples and groups sat as if they had purchased all the time in the world along with their liquor; at the gliding waiters; at the three bartenders who used shakers and bottles like magicians hired for a party; at the lighting which elicited the best from every face. She said, '*Brother!* I should get a run like this every time. You're probably spending more on our suite than Robin gets for his year's budget.'

'I've always wanted to stay here,' Peter Blackmore said. 'My mother sent me a postcard from here once, when I was about six. My father was playing polo out on Long Island. He was captain of the Jamaica team. I suppose her job was to see the American teams took the field too tired to play rough. She was very good at that.'

'Are we getting bitter and twisted?'

'Christ, no! That's the way they liked to live. I used to get a lot of postcards. From all over the place . . . Buenos Aires, the Riviera, New Delhi, Hurlingham, Mexico, Dublin, Budapest . . . Geography was my best subject at school.'

'I suppose it never occurred to them to take you along. Your geography would have been even better then, I mean.'

'There you suppose wrong . . . It did occur to them. But they were people of strong character. They resisted the temptation . . . Like the desert saints when pretty girls came to them in their dreams.'

The waiter brought their drinks as Peter Blackmore spoke; placed the glasses as if conjuring them from the table-top and vanished. Jassy Vane raised her glass, moistened her lips without drinking and looked at Peter Blackmore with shiny, reflective eyes.

She said, 'You frighten me a little, you know. I know Robin and I know Helen, and I even know me a little . . . But you are a special breed of cat . . . What would happen, Peter, if you ever had to act against me? If you ever had to make a choice between me and . . . and *something* you had agreed to finish?'

Peter Blackmore drank half of his Manhattan. From the inside pocket of his jacket he took a packet of Rothman's filter tip, but the cigarette he extracted was hand rolled, and the smoke hung heavy and sweetish when he lit it.

'I would kill you,' he said, after a careful, unaffected moment of reflection. 'I wouldn't want to, but if I had to, I would. You people shouldn't have dug that bit out of me, you know. Two years ago, I couldn't have killed anybody. I was a decent hypocrite. Now you've made an honest man of me, and you'll have to answer to God for that. You should have left me alone with my conscience . . .'

II

They finished their Manhattans in silence. Peter Blackmore slumped in his seat, resting on the middle of his spine, his long legs stretched under the low table, his long, obstinately cleft chin sunk on to his tie. Jassy Vane was half turned towards him, holding her glass by the stem with both hands and turning it constantly between sips.

She said, 'Don't look like that.'

'Like what?'

'Like you're looking now. It doesn't go with your sort of face.'

He lifted his chin and glanced at her and smiled with a remoteness that was more chilling than no smile at all.

'I was thinking.'

'I know. And I wouldn't buy any of it. They gave you a rotten time, didn't they?'

'Who,' he asked in a tone as remote and impersonal as his smile, 'gave me a rotten time?'

'Those crummy parents of yours for a start, and—whoever else brought you up when they were sending you postcards.'

'Oh, sure. I was really a case for one of those societies that prevent cruelty to children. All they ever gave me was a big house, a trained nurse, a couple of tutors with about fifteen degrees between them and so much money I could finance a small war if I wanted to. It's enough to break your heart, isn't it?'

'And now,' she said, quietly, looking into her drink, 'we're finishing the job they began on you. In another couple of years there won't be much left of the Peter Blackmore we picked up. I'm going to miss him.'

'Stop crying into your beer,' Peter Blackmore said. His heavy-boned face was suddenly vivid with a disconcerting transition to gaiety. 'You people didn't pick me up. I joined. Sooner or later, we'd have found each other.' He signalled for the waiter again and ordered a second round of Manhattans. When the man had gone, he shot the cuff of his shirt and glanced at his watch. 'I'll telephone the old gentleman now,' he said. 'He should be home by this. Unless you want to do it. He might be more responsive to a bit of sex on the hook.'

She shook her head. 'No. From what our people tell us, he's one of the old school. He's going to be cagey, whichever way we approach him; and if a strange woman telephones asking for an appointment, God knows what he's going to start imagining.'

'O.K.' Peter Blackmore rose. 'It shouldn't take long. I'll be back in a minute.'

'Play him gently. If he decides he isn't going to see us, he's too big for us to pressure.'

'Not too big,' Peter Blackmore said, turning at the entrance to the alcove. 'Too *old*. When you're as old as he is, there isn't a goddam thing anybody can make you do that you don't agree to. Except kill you . . . And even that may involve a sort of covenant.'

He crossed the carpet, entered the lobby and approached the public telephones. Unlike the modern helmets into which one sticks one's head and hears every conversation except one's own, the booths had been designed for total privacy.

Peter Blackmore took a card from the breast pocket of his suit, put it on top of the coin box, and dialled the operator. When she answered, he read her the Westchester number on the card.

'That will be thirty-five cents, please.'

He pushed a quarter and a dime into the slots. On the third burr, the receiver at the other end was lifted.

'Good evening. Mr. Robert Dalkeith's residence. May I be of assistance?'

It was the precise and tailored voice of a nearly extinct species: the English upper servant which only a few Americans and the best British Diplomatic posts could any more afford.

'Good evening,' Peter Blackmore said. 'May I speak to Mr. Dalkeith? Peter Broome here. From Jamaica. I believe he's expecting a call from me.'

'If you will excuse me, sir, I shall inquire if Mr. Dalkeith is able to come to the telephone. If you would be good enough to give me your number, sir—in case Mr. Dalkeith cannot take your call immediately.'

Peter Blackmore named the hotel and heard confidence and approval enter the voice at the other end of the wire.

'Certainly sir . . . I believe I hear Mr. Dalkeith in the hall now, sir . . . If you would be good enough to wait a minute until I inform him . . .'

It was much less than a minute when another voice said, 'Dalkeith. I got your letter, Broome. What d'you want?'

It was an old, light voice without much air behind it, but Peter Blackmore got the feeling that nothing except a total collapse of the lungs at the very end would ever make it quaver.

'I would like your permission to call on you, sir. At your

convenience. It is a matter of some urgency. Involving your firm. That is, involving some advice your firm is giving to certain investors of which I am one.'

'Don't deal with that any more, Mr. Broome. Thought they'd have told you that down at the office. Ask to see Leichman. He handles all that side of the business now ... See him ... Good night.'

'Mr. Dalkeith,' Peter Blackmore said quickly. 'I would like to see *you*, sir. I don't think Mr. Leichman would understand ... Hallo! Hallo! Are you still there, sir?'

The light, steady breath said, 'Yes. Can you come out tomorrow?'

'Yes, sir.'

'Shall I send my car for you?'

'That won't be necessary, sir. I can rent one and drive out with my wife. What time would suit you?'

There was silence, then a faint creaking like dry branches stirred by a random wind.

'Come for luncheon. About eleven-thirty. I sleep in the afternoon.'

'Thank you, sir. We shall be there at eleven-thirty.'

'Yes. I'm sure you will. Good night, Mr. Broome.'

'Good night, Mr. Dalkeith. I appreciate this. You have been most considerate.'

'I have very little choice about being considerate, do I, Mr. Broome?'

'Come to think of it, you don't,' Peter Blackmore said cheerfully. 'But thank you, all the same.'

He laid the telephone across the rest, and for a moment looked at it with a sort of bewilderment—as though he had suddenly discovered a physical feature about himself of which he had never been aware but which was now revealed accidentally in an unexpected mirror.

I shouldn't have said that, he thought. I shouldn't have

enjoyed saying that to an old gentleman I've never seen. And yet I did. I really got a kick out of reminding him that he was in as much dirt as the rest of us. Except that he got dirty by accident and the rest of us volunteered . . . But I shouldn't have enjoyed rubbing his nose in it. He has earned better company than I have become.

Chapter Nine

One of the Old School

The Dalkeith house was set in ten acres about a mile north of a small town that the middle income suburbs had not yet reached.

In five years, the fields and the woods running down to the lake would be chequered by trim, ranch type bungalows and split levels not quite big enough for the design; Sundays would be loud with the popping roar of motor mowers being ridden over small unfenced lawns by young middle-aged men with the next move farther up the state or into Connecticut already budgeted for; there would be enough children between twelve and eighteen to require two more high schools, and enough 'gap' babies for another kindergarten; the small supermarket on the maple-lined main street would have been expanded twice; the Colonial style Episcopalian church, which had been built in the 1870's, would be zealously preserved but half the men who sat on the committee raising funds to repair the steeple would attend most Sundays at the green glass, cantilevered Unitarian house of worship on the lake's edge; the country club subscriptions would have tripled, but except on three or four special occasions during the year it would be the parking lot of the Boot 'n Saddle restaurant just off the throughway that would be filled on Saturday nights; there would be at least five Negro families, three of them would have three of the most desirable houses in the most desirable development, and the father of one of these families would be president of the

P.T.A.—after his election to this office, his racial joke about the two votes cast against him would be the best one of an evening that would begin in one house and move on through five or six others until somebody's wife was discovered nearly making it with somebody else's husband on the coats piled on the bed in the guest room.

In five years, it would be the sort of community where several thousand people would be living healthier, longer, more leisured, happier lives than any comparable group in history. Guilt would be a pastime (like adultery among the aristocrats of the *ancien régime*) and half a dozen sociologists and political scientists—pornographers of the new age of scientific plenty—would have written six large books proving that they were really only fooling themselves, that they were merely functioning in an emotional cul-de-sac, a cultural blind alley.

But five out of these six academics would be living there too, having their manuscripts typed for free by women with finely trained minds seeking fulfilment, two and a half children each, and who looked younger at forty-five than their mothers had at thirty. Nine hundred and ninety-nine out of every thousand people would be working desperately towards the day when they too could live like that.

Mr. Robert Dalkeith said, 'The damn' place's filling up. Ten years ago, I used to find bear tracks in the orchard during the fall. Now the only wild life that comes down from the hills is vermin. You can always tell when too many people begin moving into a place: the vermin begin to come out of the woods for the garbage.'

'Was it a cherry orchard?' Peter Blackmore asked him.

'What? I—Oh, I see. Not bad, Broome. Didn't know your generation went in for wit any more.'

They were sitting on a garden bench of rough planed hickory overlooking a shallow brown stream. The woods across the stream were luminous with the first pale green of April. Behind them, a broad lawn sloped up to the terrace of a house which must have been designed by someone very good but very conventional. There was a cool breeze coming down the valley from the blue hills five miles to the north, but the spring sun baked them gently inside their coats.

' "Lode Invest" was my invention,' Mr. Dalkeith said suddenly to the trees across the stream. 'The name, I mean. Charlie Everett didn't approve. Neither did Tom Logan. They thought it vulgar. But I insisted, and Oswald Orr backed me up. We told them we had to move with the times. Give the public a name it could remember.'

He stopped speaking as suddenly as he had uttered. One got the impression that Mr. Dalkeith now used breath as something no longer replaceable. He had once been a big man. In the days just before he thought of calling the firm 'Lode Invest,' (when he, Charlie Everett, Oswald Orr and Tom Logan had been at Harvard) there must have been more shoulder, chest and arm to him than any but the biggest tackle on the Yale team could have found comfortable to see approaching at full gallop. Now, a lot of pale skin seemed to have crumpled on his face and hands, and the English tweed around the still massive bone structure was like excessive wrapping on a package.

'I'm sorry I had to write you the sort of letter I did,' Peter Blackmore told him, 'and I wasn't very pleasant on the telephone yesterday. I apologise for that too. But we're in a blind alley. You're our only hope of finding a way out.'

Mr. Dalkeith gave a carefully rationed chuckle.

'Oh, *that.*' He waved a large hand, all prominent knuckles and the dark splotches of physical decay. 'That letter was nicely calculated, Broome. If you'd threatened me, I'd never have seen you. Probably handed it over to the police. But you understood. Lode Invest still means something. I owe that to Oswald Orr—and the others . . . Who are you people, Broome? What d'you really want of me?'

He looked at Jassy Vane on the question. She sat on his other side; demurely provocative in a russet spring coat of mohair, a cream felt hat that looked as if it had been laid on a stage and danced into shape by Nureyev and Fontaine, cream, open-mesh stockings and a pair of those laced across, square-toed Italian shoes which seem to be designed for a thirteen-year-old bridesmaid who happens, incidentally, to be an expensive whore.

'You could call us speculators,' Jassy Vane suggested. 'We have a lot tied up in Candywine. Not money, but other things that the sort of money you people have brought in might spoil. Things that the Mafia and their friends might try to take over once they're established.'

'We didn't expect this of Lode Invest,' Peter Blackmore said, speaking to the sycamore and dogwood across the stream. 'There's all kinds of money, Mr. Dalkeith, and nobody can afford to ask too many questions about where it comes from. But Lode Investment and the Mafia . . . That's bad business, Mr. Dalkeith. A lot of things have gone damn' wrong when you find Lode Invest fronting for those boys.'

'We got too big!' Mr. Dalkeith replied. 'All sorts of people started to join the firm. People who had no business in what Oswald Orr and I had started. But Everett and Logan were greedy. If Oswald had lived, this wouldn't have happened.' He paused. Jassy Vane and Peter Blackmore waited. 'After Oswald died, I allowed all sorts of people to come in,' Mr. Dalkeith said. His words had to be caught like feathers on the breeze down the valley. 'I should have realised what was happening and pulled out in time. Charlie Everett was a rich peasant from the mid-West. Logan was Boston Irish on the make. They had me surrounded by Jews and Italians and all sorts of people before I knew it. But it was still Lode

Invest. Oswald and I had made that mean something. I couldn't let that down. I went along . . .'

He hunched over his knees and hungrily drew air in.

'You don't have to know anything more about Mayhew than we've told you,' Jassy Vane said. She put her hand out and closed it gently over the wide, huge-boned old wrist. She was a tall woman and Mr. Dalkeith was folded over his diaphragm, but when she smiled she still had to look up into his face. 'You couldn't stop anything now even if you did. And if you tried, then it would be Lode Invest that would be hurt most. All we want from you is who at Lode Invest is handling Mayhew for Candywine. We *could* find out if we really tried but that could be very—very untidy. You can find out for us neatly because you've still got the power and you've forgotten more about using power than we have learned yet.'

When Mr. Dalkeith laughed this time, he did not ration it.

He said, 'There used to be women like you once. Lots of them. I married one. So did Oswald Orr. Then all of a sudden you stopped seeing them around. Tell me, are you singular, or is the breed coming back?'

'Oh, we've always been around,' Jassy Vane told him and raised her hand from his wrist and laid her arm across his shoulders, on the chequered cloth which must have been tailored thirty years before on Savile Row, 'it's only that we had to go into hiding until they started making men like you again.'

'Like your husband here?'

'Yes. Like my husband.'

'It was the War, you know. The *real* one. The one where they killed all the officers and left too many damned corporals alive. It has taken us two generations to start breeding our sort into the book again. Yes, Mrs. Broome . . . I'll have the name of Mayhew's handler at Lode for you in two days.'

He rose and turned, looking down at them. Standing, with his hands thrust into the pockets of a coat that would never wear out but only weather, his heavy, ice-blue brows squeezed in amusement under the brim of a hat that looked as if it were either a cloth for cleaning truck windows or something to be preserved under glass in a special room in an important museum, he was like an ageing eagle on a crag, possession of which no other eagle had yet dared to challenge.

He said, 'Now, let's go up and have something to eat. You two have made me hungry. You're the first people I've wanted to lunch with in five years. I owe you something for that . . . Some day you must tell me who you really are . . . And someday you must get really married. This damn' world needs the sort of children you would have.'

Chapter Ten

A little business luncheon

'Well now, this is a real pleasure. I don't often get the chance to meet anyone from Jamaica, but whenever I do they convince me I must get there some day. You know: not just two weeks on the beach at Montego with a lot of other Americans —but time to really *see* the place and the people. What will it be?'

Martin Harriman had risen as the waiter brought them to his table, held Jassy's chair, helped her slip her arms out of her coat and drape the shoulders of it over the back of her chair, waved Peter Blackmore into his chair, conveyed his pleasure about his meetings with Jamaicans, asked them to name their drinks and seated himself again in ten seconds of calculated movement and speech that were as elegant and economical as a series of passes by a bullfighter: the stylistic necessities of a trade where the business lunch had become the preliminary to the moment of truth.

'What will it be, Mrs. Broome?' he repeated and smiled nicely at Jassy Vane. 'May I suggest a vodkatini? An old Russian professor I once did a course with told me that the reason the Russians had such a formidable capacity for sheer volume of intellectual production was they all flushed their minds out with a stiff vodka in the middle of the morning. He admitted, however, that in adding dry vermouth we Americans had improved the formula.'

'With such an academic guarantee, how could I refuse?'

Jassy Vane laughed. 'Vodkatini, please. With olive, not onion.'

'And you, Mr. Broome?' Martin Harriman asked Peter Blackmore.

'The same. We have a proverb in Jamaica, "Drink what your woman drink an' she think what you tell her to think." '

'That's good,' Martin Harriman said. 'I must remember that. I wonder what necessity of folk experience produced that one. It must come from some very crucial conflict between the sexes . . .'

'It's from the slave days,' Peter Blackmore told him solemnly. 'When the black man didn't have a masculine role to play, but the black female could fulfil herself as child-bearer, authority figure in a household, the factory of stability. Of course, the males resented this . . . Even the whites like me, who were few and drowned in a sea of femininity. The only way a man could assert his individuality was to find subtle ways of reducing the woman's awareness of independent self.'

'Fascinating,' Martin Harriman said. 'I wonder if we would find a corresponding proverb in our South, where the black woman, the black mother, was the dominant figure of domestic authority.' He smiled again at Jassy Vane, the sort of smile that underlined the fact he was so liberal he could discuss slave blackness without embarrassment, with a modern black woman.

'I doubt it,' Jassy told him dryly. 'Unless you found somebody like my husband who makes proverbs for any occasion. That one he quoted is so new even I hadn't heard it before.'

Martin Harriman laughed heartily. Pink stains of anger flushed his high cheekbones. With his dark, sleek hair, cloistral skin and wide, pale-pink, thin lips, he looked like the young Inquisitor in a bad painting by a Victorian romantic.

'You were making a joke,' he accused Peter Blackmore

'I'm full of jokes,' Peter Blackmore said. He sipped the vodkatini which the waiter had just put at his right hand and flipped open the menu with his left. 'I'll have snails,' he announced, 'and a steak Diane . . . The funniest joke I know at the moment is the one about a Chinaman named Anyo and an American named Mayhew. D'you want to hear it?'

Martin Harriman glanced once at the bleak, black mask of Jassy Vane's face and at the top of Peter Blackmore's head still bent over the menu. The twin doors to the restaurant were opened simultaneously to accommodate the entrance of five middle-aged men wearing identical grey suits and pampered pink faces: the sound of Third Avenue traffic came into the room with them.

'Yes,' Martin Harriman said, very quietly, 'I'd like to hear it, but don't you think we'd better order first?'

'I've ordered,' Peter Blackmore said, looking at the waiter. 'Snails . . . A dozen. Steak Diane and the French salad . . . What are you going to have, my dear?' he asked of Jassy Vane, in the off-hand yet paternally solicitous tone of a husband who knows what his wife would like but who realises he must also give moral support about her diet.

'I'm still making up my mind,' Jassy Vane said. 'You go first, Mr. Harriman.'

II

'You people have to be crazy,' Peter Blackmore was saying. 'At least, I hope you're crazy. If you're sane, then we haven't got a chance. Not a prayer. What are you trying to do? Prove that T. S. Eliot was wrong and that the world *can* end with a bang?'

They were leaning against the balustrade of the United Nations' garden with their backs to the East River; after their lunch at the small, good place on Third Avenue, where they had talked only of things anybody could listen to, they had walked across to the new tower where Babel was simultaneously reduced to the few languages understood by the majority of those who represented the last hope of mankind. As they watched, hope was going up the broad steps to the main lobby or coming in through the flagpoles at the First Avenue entrance for the afternoon session: hope was dressed in saris, bright African togas, Nehru jackets, standard, western, dark three-pieces. The faces of hope—whether they were black, brown, white or yellow—whether they were male or female—all had the bland, antiseptic synonymity of creatures from some zoological laboratory; as if what daily took place inside the tower were not the endless speeches but permutations of incest designed to breed a new species capable of solving esoteric problems which had little in common with the older, simpler concerns of the world outside the controlled experiment. Or perhaps they were the devotees of a new order of contemplation? Holy men and women who by ceaseless incantation of the phrases *Human Rights, Four Freedoms, Peace, Justice, Plenty, Equality* would one day touch the Infinite power that would restore life to the violently dead, fill out the shrunken bodies of the starving, translate the incoherent pleadings of the tortured into confident opinion? And, indeed, watching the delegates from Asia, Africa, Europe, the several Americas—how many countries were there now? One hundred and twenty; one hundred and thirty?—as they entered their temple for the afternoon's ritual of committees and plenary session, it was difficult to distinguish differences of race or colour or even culture. They were all transfigured in the same light of fatuous and self-satisfied sanctity.

'What interests me,' Martin Harriman said, 'is how your outfit got hold of Anyo.'

121

'Does it interest you enough to buy it?' Jassy Vane asked him.

'It might. I'm not high up enough to say, though. I'll have to ask.'

'You do that, Mr. Harriman. Everything has a price if the price is right.'

A scow wailed from the river beneath them and a muted but still manic clamour came from a traffic jam somewhere on the avenue.

Peter Blackmore repeated, in the same tones of savage astonishment, 'I still say your lads must have gone crazy. We nearly had Anyo killed when he told us that you were going to hi-jack one of your own planes and hand four hydrogen bombs over to him. We were all but sure he was lying to us again. The only thing that saved his little Chinese neck was that it was too big for a lie . . . And then a few other things began to add up and we realised what a clear, true note he must be singing . . .'

'What other things?' Martin Harriman asked. The face he turned to Peter Blackmore was faintly—pityingly—amused: the smile it wore was one of detached condescension—like that of a voluntary worker for a great relief organisation conscientiously collecting tribal lore. 'What other things added up, Mr. Broome?'

'The airstrip at Candywine for one,' Peter Blackmore said. He was suddenly no longer angry and astonished. His voice was almost casual. A party of teenagers, in the charge of a young man and a young woman who from their air of slightly bewildered dedication could only have been teachers, passed them on their way to observe that part of the afternoon's sacraments open to the public. To-night, thirty assignments would begin with the titles: *The United Nations and How It Functions* or *The United Nations: A Charter in Action*. A few of the titles would be carefully blocked out by fountain-pen; most would be typed. Like the twenty-odd transistor radios carried by the group, the portable typewriter was now a casual tool of the metropolitan young. He watched the children and their teachers mount the steps, mingling with the delegates as a group of medieval laymen would have entered a cathedral with their clergy.

'Yes,' Martin Harriman said, questioningly. 'The airstrip at Candywine?'

'Oh, Christ!' Peter Blackmore replied briskly but without heat. 'There isn't an executive jet made that would need that length of runway. And Candywine isn't being developed for the jumbo jet crowd. The safety margins for a Presidential plane are less than you have laid out there. That leaves us with only a B52 or whatever S.A.C. comes up with in the next couple of years. Then there's the shelf out from the edge of the strip: a team of half-trained frogmen could play a fast game of football in that water, it's so shallow—let alone roll a six-pack of hydrogen bombs down to the edge of the Candywine Trench like so many cans of beer . . . It was then we began to think of the *Thresher*. You've recovered everything from her down to the cabin boy's last letter from his girl friend—but not her missiles. In 1966, something went wrong between one of your refuelling tankers and a B52 above Palomares in Spain. Thirty thousand feet up. Somebody must have panicked there, Harriman, because the bombs were parachuted out too soon. They hit land instead of water and the casings broke and it nearly cost America the NATO alliance. Everybody from West Berlin to Gibraltar was feeling radioactive for a while until your publicity boys convinced them that a little radioactivity is good for the teeth, like fluoride . . . And then . . . and then . . . there was that B52 crash in Thule last year. Now that's the interesting one. It went down through the ice like a hot rivet but you still found enough pieces of it to prove there had been a cockpit fire. Somehow, though, you never found its bombs and nobody has yet explained why the telephone line between Greenland and Canada was cut by a blizzard the day before the crash.'

'You never know with blizzards,' Jassy Vane said, speaking across the lawn to where a delegate from one of the Arab countries—who had either gone to lunch late or had lingered over the meal dreaming of a return to Israel—was hurrying up the steps. 'Blizzards are no respecters of communications. Only the U.S. Postal Service takes them in its stride. Not the telephone companies.'

'You're thinking of snow, sleet, rain and hail, dear,' Peter Blackmore said. 'That's what doesn't stop the United States' postman on his appointed rounds. I think he's permitted to take refuge in a blizzard.'

Harriman was no longer smiling. He looked not like a man about to buy Manhattan Island for twenty-four dollars but like one who was wondering whether the seller knew something he didn't.

He said, 'My, my . . . What a lot of thinking you people down in Jamaica seem to do.'

'It's a pastime,' Peter Blackmore said. 'There isn't much else to occupy us. We don't have all this . . .' he waved a congratulatory hand at the Himalayan wedges of concrete, steel and glass around them that jostled for unbruised areas of sky.

'Yes,' Martin Harriman said, 'we have a great deal. Too much for a couple like you to take on. You should have thought of that, you know. You should never have told me all this . . . Now we have no choice . . .'

'Shit!' Jassy Vane interrupted cheerfully. 'We know too much. And you know *that*, Mr. Harriman. If anything happens to us, then Russia will hear everything about Candywine five minutes after we don't report in. The same goes if you decide Anyo is expendable. We don't give a damn if you take him out later on . . . But only when we tell you that you can . . . At the moment, *we* want him . . . And what we want is what you have to put up with.'

'What she means,' Peter Blackmore explained, 'is that we're such a small country we've got nothing to lose except being liberated by one of our big brothers. The only thing we have is information—and your top brass wouldn't like it at all if we told Russia that you were leaking enriched uranium from your own hydrogen bombs to China.'

'The C.I.A. would be grateful for a tip-off too,' Jassy Vane said. 'Or Navy Intelligence. From what we hear, Mayhew has a lot of the established agencies worried. What are you trying to do, anyway? Absorb the C.I.A. like the NKVD did to OGPU in Russia? Or just cut it down to size?'

Martin Harriman glanced at his watch and buttoned the light coat he had flung open while they had stood in the gentle warmth of the spring sun on the stones against which they leaned. He smoothed the sleek hair which had been slightly ruffled by the breeze off the river. The wide, too-thin lips of an unattractive pink stretched briefly in what might have been a conventional smile or a rictus of real distaste.

'All right,' he said. 'I have to get back to the office now. I've got a client coming to see me.' He smiled again, as if it was a custom his mother had once taught him a gentleman should observe, like offering one's seat to a woman in a crowded bus. 'Quite legitimate. A man who thinks *safari* camps in the Amazon headwaters may be the coming thing . . . You two haven't told me what you want from us, though. You've told me everything but that. What d'you want? What do I tell my people?'

'Just say we'd like to meet,' Jassy Vane told him. 'Like you said, Mr. Harriman; you're not big enough to discuss terms. And until we hear what you have to offer how can we decide what we want? You know our hotel. Telephone us when you've set up something, or leave a message.'

The skin stretched on Martin Harriman's cheekbones darkened once again with anger and he turned abruptly. Peter Blackmore said, 'Harriman!' and Harriman turned back. His austere, young Inquisitor's face registered something like hate as he regarded Peter Blackmore's heavier, sensual, frankly pagan features. 'Yes?'

'*Why* are your lot doing this, Harriman? Why are you feeding enriched uranium to the Chinese. They won't be able to make enough of it to count against you and the other big boy for years yet. Why are you making it easier for them?'

Martin Harriman said with astringent relish: 'You said thinking was a pastime in Jamaica, Mr. Broome. I leave you with our motives as a games problem. It should keep you and your—your wife entertained until I contact you.'

He turned again and moved across the sunlit lawn. Somehow, he seemed to throw more shadow wherever he passed than his size warranted.

They watched him until he passed under the ensigns of two countries that shared the same initial letter, adjacent flagpoles and a mutual detestation. Jassy Vane suddenly clutched Peter Blackmore's arm above his elbow with both her hands.

'I know I'm being feminine and irrational,' she said, 'but promise me something.'

'What?'

'If things ever got really final between us and that cold cat. If he was ever in a position to take us out, I mean: save your last bullet for me. Like the men in romantic novels used to do for the women they loved before the natives overran the fort.'

Peter Blackmore smiled down at her and bent and kissed her softly on her forehead between the eyebrows.

'Well now,' he told her, 'I was thinking along those same lines, myself. Only it will have to be *your* last bullet; with the second to last for *me*. I don't carry a gun, remember.' He straightened, and frowned with exasperation. 'Something's wrong again,' he said. 'I don't know what, but it isn't adding up right. There's a missing piece. Harriman was too damn' pleased with himself, when you consider what we're supposed to know about Mayhew. There's something missing still and it's so important that it's making me feel a little sick.'

She nodded. 'Somewhere along the line I got a "fiff" too.'

'A "fiff"?'

She smiled. ' "Funny internal feeling." It's a joke word Helen and I thought up in the early days; when Robin had just started us as an outfit.'

'What does this one tell you?'

'That's it, Peter,' she said. 'That's the damn' thing. I don't know. But somehow Harriman doesn't check out. There's a double-cross going on and they're going to nail us, and Anyo, to it.' She shrugged. 'Oh, hell. What's the use of letting it nag us. Don't think about it now. Let it sink in and come to the surface again. There's not much we can do until Harriman makes contact anyway . . . Shall we go to a movie? There's one at that place around the corner from the hotel.'

'That Swedish thing with all the tits and pubic hair?'

'Yes. The critics say it's one of the best things Oshkaström's ever done.'

'Is there anything in it we couldn't do ourselves at the hotel?'

'I haven't seen it, just the reviews, but I shouldn't think so.'

'Let's grab a taxi then and go back to the hotel.'

'There won't be any scenery with just the two of us. The

127

critics said that Oshkaström uses the landscape marvellously to counterpoint the sex bits. Pine trees and lakes and all that.'

'Oshkaström can shove his pine trees straight up and then jump into all of his lakes one after another. I've got a hard on that would lift a truck.'

'It's all those snails you had at lunch. A whole dozen— *plus* steak.'

'That's a lot of superstition. Like oysters. Have you ever seen a snail or an oyster with a hard on?'

'You idiot.' She laughed, suddenly, like a woman, and took his arm as they moved briskly across the lawn to First Avenue.

Chapter Eleven

Interrupted idyll

The young man who had been waiting for them in their suite said apologetically, 'I'm sorry. Believe me. I thought you'd be under the sheet.'

He had slid from beneath the old-fashioned, wide, brass bed, as deftly as a mouse out of the wainscotting, a few moments after they had fallen on to it.

Jassy Vane gave a gasp and snatched her side of the coverlet about her. Peter Blackmore sat up, began an obscene expletive, bit it off and said, 'Pass us our dressing-gowns They're on the bathroom door. We won't try anything and you can keep us covered anyway while you reach inside.'

The man from under the bed backed slowly across the carpet to the bathroom door, reached behind and turned the crystal knob of the handle with his left hand, pushed the door ajar and felt along the inside. His left hand reappeared holding two garments: a faded maroon, man's dressing-gown, a Paisley, and something transparent edged with lace.

'That's not a dressing-gown, you fucking idiot,' Jassy Vane snarled. 'That's my nightie. What's the matter? Haven't you ever lived with a woman? Or are you queer?'

'Sorry,' the man said. He tossed the Paisley across the room on to the bed; his left hand disappeared behind the door again and reappeared holding something long, pale-yellow and quilted. 'This it?' he asked guiltily. In all the time since the hole at the end of the small pistol had suddenly been presented at their two naked and entwined bodies and he had risen from the floor, spoken, and got them their clothing, he had never taken his eyes from them and the hole at the end of the pistol had only moved so that with each change in his position it still covered them. He managed to give the impression that he slightly averted his eyes while Jassy Vane sat up, shoved her arms into the dressing-gown, stood and belted it around her as if she were buckling herself into a suit of armour. Peter Blackmore who had already stood and put on his gown would not have bet a nickel that anything taking place on either side of the bed was escaping the man who had interrupted them.

He was built like a very fast middleweight; lack of height and size compensated for by the wide, sloping shoulders and slightly bowed, springy legs that would never tire. He had a lot of curly black hair and the bones under his sallow skin made attractive promontories and escarpments—as if they had been designed for a bigger man and issued to him by mistake.

He asked courteously, 'Who are you people?'

'You know who we are,' Jassy Vane said. She sat on the edge of the bed, her hands in her lap. The instinctive anger and embarrassment of a woman peeped on in the act of love had gone from her voice. 'You know enough about us to be hiding in our bedroom until the right moment.'

The man sketched an apologetic gesture with his left hand.

'I didn't expect you back from your meeting with Harriman so soon. This was only meant to be a preliminary search before we picked you up. Your coming back like this changed the situation slightly.'

'You knew about Harriman too,' Peter Blackmore said. 'That's fast work. *We* didn't know we were going to lunch with him until this morning when he rang us.'

'We know about Harriman, and the phone call from Mr.

Dalkeith telling him to contact you,' the man said. He smiled, an absent, cat's smile. 'Mr. Dalkeith may be almost a sleeping partner now, but juniors like Harriman still lunch with who he says they ought to lunch with.'

'You said "We" were going to pick us up,' Jassy Vane said. 'Who is "We"?'

'If you don't mind ... My question first. Who are you?'

'My passport's in the inside pocket of my jacket,' Peter Blackmore said. 'Hers is in her handbag over there on the dressing-table ... Peter and Jassy Broome ... Issued in Kingston, Jamaica.'

'They'll say that, I'm sure,' the man agreed. 'And I'm sure you could use them to get back into Jamaica if you wanted to. They're good enough for a hotel clerk and that means they're done with real style. I won't bother to look.'

'I believe the man is trying to tell us we're lying, Peter,' Jassy Vane said. 'What's your name?' she added suddenly.

'Einstein,' the man smiled. 'Albert.'

'May we call you Al?' Peter Blackmore asked, and they all laughed as if mirth had suddenly entered the room.

'I don't like this,' Albert Einstein told them, 'but you're going to have to meet somebody who wants to meet you. I promise you it is just a meeting to discuss certain things you and we seem to have become aware of.'

'We don't go to meetings where they send that sort of invitation card.' Jassy Vane waved at Einstein's gun hand.

'I'm sorry.' Albert Einstein's voice was still pleasant and polite, but it was not the voice of a man apologising for anything. 'You will have to come. And right now. It could be important. So important that I wish I wasn't involved ...'

'She's right, you know, Al,' Peter Blackmore told him. 'You can't make us come. You *could* have us picked up outside, in any one of a dozen ways ... I don't know who your people are, but if they can get you into a suite in a hotel like this, unannounced, then they're organised for anything. But you can't make us come. You're bluffing. If we just sit here, what the hell can you do? Shoot us? You don't want that. You want to talk to us. So you had better tell us a little more about yourself, eh, Al? Tell us about yourself and then we'll see if we want to come to your important meeting.'

When Albert Einstein grinned it was like watching the first sunlight on the side of some small but remarkable mountain: the stretched skin glinted in a dozen unexpected places on the dense, irreducible plugs of bone beneath.

He glanced briefly at his pistol and said, 'Oh, *this*,' like a woman really sure that her little black is the best dress in the room. 'It's not what you think, Mr. Broome. It's a tranquilliser, but not forever. If I were to shoot you and Mrs. Broome now you would be anaesthetised in about ten seconds. You wouldn't even be able to reach me from where you are. You'd lose interest half-way across the room. Then you'd sleep for about half an hour ... and then I'd walk both of you to the elevator and out of this hotel without anybody thinking you weren't both stiff, glassy-eyed drunk ... In a hotel of this class,' he added, like a popular young lecturer making the idiomatic illustration that always raises a laugh, 'they don't *see* well-behaved, well-dressed drunks being towed out. It's understood that you're to be invisible when in that condition. Right?'

'True enough,' Peter Blackmore said. 'It's one of the services you pay for ... but I don't believe you about that tranquilliser. They don't make anything that good.'

'Mr. Broome,' Albert Einstein said with simple pride, 'I could put two pellets from this gun into two half-starved Siberian timber wolves and take them walkies through the playground of a kindergarten. Don't let me have to prove it.'

'He can do it, Peter,' Jassy Vane said, and stood. 'We'd

better go with him fully functional. He'll take us doped up
otherwise.'

'Thank you, Mrs. Broome,' Albert Einstein said. He sounded genuinely grateful. 'I assure you, it will be much better
this way . . .' He paused, and the sun set in lurid patches of
discomfort on his high, knobbly forehead and the bluffs
and ridges of his cheeks, jaw and chin. 'You understand that
I will have to watch you dress? I mean, I can't risk either of
you out of sight from here on until we get to our meeting.'

'Oh, shit,' Jassy Vane said cheerfully, flinging open her
dressing-gown and shrugging it on to the bed behind her,
'you've seen nearly as much of me as my doctor. Feast your
eyes, you bloody *voyeur*.'

Albert Einstein unhappily and diligently watched their
every move as they collected their scattered clothing and
dressed.

'Of course,' Peter Blackmore said as he knotted his tie
before the looking-glass set inside one of the closet doors,
'if we decide to walk away from you in the corridor, or down
in the lobby, there isn't much you can do. You hadn't
thought of that, had you, Al?'

'He has,' Jassy Vane said from the woman's dressing-table
as she was about to bite on a tissue to even her lipstick. 'He'll
be closer than a Siamese twin to one or other of us all the
time. That cute little novelty he's carrying is for real, Peter.
It'll be so silent you wouldn't hear it three feet away in an
echo chamber. It we try to split the scene, he'll just push that
tranquilliser of his into the one nearest to him, pretend he
has a passed-out drunk on his hands, and drag him out.
The other one will have to follow. He knows we're not going
to start shouting for help once he's got us down in the lobby.
That we don't want that sort of publicity . . . Don't you, you
little kinky?' she asked of Einstein's reflection in the mirror
before her. 'Don't you, my little *voyeur*. I bet you go to

two a.m. movies on Forty-second Street in your spare time
. . . and send for all of those massage publications in plain
covers. Admit it, Mr. Einstein. You do. What did you think
of my panties? Or are you a boots and leather man?'

'Mrs. Broome,' the man who had called himself Albert
Einstein said miserably, 'I thought you understood. This
was an accident that became a necessity . . . I trust you don't
think that I . . . I . . .'

'Oh, shut up, Al,' Jassy Vane said as she tugged her hat
into shape and rose to look at herself in the long vanity
mirror. 'You're all right. In fact, you're so damned good, I
thought you belonged to one of the American outfits for a
while. You're nearly perfect. Just a few mistakes. All the
same, just one of those mistakes is going to be pretty expensive one of these days.' She crossed the room to the chair
on to which her coat had been flung when she and Peter
Blackmore had entered the room. She patted Albert
Einstein's cheek as she passed him, and smiled the sweet
and lethal smile of a woman who will never forgive the cause
of her humiliation. 'Nearly perfect,' she repeated. 'They
must be giving you some pretty thorough training nowadays
in that model American home town of yours. I didn't spot
you for nearly five minutes.'

Albert Einstein said stiffly, 'I don't know what you're
talking about, Mrs. Broome.'

'You do,' Jassy Vane said in a voice as light as a steel blade.
'You surely do. Worry about it, Al . . . because it's going to
get you into trouble. Shall we go?'

'Yes.' Albert Einstein said. A lot of shadow had fallen on
his face while Jassy Vane was getting her coat. 'Mistakes,'
he added, with a smile that only deepened the shadows.
'Whatever are you talking about, Mrs. Broome?'

He opened the door for them, casually keeping them always
ahead of him, his right hand in the pocket of his coat.

'*Siberian* timber wolves, for one,' Jassy Vane said reproachfully as she stepped into the corridor. 'Really, Al! They ought to have taught you better than that. "Timber wolves," yes. That's American . . . but Siberia over here is just a place people get sent to for not reading *Pravda*.'

Chapter Twelve

A better mousetrap

At the entrance to the hotel, Albert Einstein said to the driver, '417 East Sixty-Seven,' and tipped the attendant who had attached himself to the handle of the taxi's rear door.

'Nice going, Al,' Jassy Vane said. 'That was just right. How much did you give the doorman?'

'Fifty cents?' Albert Einstein asked sulkily and anxiously.

'Just right again. At a hotel like ours, its either fifty cents or maybe a dollar or you borrow the taxi fare from the man who holds the door for you. Perhaps they didn't teach you so badly after all.'

The taxi-driver asked, 'Four-seventeen East Sixty-Seven?'

'That's right,' Albert Einstein confirmed, but neither Peter Blackmore nor Jassy Vane were much surprised when h.e said suddenly at the corner of Third and Sixty-Sixth, 'You can drop us here. This'll do . . .'

'How many blocks do we walk?' Jassy Vane asked him as they stood on the sidewalk. 'If it's more than two, Al, you better call another cab, or you'll have to use that tranquilliser and call a cab anyway. I'm not walking more than two blocks after what you've done to me.'

'It is only four blocks, Mrs. Broome,' Albert Einstein said. His voice was level but tautly controlled—like that of a boy whose sexual propositions have been taken seriously for the first time.

'She's teasing you, Al,' Peter Blackmore said genially to

the air above their heads. 'She does it to everybody. She'll walk the four blocks if you want her to.'

II

The plastic-sheathed card stuck between the third and fourth rungs of the little ladder of brass read N. BROSSOKOVSKI. Albert Einstein pressed the button beside it: two long rings, a *tap-tap-tap*, and one long push during which he seemed to be trying to force the button through its casing into the hall.

From the matchbox-sized grille beside the button a voice said, 'Yes?'

'Yes,' Albert Einstein replied.

There was a buzz, a click and the door swung off the locks on its own weight. Peter Blackmore and Jassy Vane entered and Albert Einstein followed, shutting the door on to Sixty-Third Street behind him. He pointed to the narrow, acutely cornered stairs at the end of the narrow hall and kept close behind as they moved towards them. The hall was empty but well lit; the maroon carpet was synthetic but good synthetic; blue and white wallpaper was mass-produced but at a price that only those who had two hundred L.P.s and tapes, five hundred hard-cover books and subscriptions to both *Time* and *Newsweek* could afford to pay. It was the sort of building where half the apartments were empty during the four or six hottest weeks of summer and where the other half were inhabited, during those weeks, only by bachelors, husbands with families away on the edges of cool water, and by transient women.

On the second landing, Albert Einstein said, 'Here, please,' and reached sideways and pressed the button set into the wall beside the door marked 3C. After about ten seconds the door opened although they had not heard any thud of feet inside the apartment. Albert Einstein gestured them into the entrance hall that was little larger than a closet.

'Come in,' a voice said from the living-room.

They went through to the living-room. It was furnished with impersonal good taste: as though the occupier had placed an order with a recommended store after choosing from a catalogue. Only a large, leather-topped desk heaped with files and papers and with a cup and saucer surrounded by the rings of old coffee stains gave an individual touch.

A man was lying on the couch set against the wall on their right. The couch was placed so that anyone entering would have to turn to see it full on.

The man on the couch was long and grey; a heavy moustache the colour of pewter curved down well past the corners of his mouth; pewter eyebrows joined over a bluntly functional nose; thick, very straight, pewter hair straggled over the cushion behind his head and lay on his high forehead. The rims of his steel-framed spectacles were too small and his grey suit looked as though it had been slept in for a week. As they entered and turned, he raised his eyebrows inquiringly at Einstein and the small, clear green eyes behind the lenses became cloudy with attention.

Einstein said a great deal, rapidly in a language which neither Peter Blackmore nor Jassy Vane could understand. Both had watched enough newsreels and television to recognise that it was Russian.

'Speak English,' the man on the couch said, and swung to his feet. 'He says that he had to bring you back. That you returned to the hotel earlier than we had anticipated. It does not matter, really. We would have had to pick you up shortly in any case.' He extended a large, capable hand—the hand of a good mechanic or carpenter or of one who had had a lot to do with horses—to Jassy Vane. 'Saratov,' he said as they shook, 'I am Saratov.' He turned to Peter Blackmore and took his hand also.

138

'Broome,' Peter Blackmore said, 'And this is my wife. But you already know that.'

'It says "Brossokovski" on the door below,' Jassy Vane said. 'Does he know you're using his apartment? Or are you just sub-letting?'

Saratov laughed. 'Oh, Brossokovski. He comes and goes. He is hardly ever here, in fact.' He laughed again, flinging his hands up as if tossing Brossokovski back into limbo. 'You can call *him* Brossokovski if you like,' he added, pointing to Albert Einstein. 'Nikolai Brossokovski. Brossokovski won't mind.'

'How about it, Al?' Peter Blackmore asked over his shoulder of the young man behind them, 'Do you want to be Brossokovski, or would you still rather be Einstein?'

'Is that what he told you?' Saratov asked with affectionate amusement. 'Albert Einstein? Sometimes it is Isaac Newton. Or Pascal. Or Kepler. He wanted to be a mathematician. One of the great ones. He showed promise, too, but you understand that with mathematics promise is not enough. You either do something absolutely original by the time you're twenty-five or you become one of the industrious herd . . . So . . .' He gestured again.

'So he ends up hiding under beds in hotel rooms,' Jassy Vane said tartly. 'He should have stayed with mathematics.'

'Mrs. Broome!' Saratov said in a wounded tone. 'That was not our intention, as you are well aware. He has already apologised, I am sure. Won't you sit down, please. Forgive me. Let me take your coat. And yours, Mr. Broome. What will you have to drink? Scotch? Gin? Bourbon? I have some very good vodka, if you like vodka?'

He was not quite as fast as Martin Harriman in settling guests comfortably, but he brought an old-fashioned charm to the business that more than made up for the lack of speed.

They were seated, their coats neatly folded over the back

of one of the arm-chairs, and Saratov was being brisk and efficient and genial at the liquor cabinet built on to the twenty-one-inch TV and stereo-tape unit in the corner, almost before they had finished saying what they would have to drink.

The only jarring note—a minor one—in the whole amiable business was that Brossokovski *né* Einstein remained standing just behind them, his right hand in the pocket of his coat, all the time that Saratov's hands were busy with folding coats, offering Jassy Vane a cigarette from a big copper and cedar box containing five American brands and clinking glasses, bottles and ice at the little fold-out counter of the liquor cabinet.

III

'. . . it was too clear a pattern to be accidental,' Saratov was saying. 'Many rich people use Lode Invest, I agree, and not all of them are Americans . . . But your call to Mr. Dalkeith. Your visit to his house. The arranged luncheon with Martin Harriman. The place you come from . . . We realised that you must be on to something. Perhaps the same thing that we are beginning to suspect. The trouble is that you gave us so little time. We did not even know you existed before you telephoned Dalkeith. So, you see, we had to bring you in.'

They had been talking for a quarter of an hour, feeling carefully for any spaces in their exchanges which might be occupied. Brossokovski had joined them when Saratov brought the drinks, sitting in an arm-chair on their right, a little behind but not so far back that it made it awkward for him to join the conversation. Saratov sat at the end of the couch where his head had been resting when they entered. Now he looked at them questioningly.

'How many taps,' Jassy Vane asked him, 'do you have on the people in Lode Invest?'

'On all the partners,' Saratov said. 'As soon as we discovered that Harriman was a Mayhew man, we tapped all telephones, both office and home.'

It was the first time the word 'Mayhew' had been used, and it represented a kind of minor victory for Peter Blackmore and Jassy Vane. Neither felt that they should make too much of it.

'Mayhew are too efficient to use Lode Invest or Harriman's home number in any way that would help you,' Peter Blackmore said.

'Everything helps,' Saratov told him. 'The taps helped me to you.'

'You don't think Dalkeith is connected with Mayhew?'

'No,' Saratov shook his head decisively; the undersized steel rims looked more unsuitable than ever when he did that. 'He knows there is something distasteful about the development at Candywine, but he thinks it is only the gangster money. And he can't stop that. Nobody can stop money once it starts. Not potentially profitable money.'

'You mentioned Candywine,' Jassy Vane said. 'What else do you know about Candywine, Saratov? I mean, what else do you know that we don't?'

'Perhaps we are not talking of the same thing after all?' Saratov said.

'I think we are,' Peter Blackmore said. 'We're talking about the sixteen kilogrammes of enriched uranium you need to make a hydrogen bomb, and how it might get stolen. Isn't that what you're talking about?'

'Yes. In part.' Saratov leaned forward suddenly, intently. Then he looked down at his hands, sighed, pushed his glasses up on to the lowest slopes of his forehead and stood. 'In part,' he repeated. 'A small part. Crucial, but only a means.' He bent and picked up his drink—a glass of vodka—swallowed what was left of it and walked over to the window. The flapping grey trousers were not only ill-fitting, they were inappropriate: his walk had been fashioned in the oiled creases of knee-high, old leather and the flare of patched breeches. He looked down at the street through the pane. A sally of April rain, out of an ambush of sudden clouds, was flinging itself against the glass in a grey smear. He turned abruptly and flung his hands up as he had done when tossing Brossokovski into oblivion. His complexion was thick, bone-china white which never tans, but the surface had been scoured by long seasons of exposure to rain, fierce sun, cold and pitiless as a tiger's claws, the abrasive dust clouds raised by an army's feet and hooves. He looked, suddenly, old and sleepless and responsible as he stroked one end of the down-turned pewter bars of his moustache. The undersized spectacle rims stuck in the middle of his wide forehead should have been slightly ludicrous, but weren't; they were comically dignified.

He said, 'Always in this business, there are those who want too much . . . Everything . . . When enough will do . . . *Everything*,' he repeated in a hard, contemptuous whisper more eloquent than an obscenity. 'The murderous idiots . . . Unless people like us stop them in time.' He strode to the low table between the chairs and the couch and poured himself another vodka from the vase-like, pentagonal bottle into the little glass. 'Not murderous,' he corrected himself: his tone was now one of wry calm. 'But simply ignorant. Ignorant on that large, beautiful, mad scale where you believe your map *is* the country, not a guide to it. Everything flat and tidy. No ditches to break a charge; no swamps to swallow your armour; no contours to take the breath out of an assault; no forests in which you can lose a division; no distances you cannot cover with a pair of dividers . . . Only a piece of paper on which you draw big black arrows across the pretty colours that mean mud and trees and mountains, and open plains where one stupid artillery lieutenant behind a big gun can destroy a regiment ten miles away as easily as a boy breaking a stand of rushes with a stick.'

He sat on the edge of the couch, and smiled slightly, in the confidently contrite manner of one who has indulged his anger before friends.

Jassy Vane asked softly, 'What is all this about "us"? All of a sudden, it isn't "we" and "you." It's "us." I don't understand that part.'

'I think he wants to do a trade,' Peter Blackmore observed. His heavily good-looking, pampered, colonial face was thoughtful as he stared into Saratov's appraising green eyes. 'At least, that's how I read it, Jassy. And as I see it, we stand to get more from him that he's going to get from us. We're on a seller's market. I think we ought to tell him what he wants.'

'Maybe,' Jassy Vane said. She sipped her drink—a long scotch and water—delicately. 'But let him tell us a few things first. After all, *he* beat a path to our door. Not the other way round. We may only have a small mousetrap but he wants it. Isn't that right, Saratov?'

'Yes, Mrs. Broome,' Saratov replied. 'I want your mouse-trap. But do not try to sell it too dearly. I am doing you both a favour, you understand. Mayhew is not something to be taken lightly.'

'We've already learnt that,' Jassy Vane said bleakly. 'They killed one of our people. So what's new, Saratov? Like for instance who are you—and this phony refugee from the Bronx you sent to pick us up?' She jerked her head slightly in Einstein-Brossokovski's direction, without taking her eyes off Saratov.

'Now, my mousetrap,' Saratov continued evenly, 'and I

am *giving* it to you, Mr. and Mrs. Broome, not selling it, comes to you complete with a mouse. Pre-tested. A very large mouse. A rat the size of a bear, in fact.' He took the small, utilitarian spectacles off and frowned at them with mild surprise, as if he had just become aware of them stuck to his forehead. 'What would you say if I told you that Mayhew is not only an American organisation? That it is established on the other side too? Under a different name; but with the same objective?'

'When you say "the other side," ' Peter Blackmore asked him, 'you mean your side?'

Saratov twitched his shoulders, as if concurring, for the sake of the main argument, on a minor semantic point.

'If you like,' he said. 'It does not matter what you call it. Sides are taken through conviction by a few, through habit by a few more, because of proximity to conviction and habit by most. They are necessary. Without them we could not be certain of our existence . . . But there can be too many sides. The game is only possible if you do not introduce random factors.'

'Wait a minute, Peter.' Jassy Vane put down her glass on the table between the couch and their chairs. She leaned forward, her forearms resting on the discreet glitter of the stockings drawn tight over her knees. Her large, shapely hands were clasped and she rubbed thoughtfully the rectangle of topaz set in platinum which Peter Blackmore had bought her that morning—left-turning her unexpectedly into Tiffany's as they walked down Fifth Avenue—because she had remarked casually, the night before, that she was a Sagittarian. 'You're serious about this?' she asked Saratov, but her question was rhetorical; creases of puzzled concern had suddenly flawed the skin between her heavy eyebrows. 'Yes, of course. You have to be. You wouldn't feed us something as big as that if it weren't true.' She continued to rub the topaz and the band of her ring with the thumb and middle finger of her right hand. 'All right, Saratov. We'll play it any way you like from here on. We didn't know that about Mayhew.'

The dark grey head opposite nodded once. 'I did not think you did,' Saratov said. 'In fact, I was sure you did not. Until I told you just now, I was fairly certain that only myself and three of my associates knew that Mayhew was a coin with two heads—except for a few Mayhew designers here in America, in my country, and in East Germany. I think maybe in Yugoslavia also, and perhaps in Romania, but I cannot be sure. Mayhew might only be using operators in both places who do not realise what they are working for. I am fairly certain this is the case with the Chinese.' He sighed—the necessary, therapeutic sigh of one who is under great and lonely tension—and rubbed his eyelids tiredly with the fingertips of both hands. 'You see,' he explained, 'I have had to proceed so cautiously, with only the three people I could trust. Not even my own superiors know what I have just told you. That is how unsure I am of what questions I dare ask, of what I ought to reveal. If Mayhew has gone as far as I think it has then my own organisation may be infiltrated too.'

'I think the time has come round for a little frankness, don't you?' Peter Blackmore said. 'It looks as if we're going to be friends after all. Friends ought to tell each other the truth.'

'Not too much truth, Mr. Broome,' Saratov smiled faintly, with the detached pleasantness of one who would never allow a sense of humour to blunt the sad necessities of action. 'Even friendship cannot bear the weight of too much truth.' He poured himself another vodka, looked with mock reproach at their half-finished, long drinks and then without smiling at each of them. 'For your sake, I hope that what

I have risked believing is true. You will have to convince me that I have not gambled foolishly. If you are working for the C.I.A. or even for the British, then I cannot allow you to leave America alive. I am not asking for all the truth. Only enough so that we can continue as we have begun—as friends.' He raised his small glass and put it down empty.

'We can convince you,' Jassy Vane said. 'You're nearly convinced now, or you wouldn't be giving us the chance. So why don't you relax, Saratov? You've drawn us in the old card game and you either continue to play with us or you throw in your hand.'

Saratov's face opened and shut briefly on a grin of genuine admiration.

'Yes,' he said, and for the first time since they had come into the room he relaxed—as an ageing, wary cat might settle after a long appraisal of strange company. 'Yes; that is how it should be assessed . . . Now Nikolai can have a drink with us.' He nodded and Nikolai, once Albert Einstein, perhaps Brossokovski, stood and removed his coat, folded it inside out before draping it over the back of the chair at the desk, and came over to the table. He filled the other small glass on the tray from the bottle of vodka, his back to them, and returned to his chair.

'You see how much I trust you already?' Saratov said, laughing like a host.

'If you trust us so goddam much,' Jassy Vane told him, 'why don't you take that big ugly gun from under the cushion there? Yes, that's the one I mean . . . Where your hand's been resting ever since Nikolai went off duty.'

Saratov's laugh scampered about the room like a child released on to a playground. When he put the sleek, heavy Luger with its cylindrical protuberance of silencer on the table between them, nobody looked at it. Nobody needed to, since he had laid it so that the black parallelogram of the handle was free of the table's edge, more accessible to his grasp than it had been under the cushion, and that the end of the silencer was midway on the short arc joining Peter Blackmore and Jassy Vane.

Chapter Thirteen

A dozen red roses

The message from Martin Harriman came when they were at breakfast. Peter Blackmore looked inquiringly at Jassy Vane as the extension telephone burred in the sitting-room of their suite.

'Harriman,' Jassy said flatly. 'It's not Saratov; he'll realise we may have been tapped by now. And it's certainly not our lot. It's Harriman.'

Peter Blackmore swung his knees from under the folds of the table-cloth and rose from the generous round table and crossed the room to the small, Second Empire wall table on which the telephone rested beside the desk made for ladies to write shopping lists and thank-you notes on. He lifted the receiver as the instrument cleared its throat for the third time. 'Yes,' he said, 'Bl-l-oome here,' and listened. 'Yes. Thank you. Please send it up.' He replaced the receiver and turned and said to the faintly derisive face above the round table in the centre of the room, 'If you so much as breathe, I'll hit you. Straight across your smirk.' He grinned. 'Christ! How did I ever get into this? Now I feel guilty about my own name . . . Sorry about that . . . It was nearly out before I caught myself.'

'It happens,' Jassy Vane told him. 'Some very good people have been caught that way. It's why nobody likes cover names in this business. If we have to use them then we have to; but they're always a bitch unless you've lived with them so long that you've almost forgotten your own . . . Who was that?'

'The desk. There's a package for you. They're sending it up.'

'A package?'

'That's what the man said. Do you think we ought to take it? Mayhew might just have decided to get hairy.'

'No.' She shook her head. 'They can't. Not until they're sure how much we know.'

'They could be sure by now.' He came back to the table and sat and pried a piece out of the half-fleshed second kipper on his plate, put it into his mouth and took a piece of toast from the squat, Victorian silver rack between them. Chewing as he buttered the triangle of toast, he said, 'They've had time enough. Remember how quickly they got on to Patterson.'

'They knew Patterson. At least somebody knew him well enough from the old war days to get anxious about his asking questions. Nobody knows us, except that we're Mr. and Mrs. Broome from Jamaica.'

'Saratov knows who we are.'

'So? We know who *he* is. We're even. No, we're one up. Robin and Helen should be just about getting our memo on him, and he knows *that*. He can't send anything through to his outfit on us; not without tipping his hand on Mayhew . . . What's wrong, Peter? We went through all this last night, after we left Saratov and D.L.B.'d* him. If he double-crossed us now, he'd be blown anywhere he could go.'

* D.L.B. or Dead Letter Box is British Intelligence idiom for a 'dead drop', or pick-up point where messages between agents or agents and sub-agents are exchanged. Jamaican Intelligence nostalgically retains such superficial evidences of its colonial origin.

He put a bite-marked fragment of toast on to his side-plate and irritably pushed the larger plate with its burden of unfinished kipper to one side, the knife and fork askew.

He said, as he poured himself more coffee and huddled over the cup: 'I'm worried. I've been worried since last night. Saratov's all right. We had to barter with him. But we're calling Mayhew with nothing in our hands. Did you ever play deuces wild?'

'No,' she said. 'What's that? Some sort of cards?'

'Yes. It's a damn' fool form of poker. Deuce . . . two of any suit . . . can be anything you like, from ace high to two. When you're playing it right out on the lunatic fringe, you can either show your deuce face up, or hide it. Or show one and hold one. It isn't gambling, really. It's a piece of non-sense that boys play when they're learning how to gamble. The probabilities for or against you are fucking astro-nomical. There's no skill: you just take a chance. That's the sort of game we're playing with Mayhew, and for all I know they've got a whole deck of deuces . . .'

She leaned across the table, the soft, deep cuff of her dressing-gown dropping away from her wrist as she stroked the copper-stubbled hull of his jaw.

'You were brought up on agreed probabilities,' she told him. 'I wasn't. I knew about deuces wild before I could talk. That's why Robin and Helen recruited me before you. They know all about deuces wild, too. It's the only game in which people like us stand a chance against people like you . . . What's bugging you now is that you've suddenly become a deuces wild man. You'll have to learn to like it, darling. It's the only game in town.'

'I may learn to play it,' he said, and grinned at her again, 'but I don't have to like it.'

'You don't have to *like* it,' she said earnestly. 'So long as you *win* it that's enough.'

He looked at her as she leaned back in her chair smiling at him faintly with a teasing, almost maternal protectiveness. The pastel yellow of her gown softened the glow left on her emphatic face by satisfied desire and deep sleep.

Now he asked her quietly, 'Does this happen often?'

'Does what happen, sweetheart?'

'How I'm feeling now?'

'How are you feeling?'

'You know how I'm feeling. Bloody frightened. Tense and exposed. As if the next person I meet coming round the corner may be coming for me . . . That somebody I don't know and will never know may be playing with me; allowing me to think I'm running free when all the time he's just driving me into a trap.'

'It happens to everybody,' she told him. 'Sooner or later, every agent has that moment. Even someone like Saratov or that cool little swine, Anyo.'

She thought, as she said this, We have him now. Now that he's discovered he can run scared like everybody else, he'll stick with us just to prove he didn't pull out because he got the shits once.

With something close to distaste, she reflected that Robin and Helen McKay had probably calculated for this moment: for the point where the man's fierce pride would seal him to them more effectively than any oath.

On the other side of the table, Peter Blackmore stared into his half empty cup like a seer fixing his concentration over a bowl of ink.

When the bell on the door to the corridor sounded he said, 'I'll get it,' and rose and crossed the room. Jassy Vane heard him say, 'Thank you. Just a minute.' He came back carrying a long, elegant box of buff-coloured cardboard and went into the bedroom. She heard the chink of money as he scrabbled in the change on the dressing-table. He came from the bedroom with the box still under his left arm and went again to the door behind her. 'Thank you,' he said. 'No. No reply. Good morning.' He shut the door and came back to the table and laid the box on the cloth before her. The box was the size of a baby's coffin, with a Cellophane lid. It contained a dozen long-stemmed American Beauties, three in half bloom, the rest closed in a coy and velvet perfection of crimson on an ice-white pad of pressed cotton wool. A large envelope, as stiff as parchment, was laid across the stems just under the petals. On it, in handwriting like compressed lips, they could read *Mrs. Peter Broome, Hotel Van Huyten, East 64th St.*

'Well,' Jassy Vane said, 'well, well . . . Harriman may be the creeps' creep but he isn't a *mean* creep . . . You've got to admit that. Hothouse roses like this don't grow on trees, y'know.'

'O.K.,' Peter Blackmore said, 'he's got a great eye for flowers, but what's in the *billet doux*?'

She lifted the lid of the box, removed the big envelope, thumbed back its tucked-in flap and took out a stiff double sheet of notepaper with the same pinched writing on it.

Peter Blackmore read over her shoulder, nodding when she looked up at him. She turned the first sheet of notepaper and they studied the precisely sketched road map on the opposite page. The diagram was crowded into the top left-hand corner of the big, finely grained sheet—as if the man who had signed himself 'M.H.' under the six tight lines of writing on the first page had not wished to sully more of the virginal surface that he could help.

'Conscientious little bugger, isn't he?' Peter Blackmore said. 'How about it? Do we go?'

Jassy Vane nodded. 'We go,' she said. 'We've got no choice.'

'Come to think of it,' Peter Blackmore said, 'that *was* an unnecessary question. What I should have asked is: do we come back?'

'Now I was hoping you wouldn't ask that,' she said. 'It's the question on my mind too, but I was hoping you wouldn't bring it out front where it belongs.'

Chapter Fourteen

Don Capo

They crossed into Brooklyn after an early lunch, to avoid th
mid-afternoon crush of traffic, and were clear of Nassau
county and well into Suffolk by four. In Center Moriches
they stopped and had coffee and turkey sandwiches at a
drive-in. Neither of them finished the food, but they each
drank two cups of coffee. It should have been pleasant
cruising through the rolling Long Island landscape in which
the green of spring was already deeper and the air milder
than on the mainland. But neither of them seemed able to
register scenery; everything they passed lay behind a film of
Cellophane: visible but belonging to another parallel dimen
sion.

In Amagansett, Jassy said, 'I could use that drink you
offered me.'

'I don't remember offering you a drink.'

'Well, you should have.'

They stopped at a small bar on the northern edge of the
little town. Inside it was consolingly synonymous and three
young men in identical leather jackets and bleached jean
were drinking beer. There was a leaning tower of coins on
their table, from which one of them, as Peter Blackmore and
Jassy Vane entered, was replenishing the juke-box. Pete
Blackmore and Jassy Vane chose the cubicle farthest away
from the young men and the juke-box. The man who had
been leaning against the inside curve of the bar where i

urned to join the wall lifted the flap and strolled over to
hem.

'What'll it be, folks?' He was plump and sandy and had the
contented air of those who have asked little out of life and
have got it secured.

'Two Manhattans, please,' Peter Blackmore told him.

'Two Manhattans it is,' the man said and went back behind
he bar. Peter Blackmore and Jassy Vane sat in silence until
he returned with their drinks. They were grateful for the
ntrusive sounds from the juke-box. The stylised throb of
pop, all echo-chamber and electronics, required no effort:
you could listen to it subliminally.

'Where're you folks from?' the barman asked as he put
he drinks before them. His curiosity was inoffensive: the
practical inquisitiveness of a culture still assembling itself
rom a hundred origins.

'I'm English,' Peter Blackmore told him. 'She's from
Martinique.'

'I thought you were English,' the barman said. 'The
minute I heard you speak I knew that was an English accent.
was in England during the war. Near Leicester mostly,
on bombers; but I used to get up to London a lot. I never
been to Martinique, but they make a great rum. I sell a lot
of it, like in toddies, during the winter. You visiting around
here?'

'Just taking a drive,' Peter Blackmore said. 'We're staying
n New York.'

'Well, you sure picked a nice day for a drive,' the man
assured them, and went back to his corner behind the
counter.

'America,' Jassy Vane muttered. 'At least, this part of it.
One day, little green men from outer space are going to land,
walk into a bar and vanish. They'll just be assimilated by the
nearest bartender . . . That makes a great country for our

sort of business,' she added. 'So long as you don't try to run for president, you can be from anywhere.'

'You've been here before?' Peter Blackmore asked her 'On business, I mean?' And realised as he asked the question that she had never told him anything about what she had done before he had been recruited, and that he, in their most open and confiding moments, had never asked. The rules of the game he had joined were learned so easily that sometimes one wondered if it were not the only authentic game: that if what other people played was not only an image of the reality Robin and Helen McKay, Anyo, Harriman and Saratov, he and Jassy, and ten thousand unknown others, acted out every day. It had a cool and reasonable logic, certainly, that the lives of those like the bartender and of the young men nursing their beer lacked.

'Yes,' Jassy Vane said. 'I've done a couple of runs here Nothing serious; nothing like this.' She smiled over the rim of her glass, sipped at the potent, golden-brown mixture and put the glass down. 'I'm glad you're with me on this. It makes me feel confident.'

'That's more than I feel.'

'*Peter* . . . don't worry about that. The first run in a foreign country, everybody gets uptight. I told you that. It's just your nerves getting tuned to a different situation . . . What time is it?'

'Coming up for five-thirty.'

'We ought to be going. Harriman's place must be about twenty miles from here. I'd like to get there in time to see it by daylight.'

They finished their drinks, not hurriedly but in silence Jassy Vane rose, gathered her handbag and gloves, and went across to the door at the back of the room on which was set the six-inch tall outline of a ballerina in wrought iron. After a minute, Peter Blackmore got up too and went to the other door marked with a little cowboy twirling a lariat. At the washbasin in the little room he let the cold tap run free and splashed and kneaded his face. The pipe must have been laid too close to the central heating because the water ran disappointingly tepid until he turned the tap off.

When he came out he went over to the bar and paid for the drinks.

The bartender brought him the change from the cash register in a little plastic tray which he put on the counter between them. Peter Blackmore let the coins lie in the tray and the man scooped them up and dropped them into a tumbler under the counter. 'You sure got a nice day for a drive,' the bartender said with comfortable proprietorship.

'Yes,' Peter Blackmore said, 'it's been a nice day. We had a little rain at about three o'clock, but it didn't last long.'

'That's April for you,' the bartender told him. 'Me, I like it.'

'Me too,' Peter Blackmore agreed, determined not to be outbid in cosmic tolerance.

The door to the women's lavatory opened and Jassy Vane stepped out. She had freshened her lipstick and other make-up, tugged and patted her clothes with the dozen deft touches women seem to be born knowing. She looked vivid and taut and sure of herself.

'Ready, darling?' she asked.

Peter Blackmore nodded and they both smiled at the bartender.

'Come again,' he said as they went to the entrance past the three young men sitting over the dried froth and flat remnants of their beer, with the now truncated pillar of coins in the centre of the table.

Outside, the declining sun was sharing the air with a fresh burst of rain as fine as the mist from an atomiser. Their coats

were powdered with tiny drops by the time they reached th
maroon Plymouth Satellite they had rented after lunch.

It was the going home hour. As they settled in their rente
Plymouth, other cars were passing, tyres hissing on th
slickly filmed tar, wipers semaphoring combinations of tw
repeated letters across the windshields. Most of the cars wer
going north to the scattered, prosperous suburbs that la
five miles deep beyond the little town. Peter Blackmore ha
a sudden, sharp envy of the pleasures and penalties to whic
the occupants of the passing cars were returning. They wer
enjoyed or suffered in a blaze of actuarial norms, of learne
reports, of instant sociology with titles like popular song
which sold by the ten thousand in a thousand brilliantly li
drugstores. Even anxiety—about sex or money or death—
was like a club fee: you had only to look at the rule boo
to see what everybody was paying. You lived in the ope
not in a cramped world of secret warrens and occasion
camouflaged exits to the surface. As he started the Plymoutl
looked over his shoulder and pulled out into the road, he ha
an image of himself crawling down a tunnel on hands an
knees, his back barely clear of the dank roof, blind an
sniffing thick air, with every other sense unnaturally attune
to a possible challenge from the impenetrable dark.

II

The house to which Martin Harriman had asked them t
come would have been easy to find, even if he had no
indicated it so precisely on his sketch map. It was set at th
end of a dirt road in a cleft, a dent, between low cliffs o
the eastern shore-line overlooking Block Island Soun
Gardiners Island was a grey hump three miles away on gre
choppy water, and there was one pale cluster of electric ligh

about two miles to the north. From the rise where they had stopped, they could see one corner of the house: a large cottage, really, angled and austere as a destroyer, with buttresses like spars and with a lot of picture window looking on to the dune between it and the sea. The slanting light from the west made the glass opaque, giving the house a blind, melancholy appearance. Two cars were drawn close against the side of the house: a white Corvette and a big black Lincoln.

'O.K.?' Peter Blackmore asked Jassy Vane. 'Seen enough?'

'Yes. Let's go down and get it over with.'

He switched on, slid the automatic gear into drive and took the car slowly down the slope.

Jassy Vane glanced once at him as he steered the two hundred yards to the gravelled parking space under the side windows of the house. The strings of tension that had pinched his face out of shape in the bar were now loosened. He had regained the animal, almost complacent sleekness of good looks which had irritated her when they first met— until she had taken note of his always alert, candidly inquisitive eyes. She thought fondly, and with something like exasperation: Nothing will ever frighten him for long; he's had so much of whatever he's wanted all his life that he isn't afraid of losing anything; he bloody well *knows* he'll get it back.

Almost jealously she asked, 'How're you feeling? O.K.?'

'Fine,' Peter Blackmore told her. 'The way I begin to see it, Harriman wouldn't bring us all the way to the end of Long Island just to clobber us. He has the resources to do that in New York, or anywhere, if he wanted to. He's fishing, Jassy. At least, *I'd* be fishing if I were Harriman.'

He braked, put the gear into reverse and took the car back behind the Lincoln until the rear bumper nearly touched the wall of the house and the bonnet pointed towards the road.

They sat and waited, looking at the bottom step of the outside staircase leading up to the front of the house.

Martin Harriman appeared suddenly around the angle made by the walls between them and the staircase. His tonsured head and pale, severely fashioned face were incongruous above the polo-neck Playboy jersey, slim, mustard-coloured Daks and scruffy brown moccasins. He wore the casual dress of his generation and income-bracket as though it were a necessary but distasteful camouflage.

'Mr. Harriman,' Jassy Vane called to the approaching figure, leaning across from her seat and speaking through the window on Peter Blackmore's side. 'Thank you for those roses. They were beautiful.' .

Martin Harriman strained six teeth through hard lips in a precise smile.

'Not at all,' he said. 'Beautiful roses for a beautiful lady,' he added like a boy giving the responses in an examination for which he had studied hard, without belief. He walked around the front of the car and opened Jassy Vane's door. She got out and shook his unenthusiastic hand. Peter Blackmore pressed the window button to close and climbed from behind the wheel.

'Follow me, please,' Martin Harriman said and walked ahead to the staircase.

A great deal of care and not a little money had gone into the building of the cottage. The walls were cut stone and the steps were teak slabs clamped to black-painted steel rods; the banister was a steel skeleton too, with a rail of two-by-four teak bolted to the top of the uprights.

'This is a nice place,' Peter Blackmore said appreciatively as they reached the little, open landing at the top of the stairs. 'Yours?'

Martin Harriman nodded curtly, as if a spoken admission might be damaging, and pushed open the heavy door, gesturing for them to enter before him. His movements were abrupt yet untidy. There were muddy smears under his dark eyes, and in the light from the living-room as he opened the door they could see the grey of exhaustion staining his pale face.

Peter Blackmore and Jassy Vane stood on the top step of the broad, shallow flight leading into the living-room. Behind them, Martin Harriman closed the door. They could hear the click of a Yale lock and the thud of a bolt driven home. Martin Harriman passed, without looking at them, and descended the steps into the living-room. They followed.

The room was long and high. Grey field stone went up to a tent top of plain redwood ceiling. Like the stairs outside, the floor was of teak, tightly dressed and firm as the planks of a quarter-deck. There was a very good rug in the middle of the room: Navajo or Pueblo: Peter Blackmore did not know enough about American Indian crafts except to recognise the general origin of patterns. The bookshelves were cut into the walls and ran round two sides from floor to ceiling: they were nearly filled: long sets of Victorian editions merging into modern hardbacks and enough paperbacks for Harriman to have been the key figure in the publishing revolution. Enough black leather furniture was ranged around the high, wide fireplace to seat a dozen without crowding. At the end of the room away from which they were walking were a rough sawn cedar table with stout-legged refectory type benches. There was only one picture: a Wyeth, showing a meticulous spire soaring out of the subdued green of a Pennsylvania valley into a radiant sky. A Fisher 125 stereo receiver and an Akkai custom converted tape recorder with ten-inch spools were set into the low scaffolding of steel in one corner and two speakers nestled on foam rubber mats in shelf-spaces on either side of the fireplace, level with a seated listener. The drapes pulled across the glassed-in sides were of heavy, coarse linen, the colour of Martin Harriman's mustard slacks.

Above the back of the couch which formed the outer boundary of the furniture area they could see a big, handsome head of nearly white lustrous hair. A tall, comfortably fleshed young man in a dark suit that seemed to have been painted on to him was seated in the black leather sheriff chair nearest the fireplace, on the right. He was about thirty, with a florid, keen face and big, glossy black eyes that assessed them with detached thoroughness as they came up. The white head did not turn.

Martin Harriman went round the end of the couch and faced the white head.

'They're here,' he said.

'Introduce us, Martin.' The white head remained still; the voice was the sort of whisper that goes far into a room because nobody else will be speaking when it has something to say. The accent was almost American, of the urban northeast, but beneath it there were the resonances of another language and climate.

Martin Harriman nodded at Peter Blackmore and Jassy Vane, and they stepped forward beside him.

'This is Mr. Vestucci,' Harriman said tightly. 'He . . . he felt that you and he ought to meet.'

'Mr. Broome, Mrs. Broome,' Mr. Vestucci acknowledged. 'I am pleased to make your acquaintance. According to Martin you seem to have rocked my boat a little. I hope we're going to be able to get together and steady it.'

They looked down on to the lean face and into the dark eyes of bland coldness he had raised to them by tilting his prim, sharp chin up an inch. It was a face Peter Blackmore could remember seeing before: not in exact feature, but in type. It had turned to him a gaze of sightless and sublime assurance from the busts of some of the emperors—those

162

few who had managed to contain the barbarians on the
frontier, gentle their Roman wolves and yet die, full of
gravitas, in their beds; it had glowed pallidly between the
gorgeous colours of a Doge's dress in the Bellini portraits,
dominating scarlet and gold by the sheer drama of experience
on each thin-lipped, grooved and hollowed countenance; in
the galleries of the Vatican, you passed a nearly unbroken
succession of that face. It was subtle, ruthless, utterly
without illusion—and chiselled in a style that made the faces
of similar men from any other people seem slightly unfinished, one coarser stage down the evolutionary scale.

'Sit down, please,' Mr. Vestucci continued, and lifted his
slim pale hand briefly from the black leather of the fat arm-
rest. He smiled with benevolent appreciation, but from a
great distance, at Jassy Vane's matching coat and suit of
lime sharkskin; surveyed Peter Blackmore and nodded to
the other sheriff chair beside the florid young man. There
was a tall glass on the coffee table before him. It was half full
of something pale pink and grained with a few bubbles.
Mr. Vestucci lifted it and smiled again at them. 'Soda water,'
he said. 'Soda water and bitters. My goddam doctor says
he'll have me committed as insane if I so much as smell
anything else . . . Not even wine,' he added with regal
petulance. 'My own grandson gets christened last week . . .
My *first* grandson . . . And I have to drink to his future in
soda water!' He raised his glass to his lips, sulkily. 'Martin,
I'm sure our friends from Jamaica would like a drink after
their drive.'

Peter Blackmore crossed in front of the coffee table and
sat beside the young man who would one day have a heavier
version of Mr. Vestucci's face. In five years, perhaps, it
would be necessary to introduce him at meetings like this.
Jassy Vane sat in the centre of the couch, pointed her tan,
15-denier knees at Mr. Vestucci, shrugged out of her coat

and laid it beside her. Martin Harriman went rigidly to where bottles, glasses and a barrel-shaped ice-bucket in an oak casing rested on a shelf space surrounded by books.

A small snapping fire of salt-laden driftwood supplemented the central heating from the lengths of copper piping set flush into the angle between walls and floor. Mr. Vestucci contemplated the purple and green flames with their streaks of gold while Martin Harriman mixed two Manhattans for Jassy Vane and Peter Blackmore. Nobody spoke until he came back with their drinks, then Jassy Vane said, 'Thank you, Mr. Harriman,' and held an unlighted cigarette to her lips as Harriman was handing Peter Blackmore his glass. Harriman swung round, felt in the side pockets of his slacks, looked about him, took a packet of book matches from the coffee table and lit her cigarette.

Mr. Vestucci said, 'Sit down, Martin. You make me nervous. You make everybody nervous. Particularly you make yourself nervous . . . Bad things happen when people get nervous. Bad, untidy things . . . Now this lady here isn't nervous.' He smiled at Jassy—it came and went like a flake of sunlight on the surface of a riffled pool. 'She and her husband have driven all this way to meet us and *they* aren't nervous. You aren't nervous, are you, my dear lady?'

'No,' Jassy Vane told him. 'But then I'm black. If you're black you've got so many things to be nervous about already that one more doesn't make any difference.'

'I had shares in Ford once,' Peter Blackmore said. 'Just after they put the Edsel on the market. I could never be as nervous again.'

Mr. Vestucci digested their remarks for a moment—then a quiet chuckle emerged like the answer card from a computer. He felt inside the jacket of his dove grey gabardine and took out a cigar case covered with purple morocco: when he opened it they could see three slim dark tubes against cedar.

'One every six hours,' Mr. Vestucci said. He did not lean forward into the flame from the gold lighter which the young man who had been on Peter Blackmore's right was holding to the cigar's tip. 'That's what my goddam doctor allows me. Any more and he's going to have me declared a ward of the courts.' The young man returned to his chair. Mr. Vestucci drew carefully and exhaled: the smoke could hardly have passed his front teeth. He said, 'Now Martin there did a very sensible thing after you two jumped him yesterday. I like to believe you're going to be as sensible as he was.'

'Well, I don't know,' Jassy Vane said. 'We like to be sensible but maybe Mr. Harriman has set such a high standard we couldn't live up to it. What did he do that was so sensible, Mr. Vestucci?'

'He came to me first,' Vestucci said, 'with his little problem.' He chuckled again. '*You're* his little problem . . . Mine too . . . I don't like problems I can't see; that's why I asked him to bring you out here.'

'When you say he came to you first,' Peter Blackmore asked him, 'd'you mean there's somebody else he could have gone to?' He looked at Martin Harriman: the grey-white skin on Harriman's cheekbones had flushed as it had done the day before in the restaurant when he was teased: the troubled, dark eyes were dull.

Vestucci looked mildly surprised. 'Why yes, Mr. Broome. He could have gone directly to—to my partners in the Candywine Development. But then he thought it over. He thought perhaps you might know a lot more than you had told him and that I might be able to persuade you to tell it better than my partners. He . . .'

'Hold it, Vestucci.' Peter Blackmore's deliberate rudeness shook the room disagreeably, like a smashed glass. 'Just hold

165

it in your hot little hand. You may know the steps for this dance but you're beginning to lose me. We told Harriman yesterday that we didn't like what we knew about Candywine. From our side of the table it has always looked like a stacked deck, but now it's Russian roulette, with my country having to take a chance every turn of the chamber. We told him we wanted to meet his top bananas or at least somebody a bit higher up the stem than he is. Now he deals you into the game, and all we've heard is a lot of jazz about your partners. We don't talk any sort of business until we know who you are, Vestucci . . .'

'Peter,' Jassy Vane interrupted gently. 'I think Mr. Vestucci represents certain family interests in Candywine. He's acting in that capacity . . . Aren't you, Mr. Vestucci?' She smiled at him, and he nodded warily back.*

'You could say that,' he said.

'Oh, but I do say it,' Jassy Vane said earnestly. 'And I do agree that Mr. Harriman was very sensible to come to you. The way his security has been leaking since we first got on to Mayhew meant that somebody might have to answer. That could only mean Harriman. Mayhew is big enough now to have area responsibility . . . and Candywine must be Harriman's. At least, he must be close enough to the top to be answerable. They would have had to declare him redundant if he'd gone to them with the news that the uranium transfer was no longer a big secret . . . How am I reading it, Mr. Vestucci?'

* The Mafia in the United States is controlled or, more strictly, directed by 24 'families': closely knit clans from which major policies emanate. They are jealous oligarchs rather than a unified party and their relationships with the other Establishments of organised crime are too intricate to examine here. The *don capos* are the heads within the families. Most of them are as remote from the raw, sometimes lethal encounters of practical crime as modern generals are from hand to hand combat.

Vestucci drew another tiptoe whiff from his cigar and slightly raised his glass. His chin was sunk on to the top of his thorax and he still looked thoughtfully into the little flames.

'Thank you,' Jassy Vane said, and lit another Pall Mall from the quarter length of her previous one. 'Now we come to you, Mr. Vestucci . . . Why are you bailing out Harriman's boat?' She leaned forward and stubbed the butt of her old cigarette in one of the two chunky, earthenware ashtrays on the coffee table.

Vestucci said, 'You have read pretty good up to now, my dear lady. I don't think I have to spell it out for you. I've got a great deal riding on Candywine. More than you maybe imagine. It would make me very unhappy if anything happened to Candywine; if a lot of wild talk began frightening the customers.'

'Tourists are funny that way,' Peter Blackmore said. 'No matter how sweet a set-up you give 'em to gamble in, they just can't keep their minds on the game when they know a bunch of lunatics may be swapping hydrogen bombs three miles away.'

Vestucci sighed patiently, frowned at the grey cluster on of the tip his cigar, started to raise the unlit end to his lips, then reached over and rested the cigar in a groove on the rim of the other ashtray.

'It's not the same,' he said querulously. 'They don't taste the same when you got to handle them as if they were rattlesnakes or something. I pay that goddam doctor of mine five thousand a year, just as a retainer, and every time he comes to give me a check-up he's got another piece of good news for me.' His voice rose on a note of sour mimicry. ' "We shall have to go easy on the *pasta*, Mr. Vestucci" . . . "We shall have to watch our blood pressure very carefully for a few months, Mr. Vestucci" . . . "Alcohol is a no-no for us,

Mr. Vestucci" . . . "We should not really be smoking at all, Mr. Vestucci, but perhaps we can allow ourselves one after each meal if we don't inhale" . . . Where does he get with the "we" for Chrissake? He can go through a bottle of my twelve-year-old scotch like it was a Coke. And the way he helps himself from my humidor you'd think maybe the world tobacco famine was next week and he had advance information. You take him out to lunch and they have to borrow steak and lobster and potatoes from the restaurant across the street in case he cleans them out and starts eating the goddam waiters. But it's still "we" whenever I have to make like the Pope on Good Friday.' Eyes distant and comprehensive as orbiting satellites turned to Peter Blackmore. 'So the Chinese get a few extra suitcases of enriched uranium— from *us*—and they make a few more big bangs at that place I can't remember . . . It's in China someplace . . .'

'Lop Nor,' Martin Harriman said.

'Yes . . . Lop Nor . . . Where they've been testing . . . The Russians begin to get steam on the windshield because they can't figure out how the Yellow Perils are making so much enriched uranium, so quick. The way Martin tells it, they shouldn't have the resources, but they *might*. So the Russians have to move some of the muscle off us and have it ready in Asia. Just in case. Because the Chinese are way over their quota. Are you going to knock that as a proposition, Mr. Broome? You aren't going to get a better deal from the communists than me if they take over; and if you have people like Martin in there setting them up against each other, far away from here, I think you ought to co-operate. Martin's people are on *our* side, Mr. Broome. You've got to believe that. Good Americans, and a lot of them are putting up some pretty big futures as stakes if they get found out before they're ready. But they know we're losing out to the communists on this side. Look at Cuba. And they're prepared to take the risk until the rest of America realises it's time for a change and that they are the change it's time for. I really think you ought to co-operate, Mr. Broome.'

'You make it sound like a patriotic duty,' Peter Blackmore said. 'The only thing you haven't mentioned is what happens if anything goes wrong. Happens to us in Jamaica, I mean. Also you haven't mentioned why we didn't know about all this before. We had to find out for ourselves, and we can spoil it for everybody any time we want—without losing anything. We'd gain, in fact, because we'd make it impossible for your people to operate in our territory.'

'We're a legitimate business.' There was a righteous warmth in Mr. Vestucci's voice. 'Your government has given us the concession, Mr. Broome. You can look at it. It's a signed agreement.'

'All right, Vestucci,' Peter Blackmore said flatly. 'You bought a few blind eyes for the gambling. You're a benevolent association now, like the World Bank and UNESCO. But what you didn't tell the people you bought down our way was that Mayhew came with the agreement. We have some real cut-rate boys, and you must have picked them up wholesale to get Candywine served to you on a platter—but they didn't begin to know about Mayhew. If they had, you'd have been on the Huntley-Brinkley Show. They'd have just curled up and squealed and you'd still be carrying your head in your hands.'

'You didn't come all this way just to tell me what I know already,' Vestucci said. 'And you didn't make contact with Martin just to tell him how smart you are down in Jamaica. So you got to want something. O.K. That's fine. I like it when people want something. That's when you start to do business. So what do you want, Mr. Broome? I'm not saying I can supply, but I can't know for sure until you tell me what it is.'

Martin Harriman said suddenly, 'I don't like this.' His hot, suspicious gaze scurried between Jassy Vane and Peter Blackmore, probing them as if they were carrying deceits and stratagems under their clothes like concealed weapons. 'Whatever they agree to here doesn't have to be binding when they leave. You should have done what I suggested.'

'Martin,' Vestucci murmured, 'you don't seem to understand. At the moment you've got to like it. And, Martin, would they have gone to all this trouble if they didn't want to do a little business? They're bright people, Martin, and maybe they're going to ask a little more than we had figured it was going to cost. But you've got to pay people for being bright. Like I pay my doctor for being bright enough so he knows what will kill me if I don't eat and drink worse than a goddam peasant.' He turned his ecclesiastical head and bestowed a fleeting, paternal smile on Jassy Vane. 'What d'you say, my dear lady?'

'Oh,' Jassy Vane said, 'I like to talk to a person who likes to talk to a person who likes to talk business.'

'You hear that, Martin?' Mr. Vestucci's chuckle was indulgent, almost cosy. 'I knew I was going to like them as soon as I saw them. I feel about this dear lady already like she was my own daughter. As for him,' he indicated Peter Blackmore with a wave of his fingertips, 'Now, he wants us to think he's stupid. I like that. Look stupid and act smart and you don't offend anybody. I should have three stupids like him in my business.'

For the third time Mr. Vestucci chuckled. He seemed to like everybody and everything. Even the rejected cigar, which he picked from the ashtray and held to the flame produced by the florid young man who was bent solicitously over him.

Chapter Fifteen

A question of disposal

Even after midnight, one did not cross into Manhattan—any more than one entered the fanged, reaching mouth of a lion. Manhattan closed jaws behind you suddenly and you were already being digested as you went into a roar of light and the blaze of eight million lives. Only the mad, or those who created a strictly defined village of interests around themselves, could hope to preserve identity, a sense of normal human size.

Jassy Vane coasted the maroon Satellite down the ramp in the car hire agency, braked, switched off and dug her green-gloved finger into Peter Blackmore's ribs. He opened his eyes and was awake without protest or confusion.

'All out,' Jassy Vane said. 'Not bad. Three hours from Gardiners Sound to downtown. We'd still have been in the middle of Long Island if I'd let you drive.'

'Tremendous,' Peter Blackmore said and stretched. 'I'll tell the Plymouth people. Perhaps they'll give you some sort of award.' He reached across and hugged her against him and rubbed his nose against her cheekbone. 'You did all right out at Harriman's, didn't you? All the time, I kept thinking that if Vestucci suddenly decided we had to go, at least the bitch was going to die trying.'

'You were pretty good yourself,' she told him. 'I don't think we'd have left on our own if it hadn't been for you.'

He tightened the arm he had put around her shoulders,

then opened his door and climbed out. Across the sidewalk from the ramp, a stout coloured man in overalls closed the door to the office behind him and came over to the car. He nodded and said, 'Had a good day, folks?' and took the card Peter Blackmore handed him. He put his head in through the window, shone a torch on the dashboard and read, '701.3 —call it 701,' aloud, straightened and scribbled figures on the card. 'Thank you,' he said, and handed the card back to Peter Blackmore. 'Just check in at the office.' He walked round the front of the car, got into the driver's seat and took the Satellite down the blue-lit ramp to the parking area.

The clerk in the office was coloured also: a tall, coffee berry brown with tight, shiny grey curls.

He said, 'Good morning,' and looked at the card Peter Blackmore passed across the counter and then at the electric clock over the door to the street. 'Twelve-seventeen,' he said. 'We'll say midnight . . . With mileage . . .' He pushed buttons on a small calculator at his left hand. 'That'll be seventeen-sixty, sir, including tax.'

'Thank you,' Peter Blackmore said and passed his thumb along the bills in his wallet and extracted a twenty.

'Thank *you*, sir,' the clerk said and opened a drawer under the counter. 'I hope you enjoyed your day?'

'Yes, we did,' Peter Blackmore said and took the change and deposit money the clerk handed him. 'We're a little later than we'd expected, but we're going home to-morrow and thought we'd make the most of the last day.'

'You're from?' The clerk looked from face to face.

'Jamaica,' Jassy Vane said. 'We came up for a few days on business.'

'That's nice,' the clerk said. 'My old man came from Jamaica. I never been there myself but he was always telling me how great it was. I hope you folks have had a nice time in New York.'

'Oh, yes,' Peter Blackmore told him. 'D'you want this back, by the way?' He held up the insurance certificate he had filled in when he had rented the car after lunch.

'No,' the clerk said. 'It's yours. Here—I'll just put it in the basket for you.' He took the certificate. 'Good night, folks.'

'Good night,' Peter Blackmore said. 'Will we get a taxi near here?'

'Oh, sure,' the clerk said. 'Just down from here. On the corner at Third. 'Night.'

They went out. The clerk watched the door close behind them, then took a fold of thin paper from between the twin leaves of the insurance policy. He dropped the policy into the waste-basket set against the wall behind the counter beside the little desk and took an envelope from the stack on the desk-top. He put the folded paper inside the envelope, licked the flap, pressed it shut and wrote on the front of the envelope with the ball-point he took from the bakelite desk-set.

When the man who had parked the car came back, the clerk said, 'Watch things a minute for me, will you Clint?, I got to post a letter.'

'Sure,' Clint said. 'Everything's in now except 318, an' they only been gone an hour.'

The clerk took a severe black trilby and light tan coat which had been dry cleaned too many times from a peg on the wall. He put them on, left the office and walked down to the Third Avenue corner. He turned north and went two blocks to East 29th Street. Half a block along the street, going west, he stopped outside a branch of the Bank of America, took a key from the inside pocket of his coat and opened the night deposit box. He slid the envelope he had addressed down the chute, closed the box and walked back to the office.

Clint was sitting in one of the arm-chairs in the section

beyond the counter, flicking through a travel brochure on
the Alleghenies. He looked up in surprise and said, 'Man,
you musta really hustled. Post Office's all of six blocks from
here.'

The clerk went behind the counter, hung up his coat and
hat and thought, One day I'll forget something obvious like
it's six blocks to the Post Office and it won't be any dumb
nigger like Clint who'll notice, either.

He sat at the desk and clasped his fingers until his hands
stopped trembling. Sometimes he would think of telling
them in Jamaica that he wasn't going to do this any more.
There was no danger, they had said. Just post a few letters
and occasionally pass one to somebody who'd come in to
hire a car or make inquiries about hiring one. No danger at
all. But he knew different. Any job that easy where somebody
paid you two hundred a month in small bills for doing it
meant danger some time. Whenever he got the two hundred
untaxed dollars per month he would think of his son at Yale
who was going to be way up there as a lawyer one day. And
whenever he put the dollars and his son together in his
thoughts, he knew that he wasn't going to tell the people in
Jamaica anything about not working for them.

II

Peter Blackmore and Jassy Vane took a taxi to their hotel.
While he was paying, she stood beside him on the sidewalk.
As they turned to cross to the entrance she said, 'I don't see
anybody, but all the same . . .'

They went inside and he got the key to their suite and
joined her at the elevator. When they were in the suite, he
picked up the bedside telephone and asked for reception.

'This is Suite 6C,' he said. 'Yes, Peter Broome speaking.
Look, we're rather tired. No calls, please. Hold any messages

until the morning . . . Thank you . . . Good night . . . Good
morning, rather.'

They left the suite after he had hung up, took the elevator
back to the lobby and walked across to The Park Room,
which they had passed up in favour of The Retreat on the
evening of their arrival. The Park Room was larger and
lighter than The Retreat and there were a lot of formal
evening clothes among the lounge suits and short dresses at
the tables. Peter Blackmore shook his head pleasantly at the
waiter who came up with an inquiring look, and he and Jassy
Vane continued across the carpet between the bar and the
tables to the revolving door that led out on to the avenue
round the corner from the main entrance on the street. Peter
Blackmore said, 'Yes, please,' to the doorman who asked if
they wanted a taxi, and they stood close together while the
man went to the edge of the sidewalk to signal one in.

The restaurant where they had arranged to meet Saratov was
big, slick and Chinese. It was on West 54th and they could
see a large after-theatre crowd in the dining area beyond the
lounge.

There were only four people at the long bar: a big, dapper
man above a pale Scotch; a vivid younger man with the ends
of his hair resting on the shoulders of his fluffy crimson
sweater, leaning his head close to a girl with a face made for
the firelight of a gipsy camp or the sleeve of a folksong disc;
Saratov was on the last stool down from the curve of the
counter, his back resting against the wall.

Peter Blackmore helped Jassy Vane out of her coat, held
it over his left forearm while he shrugged out of his own,
hung them on a piece of spiky chinoiserie that stood in the
corner and waited while she settled herself on the stool next
to Saratov.

'Two Scotches, please,' he said to the bartender. 'J. and

175

B.; on the rocks,' and half sat on the stool before the curve of the counter, his right foot on the floor, his left elbow resting on the padded front so that he could look at both Jassy Vane and Saratov. The bartender came back with two squat tumblers stuffed with ice-cubes. The straw-coloured whisky seeped down between the cubes, and Saratov gave the barman a nod that included the glass before him. The bartender reached a bottle of vodka from the shelf under the long mirror and flourished it above Saratov's glass. 'Same again?' he asked. 'Thank you, yes,' Saratov replied. 'A double. One piece of ice.' He sipped as the bartender went back up the bar to join the two others who were not having anything to do. 'Ice,' Saratov said with distaste. 'What a waste of good vodka. I feel guilty every time I ask for it.'

'You could say no ice,' Jassy Vane told him. 'They don't have to serve it by law, you know.'

'It would make me conspicuous,' Saratov said. 'Only one cube is eccentric, but permissible. No ice at all and they might think I was a Russian spy.' He smiled at them; at least the stout prongs of the moustache twitched slightly. His suit still fitted where it touched. The thick, pewter hair was sleek with water or lotion and the steel frames of the spectacles were bright.

He said, 'I am relieved to see you back. In another half an hour I would have begun to worry. In an hour I would have had to start thinking, and to begin regretting the loss of two allies.'

' "Allies" is pretty strong,' Jassy Vane told him. 'Can't we just say "partners", or something like that?'

'Allies,' repeated Saratov firmly. 'All good alliances are temporary. Partnerships are like marriage; one side always feels badly about the divorce . . . You enjoyed your drive?'

'Yes,' Jassy Vane said. 'It was nice to get out of New York for a day. I always say if you want to meet the real Americans you have got to get out of New York. Now, for instance, you couldn't guess what a real American we met to-day.'

'No,' Saratov said, 'I couldn't guess. But perhaps you will tell me . . .'

She told him briefly, under the sounds from the dining-room and from the tables behind them. Once Peter Blackmore signalled the bartender and they repeated their drinks.

When she was finished, Saratov said, 'This changes things —a little. I did not anticipate Vestucci. What do you wish to do?'

'I told you. We've already done it. We've taken his money. At least, we've agreed to take his money, and we'll get it. Some of it anyway. Maybe it's better like this. I never liked the idea of having to negotiate directly with Mayhew. And after what you told us last night, we were plain scared going out to-day. I don't think I could have gone through with it if I'd been alone. When I realised that Vestucci was only the Mob and that Harriman had gone to him because he was afraid of his own people, I knew we had made it.'

'You are sure Vestucci knows nothing about the other side of Mayhew? *My* side?' The steady green eyes flickered with pale splinters of warmth as Saratov smiled.

'If he does then the Mob are playing it so deep and so tricky I can't even begin to figure what they'd get out of it . . . The kudos of eventually blowing Mayhew to the C.I.A.? No. Too risky. Something way out like pulling off a coup on their own? Maybe master-minding a revolution against Castro and getting back into Cuba that way? That just isn't feasible, Saratov. No . . . Mayhew offered them a very convincing story line and they've bought it. They may be big clever sharks, but that's all they are . . . sharks. Dangle a fat bait and they'll grab it, no matter what hooks there are inside.'

'They do not make many mistakes,' Saratov said. A

shadow of bitterness passed across the blunt, tidy face; the green eyes clouded. 'Forty billion dollars,' he told them, tapping the long forefinger of his right hand on the bar-top. 'Think of that. Forty billion dollars is what you permit organised crime to take in each year. Ten per cent of a nation's budget thrown to animals of no conceivable value.' He drank, and when he looked at them again his face was clear and composed and the good humour had returned to his eyes. 'If ever I might begin to have doubts of my own system, to be tempted, I only have to think of people like your Mr. Vestucci and forty billion dollars.'

'Well, he isn't really *our* Mr. Vestucci,' Peter Blackmore told him, 'and it certainly isn't our forty billion dollars. He and the dollars belong to these people here.' He waved his hand to include the men behind the bar, the young couple, the dapper man above another Scotch, the City of New York, the three million square miles of the republic between them and the Pacific Ocean.

'As do you,' Saratov said. 'You and my other ally here belong to these people too. You give yourselves a name, a nationality, but they mean no more than if the chickens in a coop think of it as *their* coop. It belongs to those in the house. Like the eggs you lay, or your lives. They will cut off your heads and pluck you and boil you into soup if they begin to feel hungry.'

'I know,' Peter Blackmore said. 'We worry about it all the time. Sometimes we tell ourselves how great it would be if we were Hungarians or Czechs or people like that.'

Saratov shook his head impatiently and drank again. 'You do not understand,' he said. 'Those things to which you refer were necessities, disagreeable necessities to save a situation. Your military lunatics and the big industrialists who pay them to keep the situation intolerable will not let us alone. A moment's inattention or carelessness on our part and they would have Germany at our throats again—to finish the job it so nearly did last time. Do you think you can imagine what a country that has lost thirty million of its people in four years looks like afterwards . . . what it *feels* about those who did it and about those who waited for the others to bleed us and bleed us before coming to our aid?' For a moment he stared into his glass, his lean, wide shoulders and long torso bent and stiff as though under a weight; he swirled what was left of the clear liquor in his glass, his face suddenly pinched and remote. Then he shrugged, tossed the remains of his drink to the back of his throat, smiled at them and raised his hand for the bartender. 'So,' he said. 'Sometimes it is better to remember aloud what cannot be forgotten.' They watched in silence as the barman did his conjurer's passes.

'You are leaving to-morrow then?' Saratov asked.

'Yes,' Jassy Vane said. 'When can we expect you in Jamaica?'

'In a week. Perhaps two. I have arrangements to secure. You are certain your people will agree to co-operate?'

'Quite certain. We need your resources. And besides . . . if things go wrong, if there was any slip up and it had to become public, we could pin it on you and the others. We could make it into another big power engagement in a small, defenceless country. You understand that, don't you?'

'Yes,' Saratov seemed absently and ironically amused. 'I understand.' The steel frames twinkled dully in the subdued lighting as he leaned his head closer to her. 'You look worried. No, not worried . . . Preoccupied . . . Is that right? Yes, pre-occupied. Are you having second thoughts? You do not wish to accept my offer?'

Jassy Vane lit a cigarette and held the match over the ashtray. She let it burn almost to her fingers before dropping it.

'I'm having second thoughts,' she said softly, 'but not about you . . . What are we going to do about Harriman?'

'Ah, yes, Harriman,' Saratov said. 'I was waiting for you to come back to him. You feel as I do, I think.'

'Yes,' Jassy Vane sighed once. When she sipped at her drink she made a face as if it had tasted badly or had no taste at all. 'He can't remain functional, Saratov. He's inconsistent and he's feeling guilty. Christ knows what's going to hit his bloody conscience, or whatever it is he thinks with, to-morrow or next week or maybe six months from now. He could blow us all . . . Oh, shit! You know we can't afford the risk.'

'I don't think we can,' Saratov said. He pushed the spectacles up on to his forehead and rubbed the little pink indentation on the flat, strong bridge between his eyes. 'Do you?' he asked Peter Blackmore.

'Suppose I said we could,' Peter Blackmore replied, 'would it make any difference? To either of you?' he added. His voice was flat and dry. Jassy Vane looked at her drink and the smoke drifting up from her cigarette.

Saratov stopped rubbing the place where his spectacles had marked him. He lowered them like a fragile, droll visor, and looked past Jassy Vane at Peter Blackmore. After a pause, he said quietly, 'No, it would make no difference to me. I do not like to think about a man's life as we are now thinking. It is better not to think of him at all, particularly if you have met him. Simply think of what he is doing or may do to your plans. If he has to be stopped then decide what is the best way. Sometimes money or threats will do; sometimes you have to be more sure. Believe me, Mr. Broome, that is the best way in work like ours. We could not live with ourselves otherwise.'

Jassy Vane said in a careful voice, 'Leave Harriman to us,

Saratov. It has to be done quickly. Like now. I can get it done by to-morrow morning. This morning, I mean.'

'You.' Saratov straightened. He said in surprise, 'You have authority to arrange for disposal?'

'Yes. Not always. On runs like this I am given discretion.'

'I see. You realise that it must be done carefully. Mayhew must be convinced that it was an accident when they investigate.'

'No, I didn't realise that,' Jassy Vane said in the same careful monotone. 'I was going to leave a note and my photograph in his pocket.'

'All right, all right,' Saratov said anxiously. 'Forgive me if I seemed to patronise. I am worried like you. I wish it was not necessary. A death often uncovers more than it secures. I have seen it so often. Sometimes I think it would be better if all sides in this work, all the agencies everywhere, agreed that there should be no deaths. That we should just try to out-manoeuvre each other like the old Chinese generals and concede victory to the one in an unchallengeable position . . . I suppose,' he added slyly, but without much hope, 'that you would not tell me what you intend to do?'

'You suppose dead right,' Jassy Vane said. 'We may want to use it on you some day . . . Don't be a hog, Saratov. You're getting a service you need and we're picking up the bill. You wouldn't like to go halves, would you? It'll cost about two thousand dollars. That's nothing to you. Our people are going to have it out of our hides.'

Saratov's smile was all apology, charm and gratification.

'Alas, no,' he said. 'I have an auditor with the instincts of a ferret. May his soul rot in hell. Not that I believe in hell or a soul, but I wish I did that for his sake. I would never be able to justify it.'

He laughed, and after a moment Jassy Vane and Peter Blackmore laughed too.

Chapter Sixteen

A matter of soul

They had one more drink with Saratov and then he left them, squeezing himself into a blue Aquascutum that made him look suddenly trim and uniformed.

Peter Blackmore said, 'You ought to eat. We haven't had anything since those sandwiches.'

'I'm not hungry. I feel like food but I'm not hungry.'

'Me neither, but let's try.'

The dining-room was still busy with the voices of people whose day began at noon. They were given a table in a corner and Peter Blackmore ordered four dishes firmly although she insisted soup and one dish would do. When the food came, she ate lightly at first, then almost greedily, and then with the pleasure of one having a little more than enough. She had one cup of coffee and a cigarette, then looked at her watch.

'I'd better be going,' she said; except for ordering and offering each other a dish, neither had spoken during the meal.

'You're not going to do anything on your own.' It was an anxious charge rather than a question.

'Of course not, you silly man. I've got to see somebody is all.'

'I think I ought to come.'

'Not where I'm going. It wouldn't be a good idea. Don't worry. This is a straight business call. I'll be back at the hotel in an hour.' Jassy Vane felt inside her handbag, took out a ball-point with PAN AM MAKES THE GOING GREAT engraved up the casing and jotted figures on a paper coaster. 'Call me there if I'm not back in an hour. I will be, but just in case.'

Peter Blackmore studied the numbers she had written and nodded when she asked, 'Got it?' She took the little disc of tissue from him and idly crumpled and shredded it. 'Fine,' she said. 'See you, darling.'

He watched the intricate sway of her hips under the long, straight back as she went to the entrance between the dining-room and bar. With an odd sense of detachment, as though listening to a friend's confession, he realised that he loved this woman. In his nearly forty years of amiable and comfortably insulated life, he had treated most of those he met with kindness, even with generosity. He had a great deal to be generous with, and not only money. But he had never given love, except for a little, to the bright, superficial birds of passage who had been his parents and whom he now thought of with a fond understanding of weakness that excluded any sense of loss. After their deaths, in a world full of conventional declarations of need, he had kept silence. Because of a sort of perverse candour that tied him to awareness of his self-sufficiency. Now, in a grotesque sub-world of deceits, treasons and deaths planned without hate, he had stumbled on his capacity to really need another. It was, he thought wryly, an irrelevant find, except insofar as it made him vulnerable and open to use.

II

Well as she knew the city, the crossing into Harlem always alerted Jassy Vane. It was like entering a beleaguered fortress. Not one about to surrender, but one where all resources had been put into the necessities of survival: into food, liquor and clothes. Colour—from her own deep-tinted black to yellowish flush of old piano keys—was not so much a flag as a heresy: a fierce and diverging conviction of grace around which the mass of white, orthodox America beat with vain hopes of expulsion, assimilation or conversion. Above all it was a fortress of the young and lean.

She had her cab stop at 125th Street and Seventh, and walked up and across to 127th near Lenox. The titled parallelogram of neon sign that used to read ANDY'S had been changed to SOUL HOLE and the poster on the notice-board outside the hall across the street was now pop art: a black Christ with IS HE YOUR GOD? above the woolly head and HE HAS YOUR HAIR superimposed across the chest of the comic-book, conventional white nightgown. Behind the plate-glass of the drugstore next to SOUL HOLE five black girl dolls in party dresses were placed like madonnas in the niches between paperbacks of black literature.

She went down the steps between the cans of festering garbage and pushed open the door to SOUL HOLE.

A detonation of noise and escaping hot air rocked her back on her heels. At the end of the room, on a low stage, five electric guitars and a mobile of drums were backstopping a sleek, oxblood brown singer who was flapping his *dashiki* shirt and taking bites out of his portable microphone as he crackled the paint on the walls and buckled the floor by sonic massage. There were a lot of crowded tables, a dim blue light and ten-tenths overcast of tobacco smoke.

Jassy Vane crossed between tables to the end of the room and past the stage. The song was coming up to its finale and the sounds from the guitars seemed to hit the body. She pushed open a door and went along the corridor past the toilets to the kitchen. It was a small bright room, clean as an operating theatre.

184

'I want to see Andy,' Jassy Vane told the big, shiny-faced black chef who was turning something delicious in a deep dish frying-pan. 'Is he in town?'

'Three o'clock,' the chef said. 'Three o'clock in the mornin'. You want to see Andy, you come to-morrow when everybody comes.'

Jassy Vane walked up to the stove, looked appreciatively into the frying pan and then up at the chef.

'Andy,' she said. 'I want to see Andy. Now you just get on that telephone up to his apartment, dad, and tell him JV wants to see him, or you're going to end up walking home with your big black balls in your hands.'

The big man's face tightened furiously and his lips parted. Then he looked at her more closely, took a long breath and turned away.

'O.K.,' he said over his shoulder. 'If you so sure. Jay Vee you said?'

'That's right.'

'I hope Andy knows,' the man said. He picked up the receiver of a wall telephone at the end of the room beside the closed doors of a service elevator. 'He's entertainin' company to-night. Special company.'

'I don't care if he's humping the Queen of Sheba,' Jassy Vane told him. 'Like you said, it's three o'clock in the morning and believe me, dad, I've had a long day.'

The man muttered into the telephone and she could see him nod and mutter again. He hung up and beckoned her and pressed a button beside the telephone: the twin doors of the service elevator slid open.

'He says to go on up.'

The chef was looking at her with a great deal of curiosity and not a little respect.

'Thank you.' Jassy Vane paused as she was about to step into the elevator. 'Sorry I made like a bitch back there. I

185

really been carrying cotton all day.' She put a ten-dollar bill into his hand.

'I unnerstan',' the chef told her. 'Some days life really leans. You don' have to do this.' He raised the hand holding the bill she had given him.

'Oh, yes I do.' Jassy Vane smiled at him. 'You can't buy good manners, but you ought to make mean talk expensive.'

He grinned at her as she pressed the UP button and the doors began to close.

Andy was as black as a shadow and nearly as thin. His balding head was shaved close, leaving stubbles of grey above the ears.

The living-room of his apartment was like the special display window of an expensive furniture store.

He was waiting for Jassy Vane when the lift doors opened, wearing a black and gold, raw silk dressing-gown that could have been part of the loot from the Summer Palace in Peking.

He said, 'Hi, Jassy . . . it's been a long time,' and led her across to the ebony and white leather bar in one corner.

'Something soft, Andy,' Jassy Vane said. 'Like ginger ale on a lot of ice and maybe a little brandy to stop me catching cold from the ice.' She settled on one of the stools as Andy went behind the bar, leaned her elbows on the bar-top and put her face in her hands. 'Kee-ry-ist, Andy,' she murmured into her gloves, 'you realise I might have had five, six children by now? One of them old enough to be getting himself arrested for riot like any decent college kid?'

Andy said, 'Here's your drink. No, your boy wouldn't be that old yet, but he'd be comin' up for it . . . You weren't meant for anythin' but lonesomes, Jassy . . . I told you that then, an' that mothahfuckin' ofay art school di'n' help.' He poured himself a Budweiser into a tall glass and leaned across the bar. 'What's with the rose-covered cottage an' kids, Jassy? You seen me twice since the ol' days an' you never showed no regrets I could see.'

'Forget it, Andy,' Jassy Vane said. 'I was just feeling low for a moment.' She sat up straight, nodded at him with a smile and picked up her glass. 'Sorry I had to spoil a party.' She gestured across the room to a closed door.

'She's a good party,' Andy said. 'She'll get better for a li'l hangin' aroun' . . . What's the job, Jassy?'

'A take-out—but it's got to look good. Really accidental. The accident case has got very sensitive friends.'

She peeled her gloves, put them on the counter beside her glass, opened her handbag and took out a 7 × 5 print. She put it on the counter facing Andy.

'This is Mr. Who,' she said. 'It's a blow-up from his college yearbook, but that's pretty much how he looks now.'

'Check,' Andy said. 'Where d'you want it done, an' d'you have any ideas—or you leavin' that to me?'

'I've got an idea, but if you don't like it, I'll leave it to you. Only thing: it's got to be done by this morning. Maybe five hours from now—and he's right out the other end of Long Island.'

Andy nodded.

'That's tight,' he said, 'but it ain't impossible. It'll raise the price, though . . . Three.'

'Gee-zuzz, Andy! They'll put me on a block and sell me when I tell them that in Jamaica.'

'*Three!*' he repeated. 'You musta tol' them I give good service when you put them on to me five years ago. You gotta pay for good service.'

'Well, sometimes.' She smiled again. 'There was a time when I didn't pay for good service, Andy.'

'Yeah.' Andy smiled. 'Those were the days, all right . . . O.K., Jassy—what you got in mind?'

III

The door swung to behind him and he went down the steps
and got into the white Corvette.

He had not intended to go across to New York to-day, but
that black woman from Jamaica had been disagreeably im-
perative when she telephoned at half-past three this morning.
And with the sudden, appallingly untidy intrusion of the
two Jamaicans, he could not take any chances. He was
committed now to keeping them happy—until the day when
they could do no further damage.

A convulsion of hate like nausea shook him as he thought
of what they represented: the decadence and squalor of a
system on its way out. A system in which all high-sounding,
empty principles ended in the realities of a Vestucci. In bed,
he knew, they would explore each other, grunting and
snuffling like pigs. Especially the woman—traitor to her race
and to the class from which she must have come. They were
the real enemies. They and their like in every country. They
and those others who had corrupted a revolution at the
moment of its triumph. Thinking of those others, he forgot
the couple he knew as the Broomes. He stared unseeingly
through the windshield into the bright, gull-loud morning
over the Sound, dreaming of the inexorable and necessary
justice he would help to dispense. A tight, absent smile
touched his face as he thought of how carefully he prepared
himself in the severely beautiful, book-lined room upstairs
for that time of judgment. His work over in the city was
preparation too. As was the strict, almost austere regimen
he followed in his daily life. No entanglements. No untidy,
softening concessions to the rotten world that would have
to be cleansed and made whole. When the time came he
would be ready.

Then he thought of Vestucci and felt his stomach contract with apprehension. They would never understand. There would always be doubt about his reliability when Vestucci talked. And he would talk as the new dispensation began to throttle him and his like. Something would have to be done about Vestucci. But not now. There would be the right time and, by then, the people whom he could command. It would have to be judged exactly. And the two Jamaicans: that flaunting black whore and her sleek, parasitical white lover. They would have to be silenced too. Nobody must be left who could testify to his one moment of carelessness and self-interest.

He drove the Corvette up the dirt road from the beach and halted at the intersection with the highway. A removal van and two cars passed going south; three more cars were coming up. He waited for them to cross the intersection because he was still thinking hard. Then he took his foot off the brake and drove across the highway and turned south for Amagansett.

The dark green Camaro that came up suddenly behind him and swung out to pass was being driven very fast, but it seemed to slow when it drew parallel. Still thinking of Vestucci and the two Jamaicans, not taking his eyes from the road ahead, he eased his foot off the accelerator, instinctively anticipating the Camaro's turn across his front. It swung in, too sharply, and he said 'Jesus!' and stamped on the brake and turned his steering wheel hard right as there was a screech of metal. 'Oh, shit!' he said as he stopped the Corvette on the soft shoulder of the road. 'Just what I needed.' He opened the pocket on the dashboard, took out the envelope containing the duplicate of his insurance policy and climbed from the Corvette.

The two occupants from the Camaro were already crouched outside their car, examining the side closely. As he

walked over to them they straightened and turned. A red
and cream Rambler passed going south as they did so, then
a trailer truck. The driver of the truck looked out, and his
vehicle slowed for a second, but as he saw what level of
accident it was he shrugged and accelerated.

The younger of the two men from the Camaro said, 'You
mean like it ain't enough to put us down in everythin' else,
man, you also gotta try to *kill* us because we get ourselves a
nice car.' He was wearing a green *dashiki* over a black polo-
neck sweater; his very young, black face was unforgiving; the
ends of a thin moustache grew into a tuft on his chin and
his hair was a bonnet six inches deep.

'Now look,' Martin Harriman said. 'It was an accident,
but it wasn't my fault. You fellows pulled in pretty hard
there.'

He was smiling—but not falsely or patronisingly. He had
searched himself thoroughly in the past and knew how
genuinely he had overcome any residual feelings of racial
prejudice, how thoroughly he understood the origins of
hostility between colours, the conditions that perpetuated it.
With pride, without false modesty, he was aware now that
he had spoken to these two exactly as he would have to any
two young white road-burners.

Two cars close together went up the road on the other
side, going north. Pale, casually curious faces, one of them a
woman's, turned briefly to the group between the Camaro
and the Corvette. There was a thud of air rushing in to
replace that pushed aside by another trailer truck going
south at seventy.

Martin Harriman said again, with affable impatience,
'Look fellows, there isn't much damage done. You've
bruised me worse than I have you. I'll have to get a new
headlight on the left, let alone beating out the bumper and
respraying. You'll be able to airbrush your job. You couldn't

have lost more than a couple of coats . . . Here's my insurance. Let's see yours and get the show on the road again, eh? I'm in a hurry.'

He stepped up closer to them, holding out the insurance duplicate he had slid from the manila foolscap envelope.

The older of the two young men looked at the paper without interest, as he might have glanced at a used bus voucher blown across his line of vision.

'You hear that, Achmed, doll baby?' he said. 'The mothah wants insurance now. He try to push the bonnet of his all-white automobile up yore fuggin' ass an' now he want yore insurance as well . . . You all want anythin' else, man?' he asked Martin Harriman. 'Like, I mean, you might fancy havin' the key to my girl's apartment or my Blue Cross or maybe I could lie down right hyeah an' you could get to kick me in the balls a li'l until you feel good again.'

He was tall and loose, the colour of the burnt sugar crust on a caramel pudding. His dark grey suit and the quiet maroon tie would have been judged conservative on the bench of the Supreme Court.

Martin Harriman flushed dully across his cheekbones.

'Of course if you're going to play it like that,' he said. 'I'll have to take your licence number and report the matter to the police. People like you shouldn't be allowed to put on a pair of roller skates. What you don't realise is that a car can be a lethal weapon. It ought to be a criminal offence for you to even come near a covered wagon, let alone . . .'

The younger man cut across his honest anger in a voice like fallen leaves drifting over dank stones. 'Oo-ooh, *man*! Now he's getting down to it. How you goin' to finish about us *people*, Mister Charlie? You doan' like that yore nice white car got to drive the same road with ours? You want we should wait until you finish drivin' for the day?'

'Don't be . . .' Martin Harriman started to say, and was

going to add 'ridiculous', in a tone of contempt between equals, when the younger man pushed the point of a switch-blade knife between the two top ribs on the left, near to where they joined the sternum, and twisted the six-inch edge inside Martin Harriman's body until it found and severed the aorta. At the same time, a blade of similar length and sharpness operated by the older man was cutting a piece of his liver adrift from the main organ.

A word that might have been 'Wait!' gurgled in Martin Harriman's throat as the two men withdrew the blades.

He stood erect for as long as it took them to get into the Camaro. Then he folded over the bonnet of his Corvette and shrank to the ground, leaving a wide red smear on the white duco as the Camaro was flung expertly down the road. Two drivers coming north saw him fall but did not stop. The small, grey man in the small, yellow delivery van of a cake company, who had seen it all from four hundred yards up the road as he came south, did stop.

By that time Martin Harriman was dead. And the man who had stopped got it all wrong, anyway, when he told the police about it. As he had seen it, three Negroes, all in Afro dress, had been chasing Martin Harriman up the road and stabbing at him. Harriman had turned to face his attackers and had hit one of them with his fist. He even got the car in which the three murderers had driven away wrong. Until the police found it abandoned in a sidestreet in Amagansett, he insisted that it had been a Cadillac.

Part Three

Chapter Seventeen

Situation report

'. . . no doubt that Mayhew has deeply infiltrated both the
C.I.A. and the K.G.B. As far as Candywine is concerned,
all our contacts in the above organisations must now be
regarded as insecure. We must also be extremely careful as
to what we relay to the British High Commission. Mayhew
almost certainly has a "double", perhaps two or three, working in M.I.6 and/or M.I.5. Our contact, Wisdom, in Special
Branch (Scotland Yard) has been briefed on this possi-
bility . . .

'Saratov is not prepared to answer for his own superiors
in the G.R.U., but feels it is unlikely that there has been any
large-scale penetration of that branch of Soviet Intelligence
by Mayhew . . .

'. . . that this re-emergence of what we can only call international Marxism is not unexpected. The Minister will recall
my verbal and unrecorded report to the Cabinet in special
session in the October after Jamaica became a sovereign and
independent nation. At the time, I stressed that the essentially
nationalist deviation of the Stalin era, the repudiation of
Stalinism by Khrushchev (Twentieth Congress of the C.C.
C.P., March 1956) and the subsequent liberalisation of atti-
tudes in Russia and between Russia and the West did not mean
the end of the international revolutionary dynamic. That
many who were compelled by fear to agree with Stalin, or
who appeared happy to agree with Khrushchev, or who had

been demoted because of change, might well be preparing a counter-reformation. And that the developing nations—like Cuba or Jamaica—were favourable areas from which to operate. I did not anticipate, however, the fact that doctrinaire Marxism had gone underground so thoroughly in the United States and that there would be a highly organised alliance established between these elements in the U.S.A. and their counterparts in the U.S.S.R. . . . unlikely that Chinese Intelligence yet realises the dual nature of Mayhew's operation . . . all evidence indicates that the approach to China was made from Mayhew (U.S.A.) alone . . .

'. . . destruction of confidence and capture of function from within, not overt revolution, are the objectives. Attainment of these objectives will be easier, of course, in the Soviet Union than in the United States; but even in the latter country, a judicious manipulation of "arranged" crises by Mayhew could put its own people into an ever-increasing number of unchallengeable positions of executive power, from which the financial resources of government could be deployed. The methods by which all present governments maintain themselves are so similar that any radical change of policy can well pass unnoticed until it is achieved . . .

'. . . Saratov is now convinced—and we are prepared to agree on the argument he has submitted—that Mayhew was responsible for the assassination of President John F. Kennedy and is now planning the removal of the late President's brother, Senator Robert Kennedy. There is incontrovertible proof that a serious disagreement arose between Mayhew (U.S.A.) and Mayhew (U.S.S.R.) over the strategic necessity of assassinating President De Gaulle of France. Two attempts on the life of this Head of State mounted by Mayhew (U.S.A.) have been aborted by Mayhew (U.S.S.R.) working through the French Communist Party . . .

'. . . no disagreement, however, arises over Candywine. This is a joint operation . . .

'. . . in the U.S.S.R. the total absorption of the G.R.U. by the K.G.B. is one of Mayhew's top priorities . . . we have been fortunate that Saratov's first loyalty is to the Red Army and not to the politicians of the Praesidium . . . The following appendix contains the profile on Saratov relayed to us by Wisdom of Special Branch (Scotland Yard) . . .

'. . . ir Mishka Lepyernev.

BORN: April 17, 1902, Kol Kysima, Uzbekhistan.
(Note: Date of birth is a significant data piece on this subject, as he believes in the influence of the signs of the Zodiac and has frequently boasted of being a Taurus as was Alexander the Great.)

ANTECEDENTS:
Father: Sergeant of Artillery (Grand Duke Michael's Own—116th Horse Artillery). Killed in action at Boroslivik, June 1915.
Mother: Katya Alexandrovna Chevazc: Georgian, probably Jewess; died of starvation, 1942, during the siege of Leningrad.

PERSONAL HISTORY:
Education: Regimental School, Kol Kysima, from September 1907 to June 1914. Café kitchen assistant, Moscow, from June 1914 to April 1917. Member of the Communist Party from October 1916. Led four hundred plus Moscow waiters and kitchen staff to welcome Lenin at the Finland Station, Petrograd, in April 1917. Joined Red Army as Private of Cavalry in January 1918. Squadron Commander in Archangel, August 1918. Wounded in action at Tryzem against British Naval Brigade in September 1918. Recruited by Berzin in February 1921 for recently formed G.R.U. "Illegal"

in Budapest, Vienna, Johannesburg and London as tobacco salesman for Turkish company from 1926? to 1939. Recalled to Russia in January 1939. (NOTE: Saratov's prolonged absence from Russia almost certainly saved his life during the Stalin purges—particularly after his mentor, Berzin, was shot in 1937.) Lieutenant-Colonel of Cavalry from June 1942 to December 1944. Wounded three times in action against the Wehrmacht. Order of Suvarov for leading counter-offensive against 17th Panzer (S.S.) Brigade at Boroslivik in June 1944. (NOTE: This is another significant data piece on the subject, as Boroslivik is the place of his father's death in action and he has confided to Wisdom of Special Branch—while under alcoholic influence—that he spent three days trying to find his father's grave after his own victorious engagement.) No trace of marriage or of any other deep emotional attachment has been found on this subject . . . Promoted Colonel in G.R.U., Special Activities (North and Latin America) in 1957 . . . operated as G.R.U. "illegal" in New York since then . . . cover of Polish ex-Cavalry colonel now functioning as broker of Slavic antiques . . .

SPECIAL QUALIFICATIONS:
Perfect Polish; fluent in French, Spanish and Turkish; English very good, but accented . . . Extensive knowledge of world tobacco trade. Has contributed several articles on the use of cavalry to Russian military journals: chosen by General Staff to translate and abridge Fuller's *Armoured Warfare* for use in training of Red Army non-commissioned officers . . . Authority on *ikons* of the 16th and 17th centuries . . .'

The minister looked resentfully up from the file he had been studying when McKay was shown into the office.

He said, 'This is a very disturbing report, McKay.'

'Yes, Minister,' McKay said and waited in silence, settling back comfortably in the chair drawn up before the big desk.

'I don't understand it,' the Minister said irritably. 'I mean, all this business about the C.I.A. and the K.G.B. and the G.R.U. and the Stalinists. Communists are communists, aren't they? My government has gone on record that we are opposed to communism in any form. We are with the West.'

'Yes, Minister,' McKay said.

'Then why are we—why are *you*—working with this—' he glanced at the file under his thrust-forward chin, his lips moved silently '—this Saratov?' he said. 'He's a communist, isn't he?'

'Yes, Minister.'

'I don't understand.'

The Minister no longer looked irascible, simply sullen and childish. His bright, flawless face—the face of a wall-plaque stamped out on an assembly line for a million homes without taste—wore thought incongruously; rather touchingly, like a small boy trailing a man's sword. Even the wings of grey hair framing the glossy dark skin of his temples looked spurious, as if they had been applied by a deft, hack brush.

'Is Saratov on our side?' he asked.

McKay sighed, without sound. Almost any interview with the burnished, empty figure across the desk was the occasion for many soundless sighs.

'Not exactly,' McKay said, 'but we need him for Candywine. As far as Candywine is concerned, he is on our side . . . He is G.R.U.—that means *Glavnoye Razvedyvatelnoye Upravlenie*, Chief Intelligence Branch of the Red Army's General Staff. G.R.U. does not always see eye to eye with the K.G.B., the political arm of Russian Intelligence—I have explained the difference to you before this, Minister—

Anyway, we need Saratov in this operation. For the moment he is on our side. You might say he is on everybody's side except Mayhew's.'

'But Mayhew is a communist group. That's what you've said in your report.'

'There are varieties of communism, Minister. Mayhew is a revival. A survival, rather. It would like to bring communism back under a more central control, if you understand me.' He smiled hopefully at the impenetrable symmetry that regarded him without a flicker of comprehension. 'Just as the Catholics, say, four hundred years ago, tried to bring the new Protestant churches back to Rome. Well, not quite the same, since these new Catholics have to operate from within the new reformed churches, but you see what I mean.'

'I am a Catholic,' the Minister said stiffly. 'My wife is a Methodist.'

'Of course, of course,' McKay said apologetically. 'That's exactly what I mean, Minister. That's why I said "four hundred years ago." The situation is quite different now, yet it is the same.'

He waited while behind the high, broad brow, one small slab of thought was formed and another lowered laboriously into place on it.

'Oh, yes,' the Minister said finally. 'Yes, I see . . . but I don't like this. I don't like this at all. Why are we in it? . . . And we *are* in it,' he added triumphantly, flipping back three pages in the file and tapping a manicured nail in the middle of a paragraph. '*Your* people had this American, Harriman, killed. You don't say so in so many words, McKay, but I can read between the lines. I can read between the lines. This could embarrass us, Commissioner. This could embarrass us very seriously.'

'No, Minister,' McKay's neat, furrowed face was suddenly

no longer polite and encouraging. 'I must beg you to trust my discretion on that. Mayhew made a serious error of judgment when they recruited Harriman in the first place. They made an even more serious mistake when they decided to use him as their operator with the Mafia. He was a fanatic, an insecure zealot looking for some final authority to worship. He would have made an ideal functionary in a settled situation, but he didn't have the nerve for this sort of game. Sooner or later he would have broken under the guilt of having bungled the job and confessed to his superiors in Mayhew. Our biggest stroke of luck so far was his going to Vestucci instead of to his own people after our agents began to pressure him. If we had left him functional after that, he could have blown everything. Mayhew would have phased out of Candywine quietly, and we'd be back to where we started . . . Don't worry, sir. It was a very neat job. An interracial killing over an automobile accident . . . In America to-day that's expected. Mayhew will make their own investigations, of course, but I don't think they'll get any further than the police have.'

The Minister said hurriedly, 'All right, all right, McKay. You don't have to tell me any more . . . What do you want now?'

'I want us to leave things exactly as they are, Minister,' McKay said flatly. 'I want Mayhew to proceed according to plan. Some time between now and the end of the year, they're going to put a B52 bomber down on the airstrip at Candywine. They have told our Peking contact that they're going to hijack it, but I don't buy that. I think they must have an agent, probably more, in Strategic Air Command. It would fit their pattern of sensitive area infiltration. When that plane comes in there's going to be a Chinese submarine waiting at the edge of the trench, and our Peking contact waiting with his people on the strip itself. What's supposed to happen then, we can't be sure, but we can assume that after they've unloaded the bombs neither the plane nor its crew are going to be heard of again . . .'

The Minister said, in a small, creaking voice, 'And you are seriously proposing that this government allow that to happen on *Jamaican* territory . . . You must be mad, McKay. You must be stark mad.' The facile distinction had drained from the handsome face. He looked, suddenly, like a human being.

'I am proposing that we allow everything to proceed as planned up to where the bomber is put down,' McKay continued without a change of inflection. 'After that I propose we should begin to take over. How we take over and what we do afterwards depends on the further information we shall get from our Peking contact. He hasn't told us the whole story up to now. Not that he should have,' McKay added approvingly. 'That would have been expecting too much.'

'Did you hear what I said, McKay?' The anger, flourished in the Minister's words, was curiously insubstantial, like a plastic revolver. 'Were you *listening* to me? I said that anything such as you propose is out of the question. Out of the question. This whole matter should be turned over to the Americans immediately. I shall recommend that to the P.M. —and to Cabinet, in the strongest terms. The strongest possible terms . . . It very much looks to me, Commissioner, as if you are in need of a long rest—perhaps retirement. The volume of work you have had to undertake since Independence seems to have been too much of a strain. I shall recommend that also.'

McKay said evenly, almost consolingly, 'Of course, Minister, it is your prerogative to ask for my retirement at any time, and I understand your agita . . . your concern in this matter. But I beg you to believe, sir, that I have weighed

the matter carefully. At least, I must request that my report
and recommendation are presented to the Prime Minister.
For his consideration only. *Before* it is discussed in Cabinet.'

'Is that a formal request?'

'Yes, sir. I am invoking the special procedure clause.'
Maybe, McKay thought as he spoke, I *don't* treat the little
bastard with enough respect. But he's such a fool; and God,
does he hate my guts. Always has since I warned his boys
off the course about selling contracts. I should have kept my
bloody trap shut: it has only made the real work more
difficult. 'Naturally, Minister,' he said, and smiled like a
jovial skull at his master, 'I appreciate your objections on the
matter. You would be doing less than your job if you did
not object, and I shall make a special point of emphasising
them when we see the P.M. But I do feel, sir, that this is a
case for his final decision. You and he will be well within
your rights, if you inform your colleagues *after* a course of
action has been decided on.'

But the Minister had withdrawn sulkily now to an
Olympian aloofness. He said distantly, 'Very well, McKay.
Your report and recommendation will be forwarded. You
will be summoned.'

'Thank you, sir,' McKay said with a hearty deference
which, he realised, was probably the year's worst acting in a
land of amateur theatricals. 'I knew you'd understand.'

He rose, and automatically felt for his cap and stick before
remembering that he was in plain clothes.

'Will that be all, Minister?'

'Yes,' said the voice from above the clouds.

II

In the parking yard at Police Headquarters, McKay dis-
missed his driver for the day. He went up to his office,

signed the letters which had been typed during his absence and rang for his secretary.

She was a little, cat-faced, brown girl who moved with an elegance that made her uniform look like an ingenious creation by one of the more avant-garde designers. She held the rank of Inspector, and occasionally took a sadistic pleasure in telling McKay how much she could earn in commerce if she ever decided to leave the Force.

Now, as she took the file of letters from him, she asked, 'How did it go?'

'I had to drag him,' McKay told her, 'kicking and screaming, but we're on our way. The P.M. will clear us for action.'

'Don't you think perhaps our noble Minister may be right? That we *have* bitten off more than we can chew this time?'

'The damn' thing, Joyce,' McKay said, 'is that I know he may be right . . . How many years to my retirement?' he added.

'Six. Why?'

'This operation is going to age me at least five—so I'll be able to put in for the shelf next year. I was never designed for this. When I first started out as a copper, it was a big week when we had two arrests for *ganja* growing and one jealous husband on the run after carving up his wife. During the war, we nailed one chap the Germans landed from a submarine to smell out the convoys gathering in the harbour and we carried on as if we were M.I.5.' He gave a histrionic chuckle. 'And now look at us—they'll be writing spy stories about us before you know it.'

Joyce sniffed with derision.

'You love it,' she told him. 'Talk about kicking and screaming. When they really decide to retire you, they'll have to lift you out in a cage . . . Where do we go from here?'

'Back to the source,' McKay said. He leaned back in his chair and swivelled round to rest his eyes on the blue hills behind the city. He said, without looking back at her, 'Anyo will have to be contacted, and this time he's got to tell us everything. Date of transfer, if that's been fixed yet. The people he's going to use here. His new contact in Mayhew. The exact method of operation. The whole works . . . My word, I'd give a month's pension to see his little Chinese face when we tell him just where he figures in Mayhew's scheme of things. We can't bring him back here, though. Not so soon. Mayhew are going to be edgy after Harriman, no matter how convincing Jassy's people made it look. If we bring Anyo back in again, we just might start the one bit of addition in one bright mind that could work out badly for us. He'll have to be contacted down there. I'll give the D.L. for him to-morrow, after I've seen Blackmore . . .'

'*Blackmore!*' Joyce breathed explosively behind him. 'You're sending in Blackmore? He's never done a run alone. Commissioner, is this wise?'

'And you can stop slitting your damn' cat's eyes at me,' McKay said, without turning round. 'I said Blackmore and I meant Blackmore. He's bright and one day he's going to be the best thing that ever came our way. If I brief him right, he'll do the job. Anyway, we've got nobody else. What with Roper playing revolutionaries in Havana and Woodville at that Black Power school, we're nearly out of possibles.'

'Why not send "Wonder Woman"?' Joyce asked.

'I've told you not to call Jassy "Wonder Woman." She's very good, and you know it . . . Besides, she is over-exposed. We've been using her too often recently.'

'She *is* over-exposed,' Joyce conceded sweetly. 'Those skirts . . . At her age . . . And she has been well used . . . Will that be all, Commissioner?'

'Yes,' McKay said distantly, from above the clouds, 'that

205

will be all, Joyce. I'm going off now. I'll give you the D.L. for Anyo first thing to-morrow.'

He listened to the muted but triumphant beat of Joyce's heels across the floor and waited for the victory crash of the door between his office and hers.

Chapter Eighteen

Meeting on the Orinoco

The steamer hummed faintly as the water divided its force on the bows and rushed along the sides. Every day now, far up in the Parimas, and along the Guyana highlands flanking the river's middle course, the rain clouds would pile, grow uncontainably pregnant and burst over a thousand tributaries, adding countless gallons that were half water, half mud to the main stream. Here, in the narrow Macareo Channel, thirty miles from the sea, it was like pushing up through a thin solution of blackstrap molasses. The sky above the huge estuary was hard and glaring, the colour of a dirty silver tray in which was centred a brassy disc of sun; the dense forest, gluttonously sucking life from the deep silt of the islands between the wide, looping ribbons of water, was grey-green, stretching as far as one could see across a landscape without depth or relief. The heat was like the inside of an oven: one did not sweat freely, but oozed a film of mingled water and body oils that pasted the clothes to the skin and the skin to anything it touched.

Peter Blackmore shook out the folds of a clean handkerchief, wiped his face and looked with distaste at the grey stains on the white linen.

He decided then that he had seen all he wanted or needed to of the Orinoco Estuary. At dawn, as they had weighed in from the Gulf of Paria, there had been a half-hour of haunting promise: a hallucinated glimpse of the soul's enrichment behind the lifting mists, ascending the dark glitter of water that snaked into the obscure heart of a nearly unexploited continent. In the surgical light of noon, one was left with a lot of muddied water, coarse vegetation, harsh-voiced parrots and a random collection of priests, engineers and mining men going up to the mill at Puerto Ordaz or the iron deposits at Ciudad Piar, prospectors, ranchers, cowboys and drab Indians or near-Indians whose only distinction was that they spoke Spanish all at the same time, unceasingly. The little steamer was as crowded as a tenement in a slum.

He crossed the six feet of deck from the rail and pushed open the door into the small lounge. Four fans, one at each corner, stirred a tepid maelstrom around the bar. At one of the small, square tables, three dried, hawk-faced ranchers from the grasslands up river, their heads close together, conversed like actors. A plump, very white American in a grey Dacron jacket and loosened tie glistened above a heap of papers. Two Dominicans in cotton habits and a squat, indefinable, yellow man in an expensive dark suit sipped tiny cups of coffee at a third table.

'A beer, please,' Peter Blackmore said as he sat on one of the four stools at the bar, and added, '*Buenos dias, señor. Una cerveza, por favor.*'

He had been taught Spanish, as he had been taught French, with expensive and exclusive care at the age when all sounds are democratically accessible to memory, but he resented having to speak anything but English.

He sat over his beer—like all local brands in tropical America it was excellent—nursing it swallow by swallow and sulking. Sulking about the bland assurance on Robin McKay's part that he would accept the suggestion, which was more of a directive, that he would be on board an Orinoco river steamer within forty-eight hours; sulking about the tender, but briskly maternal finality with which Jassy Vane had helped him to pack when McKay had given the order; sulking about the demanding intrusion of others into a life that he had always conducted, since he was sixteen, according to his own tastes and inquisitive whims.

When the man he had known in New York as Albert Einstein pushed open the door and walked up to the bar, he managed to give him only the idle glance of the drinker in residence to the newcomer, but the day suddenly seemed much less hot. There was a gentle pricking under the skin of his face, arms and legs, and for a moment his breathing quickened. Somewhere, somehow, things had gone sour. Einstein had no business here. Was not even supposed to *know*. Nor could his presence aboard the steamer be coincidence. One no more allowed for coincidence in this calling than one believed in fairy tales. All the possibilities of the other's purpose were tumbling over each other in Peter Blackmore's mind as Einstein settled on the stool beside him.

Albert Einstein was hung grotesquely but functionally with four different sizes of camera, and a leather holdall the size of a hatbox; he was sweat-patched and bouncy and made a great deal of extrovert noise as he unstrapped himself from his equipment and put it on the bar.

'That's it for now!' he said loudly to the uninterested barman. 'This light, you might as well be shooting into arc-lamps . . . Man, I've been in some hot places, but this is something else again.' He pressed sweat out of his curls and dried his palm by flapping his hand in the air. 'What d'you have that's good to drink on this boat? Like I'll take anything so long as it's cool and long and alcoholic.' He peered without embarrassment into Peter Blackmore's beer. 'What's that you drinking, friend? Beer? Well, that'll start me off at any rate. One beer, bartender, *if* you please. Beer. *Comprende?* Like he's having.' The barman opened one of the brown, squat bottles, poured the beer and aloofly set the glass down in front of him. Albert Einstein said, 'Ah!' very loudly, and half drained the glass in one swig and put it down. He turned to Peter Blackmore and said, 'Good. *Bueno.*'

'Yes,' Peter Blackmore said, looking ahead of him.

'*Say*, you speak English. Well now, that's nice. Didn't expect to find anybody I could have a real talk to this far from Caracas. I'm doing a spread for *Paris-Match*. Free-lance job, so it's got to be better than good, and the *Match* only buys the best. Musta made two hundred exposures since morning and maybe I'll get to print one. But that's the way you've got to do it if you're going to beat the competition. And you'd better believe the competition a free-lance has these days. Some of the kids know how to use cameras before they learn to write, for Christ's sake . . .' The remorseless, cheerful confidences ricocheted from wall to wall of the little cabin. Invisible but palpable shutters came down between the two men at the bar and the others. One of the ranchers raised his hand with the forefinger pointed down at the glasses on his table. The bartender poured Fundador into three clean glasses, put them on a tray and carried the tray across the cabin to the table. He seemed glad to go. The rancher who had ordered said something in a voice that didn't carry to the bar and the bartender replied on the same pitch. They all laughed, and it did not appear as if the bartender was going to hurry back.

Albert Einstein raised his glass and drank some of what remained of his beer. He said, into the inverted cone of the glass, 'You're in trouble, Mr. Broome. You and your Chinese friend. He's being tailed. If I've sweated this morning it's not with taking pictures. It's because I've been waiting for him to try to make contact. When are you supposed to join up?'

'Bulfinch,' Peter Blackmore murmured to his reflection in the mirror at the back of the bar area. 'The name's Bulfinch.

With one "l". I don't know what the hell you're talking about.'

Albert Einstein breathed heavily down the froth-crusted walls of his glass. 'For God's *sake*!' he said. 'Whatever you do now, don't get smart. We have had a spot on you since you left New York. And another on the Chinese. It's damned lucky for all of us that we did. If we hadn't, we'd never have known you were leaving Kingston the same time he was leaving Caracas. I shit you not, Mr. Broome, you and he are going to end up with your guts spilled over half of Venezuela if you're not careful.'

'Bulfinch,' Peter Blackmore repeated. 'Bulfinch is the name. My cabin is 14.'

'I know *that*,' Albert Einstein said. 'I knew that before I boarded this tub in Port of Spain. Half an hour O.K.?'

'Yes,' Peter Blackmore told him as the waiter began to return, reluctantly, from the ranchers' table.

II

'So that's what your people mean by co-operation,' Albert Einstein said bitterly. 'You're supposed to be working with us and you go and set up a sweet little meeting on the Orinoco with the party of the third part and we don't get even a memo on it. Not so much as a goddam postcard. Oh, great . . . *Great!* My boss was really touched by your consideration . . . The way you wanted to save him the worry and all. He was so touched, he had me practically off the can and down to Port of Spain before I'd had time to wipe my ass—just to tell you how much he appreciated your efforts to spare him any headaches . . .'

'Al,' Peter Blackmore said, 'you're a ham. You ought to get some sort of award, but they don't make anything cheap enough.'

Albert Einstein's lumpy, boxer's face, already shiny with the humid heat, gleamed brighter with a smirk of self-congratulation.

'Fuck you for a critic, Bulfinch,' he said happily. 'I was damn' good in there. You've got to admit that. I'd have fooled *you* if you hadn't known . . . And don't change the subject. Why didn't you tell us about this little rendezvous?'

'And talking about co-operation,' Peter Blackmore added, 'what about the tag you've had on me and my . . . my wife . . . since we left you in New York? Also the watch you seem to have mounted on my little Oriental friend? I suppose that's a sign of trust between allies.'

'Routine,' Albert Einstein said, and slapped away the question with the back of his hand. 'You'd have done the same to us if you had the resources. Our monitors didn't even know why they were watching you and the girl and the Chink. They only had to report in every time any of you so much as changed your underwear . . . And it paid off. *That* you've got to admit. You and the third party would be sailing straight into a lot of grief now if we hadn't decided to keep a protective eye on you.'

' "Protective",' Peter Blackmore mimicked. 'What you mean by protective, Al, wouldn't reduce my premiums on any insurance policy.' He paused and added uncomfortably, 'This tail on An . . . on the Chinaman—is it Mayhew?'

'We've got to believe it is,' Albert Einstein said. 'It may be another department from my country; it may be Taiwan; or the local Fidelistas. It could even be his own service checking him out. Christ, it could be anybody. But for us— for you and me—it's got to be Mayhew. All we know is that he had a tail fastened on him two days after Harriman didn't finish his journey on Long Island . . . We're not blaming you for that. It was a neat job. Better than we could have pulled at short notice . . . But it has made Mayhew nervous. They're nearly convinced but they're not satisfied—if you know what I mean.'

'Yes.'

Peter Blackmore was lying on the bottom bunk, propped up on two pillows the size and consistency of ship's biscuits. He had to lie because less than half a yard separated his face from the bottom of the upper berth. Albert Einstein sat in the cabin's only chair, two feet away because that was as far as one could get before the chair was stopped by the bulkhead. In an excess of mutual consideration, they had turned the cabin's single ventilator vent so that the draught of air came straight down between them, cooling Albert Einstein's kneecaps and tickling Peter Blackmore's elbow as he lay with his hands clasped behind his head. In the clouded green of the propped open porthole glass, the reflection of the browny-black, swollen river six feet below swirled and roiled.

'You and the Chinese,' Albert Einstein said, 'you were going to meet here, on the boat?'

'Yes. He's aboard now. He picked it up at Puerto de Hierro. We're both going on up to Ciudad Bolivar.'

'I know he's aboard,' Albert Einstein told Peter Blackmore. 'So's his tail.'

'How did you find out he was being tailed?'

'I *told* you. He couldn't wash his hands without our monitor knowing. It took us only twenty-four hours to realise we were watching two people.'

'Thanks for passing that on to us,' Peter Blackmore said with elaborate sarcasm. 'You really kept us in the picture there, didn't you? It seems to me, Al, that you people nearly blew the whole thing by not telling us about that. Suppose we'd planned to make contact early? This morning for instance?'

'We couldn't tell you before.' Albert Einstein was looking

slightly abashed. 'If we'd told you about him, you'd have probably figured we were on to you too.'

'All I can say is you cut it pretty fine,' Peter Blackmore told him. 'All right, you're the big professional . . . What do we do now? Maybe you'd like me and my contact to just go sailing up and down this river until his tail dies of old age.'

Albert Einstein grinned at him and, after a moment, Peter Blackmore grinned back.

'So how about me making contact for you?' Albert Einstein asked.

Peter Blackmore began to sit up quickly, remembered in time the bottom of the bunk above him and sank back.

'You must be out of your tiny pointed mind,' he told Einstein. 'Pass my man over to you? Oh, come on, Al . . . I may be an amateur, but even I realise that one doesn't do that. For all I know, this is exactly what you and your boss have been setting up ever since you rumbled us in New York. Some plan of your own in which we get a screwing and maybe an apology later on. Or perhaps I'm to be a clay pigeon. The expendable factor in something I don't begin to understand. You can stuff the idea of making my contact for me.'

Einstein stood and leaned his forearms on the upper bunk, and looked down at Peter Blackmore.

He said, 'You're right not to trust me. A suspicious mind is the first requirement if one is to last in our job. But rules and requirements have to be broken. I may be setting you up as you said, but you've got to take the chance. We have no alternative now if we're going to tip your contact and keep his tail occupied until we get to Ciudad Bolivar. You understand? His tail's got to think *I'm* who the Chinese is meeting.'

Peter Blackmore studied the alert, taut-skinned face above his. It seemed to plead the truth, but how could one be sure? Truth in this business was not even like Kipling's naked lady

214

fished from the sea and decorously clothed before being brought into the open. Truth was most often only the lie closest to what was really the situation.

'All right, Al,' he said finally. 'I'll buy your deal . . . At the starboard rail, just forward of the bridge at six-thirty this evening after we've cleared Puerto Ordaz. Join him there and tell him Bulfinch sent you. He won't give you the time of day otherwise. Clue him in on how the situation has changed and say I'll wait for him to make contact in Ciudad Bolivar.'

'Check,' Albert Einstein said. He turned and looked out of the opened port. They were both silent until Peter Blackmore spoke what was on both their minds. 'The tail? What do we do about the tail?' The words followed heavily on each other, as if he was suddenly very tired.

'Yes.' Albert Einstein glanced over his shoulder: an embarrassed look in which there was something furtive and sad. 'Well now . . . I don't feel he should take anything back to whoever wants to hear from him, do you?'

'No,' Peter Blackmore said. 'No, I guess not. That just wouldn't be right procedure on our part, would it?'

'It's never pleasant when it has to be done,' Albert Einstein said, 'but if we see it must be done, then we owe an obligation to those we work for.' Almost shyly he added, 'It is our only honour.'

'Oh, shut up,' Peter Blackmore said savagely and quietly. 'We're going to do it, but for God's sake let's not pretend that it's down there among the Ten Commandments and the Beatitudes if we look hard enough.'

'Yes,' Albert Einstein sighed. 'I see what you mean . . . You will have to pull it off, you know. Once he sees me making contact I've got to make like he's invisible. I'll finger him for you, but you will have to take him out.'

'I realise that,' Peter Blackmore said. 'That was obvious

from the time we agreed on you making contact . . . D'you have any ideas?'

'A lot . . . but none of them suitable. This will have to be another accident . . . anything overt is out.'

'Fine. Well, I have an idea. You'll have to help a little, but the actual work will be done by me. If we time it right neither he nor anybody else will even know it's happening until it's all over. You ready to hear it?'

'Yes,' Albert Einstein said.

Chapter Nineteen

An obligation discharged

At Ciudad Bolivar it was raining: flights of thin lances coming out of the night from the huge grasslands, the *llanos*, behind the city and hissing into the river around the ship. The edges of the awnings over the decks wept into the scuppers, and an occasional gust would break on the stretched canvas or on the broad wooden rails beneath and come in like driven mist.

The little steamer nosed into the long cement wharf before the big, open-fronted shed. The whistle yelled into the black, wet sky; a bell jangled on the bridge; and the ship stopped broadside on to the current. As it began to lose way downstream, the bell jangled again; the beat of the engines quivered in the planks; and the stern began to swing round against the flow. A man in a gleaming black slicker and yellow plastic rainhat stood at the bridge rail and shouted at a man in the bows, turning to shout towards the stern. Two flung lines arced brokenly against the floodlight beams on the masts and on the dock; there were shouts from the wharf; another shout from the man on the bridge; the bell sounded for the third time, and the ship began a tentative crab crawl towards the cement wall of the dock rising out of the swift, foaming sludge of the channelled river.

Peter Blackmore stood with his back resting on the outside bulkhead of the little lounge, his canvas Gladstone bag on the deck between his feet, and tried not to look too frequently at the man he was going to kill—to try to kill—in the next few minutes.

It was necessary to look, however. More than necessary: it was—it was seemly. One had to build a human pattern, however inaccurate, out of all the desire, care, pain and accident that might have gone into making the gaunt, saffron-coloured, freckled face, crinkly brown hair, lugubrious Adam's apple, long, thin body jointed like a draughtsman's ruler. He looked like the sort of man, too young yet to be resigned, too old now to believe any more in ambition, whom one met in a hundred outer offices: one desk among the many, beyond the frosted glass of doors with names on them. Peter Blackmore hoped that he was highly trained. An expert. Professional. With a sense of gratitude, almost of absolution, he told himself that the man must be: no amateur could have tailed someone like Anyo for so long without arousing *that* professional's suspicion.

There was a gentle thud as the ship nudged itself alongside and the old truck tyres hung across the face of the concrete pier cushioned the force of two thousand tons coming to rest. Two sailors had already flung back and secured the hinged section of rail and were now lowering the gangplank: one of them riding the bottom step to the dockside as the other paid off the rope through the block.

There was an immediate rush and jostle for the opening in the rail at the head of the gangplank: a purposeful confusion of bent backs and thrusting shoulders in gabardine and plastic, of bobbing heads, some bare, others shawled or hatted or covered by handkerchiefs knotted at the four corners. An immense, middle-aged woman in black breasted her way through the crowd like a Cunarder in a flotilla of yachts; a short, elderly *mestizo* without shoes passed Peter Blackmore, carrying a large goat under one arm, a cardboard suitcase under the other and a solemn little girl, her arms around his neck, on his back; the two Dominicans flipped open identical green cotton umbrellas as they passed from the shelter of the awning.

The saffron-coloured man made no attempt to join the shoving crowd around the opening in the rail. He strolled back and forth, five yards down the deck from Peter Blackmore, carrying a fibre and composition attaché-case and wearing a faded grey raincoat, tightly belted. It was too short for him and flounced incongruously, like a girl's skirt, with each stride.

The door leading from the little lounge was held open from within and Anyo came out; Albert Einstein followed. Anyo was buttoned neatly to the neck in a white, rubber raincoat of the kind no longer made; a black felt hat, the brim pulled down all round almost concealed his face: he was a figure of gnome-like dignity. Albert Einstein was laden once more with his cameras; he was dishevelled and sweaty and eager. As they passed the patrolling figure, Einstein looked down at his festooned body, took inventory, uttered an exclamation of annoyance and darted back like a fox-terrier to the door of the lounge. He barked an explanation over his shoulder to Anyo, his words half lost in the sounds of disembarkation, '*Forgot . . . goddam flash case . . . Join you,*' and dived through the doorway.

For a moment the saffron-coloured man seemed uncertain: an almost imperceptible halt in his measured stride. He glanced back at the lounge and then, as Anyo reached the edge of the thinning crowd at the head of the gangplank, he continued his walk. When Anyo's white raincoat had been swallowed by the dark press of bodies, he drifted over and became part of the disembarking crowd too.

To Peter Blackmore crossing the deck after him there came a flurry of alarm. It seemed as though they might have miscalculated. The man, for all his ungainliness, was insert-

ing himself between bodies like water finding its way between
rocks. Once he crossed the little platform at the head of the
gangplank there would be nothing they could do. Peter
Blackmore pushed himself against the backs separating him
from the man, using his weight and height as unobtrusively
as he could. In most countries he was always taller by a few
inches, heavier by many pounds than the average: here in
this half-Indian land the differences were considerable.

He passed through the gap in the railing, felt the grating
of the platform beneath his feet and the dabble of rain on
his face; on the first narrow step of the gangplank a very old
woman clutching to the arm of what might have been a son
or grandson had paused for recuperation; halting the descent
of disembarking passengers; the saffron-coloured man stood
near the rope which, strung through stanchions, railed off
the little square of grating. As Peter Blackmore shuffled up
beside him, wielding his heavy shoulders, the man moved
by reflex, his gaze fixed on the crown of Anyo's hat half-way
down the steps. Below them, a narrow channel of swift
water between the ship's side and the face of the quay
widened momentarily as a random surge of current pushed
the vessel, shaking the rickety structure of the gangplank;
the bow dipped slightly as the mooring hawser reined it in;
the platform swayed.

And in that moment, Peter Blackmore, his right arm stiff
along his side, thrust his hand between the man's legs, closed
it round his left thigh and, using the crotch as a fulcrum,
heaved with a strength he had been concentrating towards
this action for hours. He was already two steps down the
gangplank as the man hit the waist-high rope around the
platform, balanced for an instant with hands scrabbling
among the streaks of rain and toppled into the space between
the pier and the iron hull as the ship once more heaved
gently into the cushioning tyres. On the platform above,

Albert Einstein was having great trouble getting into his raincoat. He had been trying to put it on ever since he had followed in Peter Blackmore's wake through the crowd. Bulky and awkward in his lush growth of cameras, he had managed to wrestle the coat into a screen between the second's action by the rope railing and the people behind.

He, too, was already off the gangplank's head and on to the steps before the first shouts came from the pier and figures began to run to the edge, to kneel, peering down.

Peter Blackmore had nearly reached the lower platform slung just above the quay before the girl who had waited irritably behind Albert Einstein's struggles with his raincoat looked into the gap between the hull and the face of the pier to see what was attracting so much attention below.

It would have been conspicuous, then, not to stop and look back at a girl who stood and screamed and screamed around a mouthful of tightly bitten knuckles.

Equally conspicuous, after that, not to follow her gaze to where two soldiers in oilskin ponchos shone their flashlights on something that was swept down the current into the darkness as the hull tried to drift free into the stream again.

Chapter Twenty

I'm all I've got

Two nights later in Jamaica, he said to Robin McKay: 'Anyo agrees. He'll take one bomb—if we make it look good enough for him to convince his people.'

'I thought he would agree. But he must have asked for more than one, surely? We can blow him to anyone we fancy whenever we like, but he's in a bargaining position now. We need him. I'm surprised he didn't ask for two.'

'He did, but his heart wasn't in it. He was pretty shaken about Mayhew playing both sides. I could see him asking himself where that left China if Mayhew ever pulled their real coup. And he'd lost face over the tail. He'll take one bomb.'

Peter Blackmore had flown in earlier on a Viasa flight from Caracas. There had been no one to meet him, and he had not tried to telephone anyone. He had taken a taxi up to the service station at the foot of Stony Hill where he had left his car and driven on to his house. On his way to the bed-room he had taken a large sirloin from the deep freeze and opened a bottle of Gevrey-Chambertin.

After a long shower—very hot while he soaped himself three times and shampooed as though washing out lice; then cold, during which he poured and drank swiftly two large brandies from the bottle on the lid of the lavatory cistern—he had gone to bed.

He had slept until near midnight, woken and gone out to

the kitchen in his dressing-gown. The steak had thawed enough for the grill, and the wine, when he smelled a little in a glass, had breathed nicely. While his steak was grilling, he took a loaf of French bread, an iceberg lettuce and three onions from the refrigerator. He also drank two more brandies: smaller ones than those he had swallowed while in the shower. The scent of a fatly rolled *ganja* stick mingled with the odour from his cooking steak.

McKay had driven up when he was half-way through his meal and let himself in. Peter Blackmore had looked briefly from his food when McKay came into the kitchen, but continued eating and taking a lot of the wine. McKay found the whisky in the cellaret under the draining-board, poured himself a drink and sat down on the other side of the Formica-topped table while Peter Blackmore ate with the exclusive concentration of a dog.

When Peter Blackmore had finished, McKay asked, 'Feeling better?'

'Yes,' Peter Blackmore had said, and leaned back in his chair and poured the last of the wine. 'Much better. I haven't eaten in two days.'

'That's not good,' McKay told him. 'You should have eaten something. I mean it, Peter. Another time you may not be coming back home. You may be stuck in a damn' awkward situation on strange ground, where you'll need a fast mind and all your stamina. Not eating doesn't help.'

'He knew,' Peter Blackmore said slowly, looking down into the wine. 'Just before I put him over, he must have realised . . . I saw his face when he hit the rope . . . he knew he was dead . . . then there was that damned woman.'

'What woman?' McKay asked.

'The woman who saw him in the water before the current carried him under. She was screaming. Then she began to cry. For all I know she may have been pregnant.'

223

'Yes,' McKay said, 'he couldn't have been pretty.' He had looked at the impassively sullen face across the table from him and added quietly, 'You've got to stop thinking about it. You just have to put it into a place where it means nothing more than a filthy job well done. If you don't, you're going to be in bad trouble . . . He was a professional, remember. He knew what the consequences were if he slipped up. Given the chance, he'd have done the same to you.'

'I thought of that,' Peter Blackmore had said then. 'I've been trying to sell myself that idea ever since—but it doesn't help much.'

II

Now, sitting in the big, functional living-room, Peter Blackmore was saying, 'It's a very cute set-up, you see. Simple but effective. If we hadn't come into the picture they'd have pulled it off without a trace. They haven't told Anyo everything, of course, but they've had to brief him sufficiently so he won't foul up . . . They have two of their people on the bomber. The two defectors will bring it into Candywine. That makes one of them a pilot, I suppose. One of the pilots . . . No, Anyo hasn't been told anything about how they do it. The only thing he's been told is what happens to the rest of the crew when they land. After they've unloaded and the Chinese frogmen have taken the bombs out to the submarine, the defectors take the plane out again. They're to get destination orders after they land.'

'Who gives them the orders? Not Anyo?'

'No. The top banana on the ground team that Mayhew is assigning to Anyo. They're going to be put in as casino people: croupiers, table attendants, the usual muscle men registered as administrative staff.'

'That's taking a risk, isn't it? I mean, the day that Candywine opens for gambling the F.B.I. will have their chaps living in round the clock. To try to pull something like this with the F.B.I. sitting in your lap takes a lot of cool cheek.'

'The F.B.I. will be watching the tables and where the money is going. All they're interested in is who they can nail for tax evasion. Mayhew could gang bash his sister on the dance floor and an F.B.I. man wouldn't register.'

'Yes,' McKay said, 'you've got a point there.' He rubbed his eyes, massaged his seamed face and, leaning on his elbow, poured himself another drink from the bottle on the floor beside the divan where he reclined propped up on half a dozen cushions. Peter Blackmore frowned at the record he had just taken off the Garrard turntable, reversed it and laid the needle into the first groove, on manual. Copland's "Tender Land" breathed fragrantly through the room. McKay said, 'You get a lot of points, Peter—for somebody who isn't trained . . . These two defectors? Where are they supposed to go? I mean, you can't dig a hole in a beach somewhere and bury a B52 . . . That's a bloody great slice of aeroplane to get rid of.'

'I don't think they're going to go anywhere,' Peter Blackmore told him. He came back to his chair and folded heavily into it. His eyes were bright and dead and steady as he looked across at McKay. 'I think they're supposed to get out across the Atlantic or the Pacific and then something is going to happen that will take care of the plane and them, and nothing left except a few pieces floating which may or may not be spotted.'

'That's roughly what I was thinking,' McKay said. 'Why haven't those two defectors thought about it too?'

'Because this is a crazy world,' Peter Blackmore said, 'in which people will believe any shit that's put on them if it's the shit they need to make them feel nourished and strong and valuable . . . I don't know what our particular shit is,

Robin, but we believe in it. We believe in it enough for me to commit murder, and for you to feel that murder was the only way out of some idiot situation that nobody understands but which everybody enjoys because it gives us the excuse for committing more murders.'

'Are you drunk?' McKay asked dispassionately.

'A little. I had four or five brandies on the plane, and then a bit here before I ate; and the wine. Why?'

'I thought you might be drunk. You hold your liquor very well, but you sounded as though you might be getting drunk. You'd better go to bed ... I want to see you to-morrow, if I may. I think you ought to consider being trained. You're very good. We really were in luck when we got you in. But you need training. I'd like to tell you about it to-morrow. It'd only be two months. Not here, but a pleasant climate. Interesting people. You'd enjoy it ... You're half-way there, already. It's only the details that need filling in ... Codes and ciphers, for example. And weaponry. Procedures. That sort of thing. It's a profession like any other, you know, Peter. You have been a lucky amateur up to now, but you have to acquire the craft.'

'No, McKay.' Peter Blackmore could hear the buzz of liquor and feel the soothing mist of the *ganja* descending in his brain. Soon he would sleep. But his voice was unslurred and decisive and his heavy eyes did not waver as he looked at McKay. 'I'll learn anything you and Jassy and Helen want to teach me as we go along, but I'm not going to any of your special schools. That was never part of the contract.'

'You realise that it makes you vulnerable? Unnecessarily so?'

'I prefer it that way.'

'And that it might endanger others who depend on you in an operation?'

'I never asked to be taken on, McKay. I joined, but you

226

invited me. Something happens to people who take your fucking codes and procedures seriously. They either lose something or gain something. I can't decide which. Either way, it's nothing that I want to be like.'

'Suppose we talk about this to-morrow. When you've had some sleep.'

'No matter when you catch me, McKay, the answer is going to be the same.'

'Yes.' McKay rose, and looked down pensively at the big, self-contained figure curled in the leather arm-chair. After a while, he smiled briefly. 'Yes,' he said again. 'I didn't really have much hope but I had to try. You know that you're a self-satisfied, self-centred, egotistical bastard, don't you?'

'Yes,' Peter Blackmore told him cheerfully, 'I'm all of that—but then when you come right down to it, I'm all I've got.'

Part Four

Chapter Twenty-one

Mr. Vestucci gets the message

The exterior walls, parapets and entrance to the old fort had been retained: a shell of hand-cut limestone six feet thick. Inside, pink and white leatherette, nylon carpeting, looking-glass walls; indirect fluorescent lighting, parquet flooring of Caribbean hardwoods, and Victorian chandeliers had been assembled in a decor of antiseptic luxury. The fittings and fixtures would never wear and become shabby. They would be disposed of like ingeniously designed cardboard containers.

Only the tables, machines and equipment for gambling gave a sense of solidity: functional, uncompromising of purpose, austerely handsome like the heavy weapons of war.

Peter Blackmore and Jassy Vane stood on the balcony above the main floor. Below them the last of the electricians, plasterers and carpenters were at work in corners, at random points along the walls, up on step-ladders, putting in the finishing touches.

'Well, you've got to say this for these lads,' Peter Blackmore said, 'they don't pare any cheese. I wonder how much all this has set them back.'

'About the first week's takings I should imagine,' Jassy Vane said. 'After that their only problem will be finding goons strong enough to lift the money bags.'

The air-conditioning had not yet been turned on, and it was a warm day, but the man who had met them on the jetty of the yacht basin, escorted them through the grounds, and who now lounged against the railing of the balcony five yards away, kept on his coat. He was lean and tall, with a lot of dark hair slicked back without a parting, and he had the sort of face that would have handicapped him badly in the used car business. In the ten minutes that Peter Blackmore and Jassy Vane had been waiting to see Mr. Vestucci, he had not offered any conversation.

A door covered with padded beige leatherette opened behind them; cool air, smelling of electricity, surged across the warm balcony like a small wave running up a beach; Mr. Vestucci followed it. He was dressed in slim white slacks of a weave so fine they could have been drawn through a wedding ring, green espadrilles and an emerald green, raw silk sports shirt with the ends knotted across his stomach. Against the burnished mahogany tan of his face, his white hair looked nearly blue, like sculptured ice.

'Mrs. Broome . . . Mr. Broome,' he said, coming forward and taking Jassy Vane's hand in both of his. 'A pleasure . . . Please forgive me but you know how it is when you're preparing for an opening . . . Problems. Nothing but problems. Yesterday, fifteen hundred square feet of carpeting I'd selected myself for the roof bar is supposed to arrive. I have a goddam faggot of a decorator who is only costing me a hundred dollars a day, *expenses*, let alone his fee, waiting for it—and the sooner I can get him out of Candywine the more I'll like it. I can tell you, he's going to seduce every goddam waiter in the place if he stays here another day, why he's even made a pass at *me*, and me a grandfather. So what happens to my carpet? It's in Peru. The goddam airline overflighted it. Christ knows when it'll get back to Montego. And this morning my chef tells me that his mother's thinking of starting a restaurant in Zurich and wants him to come and cook for her. I never knew chefs had mothers. Sure, I've got him under contract—but you ever tried to hold a chef to a contract he wants to break? You end up keeping a doctor on retainer with a stomach pump . . .'

He had ushered them through the padded door, along a short passageway and into an office as he spoke. The office was on the west side of the fort, where the wall was built up from the coral platform at the water's edge. Along the side of the room that overlooked the sea, the old stone had been knocked out and replaced with a floor to ceiling picture window backed by narrow aluminium louvres painted pastel green and hung on cord; a grey steel desk and a high-backed swivel chair in black leather were placed dead centre of the picture window, facing into the room; six tall filing cabinets and a secretary's desk and chair were set against the north wall; at the other end of the room there was a home bar, two long, deep settees of green leather and three arm-chairs in slip-covers patterned with exuberant pineapples; the off-white, wall to wall carpeting gave under the feet like moss. The door to the office was a little less heavy than that on a bank vault, and let into the wall above it, inside, was a 27-inch television screen.

The florid, glossy young man whom they had seen at the house on Long Island was working at the secretary's desk, holding a big sheaf of what looked like bills under his left hand, turning them up by their lower right-hand corners between forefinger and thumb and jotting figures on to a sheet of foolscap. He was lightly but neatly dressed in a pair of white shorts, blue yachting shoes, and a shoulder-holster. He glanced up, briefly nodded, and turned to his work again. It did not seem to embarrass him this time, any more than it had done the last, that he was not introduced.

Mr. Vestucci stopped the small talk when he shut the heavy door between the office and the passage. It was half past eleven in the morning and there was a lot of hard white glare bouncing off the brilliant sea immediately below, even

though the louvres were half closed, but he seemed to feel
the need for more light. He flicked three switches by the
door and the concealed fluorescent tubes flickered for a little
and then began to compete steadily with the sunlight. Over
at the secretary's desk, the young man bent over without
taking his eyes from the foolscap sheet of figures and depressed a knob on something that looked like half a chrome-
coloured telephone attached by a flex to a small, cream-
enamelled box with two switches and two dials. Peter
Blackmore frowned quizzically and Jassy Vane said, nodding
at Mr. Vestucci, 'He's not sure that he isn't being bugged.
Fluorescent lighting will confuse most mikes.' She jerked her
thumb at the half telephone and box beside the young man.
'That's a sonic massage unit. Ultra high frequency sound
waves. Three minutes of that on a torn muscle is worth about
three weeks of manual therapy—if you get it right. Five
minutes at high pitch could turn a weight-lifter's biceps into
soup. It's a crude scrambler but it works on anything small
and sensitive. At least we hope so . . . Isn't that right, Mr.
Vestucci?'

'Yes,' Mr. Vestucci said absently. 'That's it, Mrs. Broome.
You get somebody like me and you get people who'd like to
know what he's saying—all the time—to anybody.'

Behind his coldly disciplined front, Mr. Vestucci was
tense. And beneath the lustrous tan, they could see an ageing
man, worried and suddenly feeling the years at his back.

He led the way to the upper end of the room, sat in one of
the arm-chairs and gestured cursorily at the settee opposite.

'I got your message,' he said as Peter Blackmore and Jassy
Vane sat. 'I didn't like it, Mr. Broome.' His voice crossed the
space between them like a snake through dry grass.

'I'm sorry,' Peter Blackmore said without apology. 'What
didn't you like?'

'It was full of nothing,' Mr. Vestucci said. 'At least it was

full of the sort of nothing that's trying to hint something. I
don't like that. I've learned that sort of nothing comes expensive.'

'You run an expensive show, Mr. Vestucci,' Jassy Vane
murmured. 'A little bit more won't hurt.' She had on a mid-
thigh, wrap-around beach coat of soft, yellow towelling over
the bikini she had worn aboard the cabin cruiser they had
hired in Montego Bay that morning. Now she snuggled
back into the settee and stretched out her long legs and smiled
at Mr. Vestucci. Her silver painted toenails smiled, too, from
her single-thonged sandals.

'And I don't like *that*.' The gliding snake suddenly reared.
'That sort of smart talk I particularly don't like. We made
a deal out there on Long Island. A straight deal. Your people
get a piece of the percentage, *which* we've been paying since
July although we don't open till next month. O.K., I'm not
knocking you for using what you had on us to make a deal.
If you see a chance to make something and you don't make it,
you're going to end up shining shoes in the john of a hotel
some place . . . And I know from I saw you out on Long
Island that you're the law. Maybe not the law wears a blue
uniform and swings a stick in the park, but law . . . That's
O.K. too. The way things are, I make plenty of arrangements
with the law—to our mutual advantage . . . So—I'm here
since August, getting this place ready, and I don't see you.
I don't *hear* from you—until I get some crummy message
. . .' Mr. Vestucci slid the fore and middle fingers of his left
hand into the breast pocket of his shirt and lifted them out
with a visiting card held between the tips . . . 'a message,' he
repeated, and quoted from writing on the card's blank side,
' "to reconsider investment plans." What does that mean,
Mr. Broome? We agreed on your investment: no interference.
And we agreed on our return: twenty grand per month, paid
into where you said. So what's all this now about reconsider-

235

ing investment plans? You got a good hand, Mr. Broome, and I'm not blaming you for playing it for all you could get, but don't crowd your luck. That's not smart, and I figure you to be smart. You and your little lady here. And if you're smart, then you work for smart people. They ought to know you don't try to break the bank except in the movies.'

The face opposite them retained its serenity, but it had become as raw and pointy, while he spoke, as a newly sharpened pencil.

'No, we wouldn't try to do that,' Peter Blackmore told him. 'We know better than that. But we thought you might be interested in buying a little information from us. If you don't want it, we'll just go back to Montego Bay and stop taking up your time.'

'Yeah,' Mr. Vestucci grunted, 'you could do that, but you won't. What information do you have that you think I'd want to buy?'

'From where I sit,' Jassy Vane said, speaking to her bright toes, 'I'd say it's information that could keep you out of jail, Mr. Vestucci. Not that going to jail,' she added thoughtfully, 'might not be better for you than what your partners would feel like doing when they found out how you'd allowed yourself to be taken for a ride.'

Under the fine glaze of his tan, a turgid flush darkened Mr. Vestucci's cheeks; the wide thin lips hardened, momentarily, into scar tissue; he said slowly, 'That sounds like information I ought to have, Mrs. Broome. I'm not saying it is true information, but if somebody has it, I ought to have it too.'

'That's about how we thought you'd see it,' Peter Blackmore said. 'Loose talk can do a man damage even if it isn't true.'

'Who's talking?' Mr. Vestucci asked. 'And what are they talking about? You got something I need to know, Mr.

Broome, you know I'll buy—at a fair price . . . but don't play it cute. At my age I can't afford cute players.'

'Nobody's talking yet,' Jassy Vane said, and they could both see the sudden flare of quickly controlled anger behind his eyes as he was forced to turn his attention to her. 'But when they do talk it will be about Mayhew and how a big, way up operator like you ever allowed himself to buy snake oil in a penicillin bottle. You've been conned, Vestucci. They've taken you and your friends about as high as you can go and you won't even know it until you find yourself coming down without a parachute.'

Mr. Vestucci did not reply, For a minute, the opaquely surfaced dark eyes registered Jassy Vane, then Peter Blackmore, then Jassy Vane again. He got up and went past them to the grey steel desk. From behind, the only indications of his age were the broad-based U of white hair above a brown neck and a slackness of buttocks beneath the moulded slacks. He pulled open the top left-hand drawer of the desk and took out a flat, narrow cigar case covered in purple morocco. The young man at the desk made a protesting noise and Mr. Vestucci impatiently waved it aside as he bit the end from the dark tube and spat it on to the carpet. 'My goddam doctor,' he said. 'He's told me it's one a day now or he's going to have me up before a Senate investigation committee.' He scrabbled inside the opened drawer, petulantly slammed it shut, opened the drawer below, searched that, and then, with a furtively casual air, lifted the edge of the carpeting under the window behind the chair and straightened, holding a gaudy envelope of book matches. He struck a flame and drew the first puff like a man swallowing the first inch of a sword, for the first time, on a bet.

He snapped the thumb and middle finger of his left hand, and the young man at the secretary's desk rose and came up beside him.

'Ask them what they're having,' Mr. Vestucci told him.

The young man went to the little home bar and emptied a Schweppes soda water into a tall glass around four cubes of ice on which he had sprinkled Angostura bitters. He poured two Tuborgs into glass-bottomed tankards, put everything on a round, silver-rimmed, ebony tray and brought the drinks over to them.

'Tell me about Mayhew,' Mr. Vestucci said.

Chapter Twenty-two

Aerial interlude

The great bomber seemed to hang between the dome of a gigantic black circus top studded with unwinking bulbs and the moonwashed floor of some limitless wool shearing shed. Three thousand miles north-west of it, on a huge screen in a bunker beneath an Ohio field, a moving dot traced the speed with which it hurtled into the night. There were many other dots of light on the screen and eight men, all officers, seated in deep swivel chairs before it, watched the dots as they crawled, at varying distances from the centre, to every point of the compass. Occasionally one of the officers would swing round in his chair and hand a slip of paper to one of the sergeants or corporals who sat behind them. The sergeant or the corporal would take the slip across the wide floor to the flight of steel steps leading up to the platform which ran the entire length of one wall ten feet up. In the centre of the platform opposite the screen there was a desk and chair and placed before the desk, almost at the edge of the unrailed platform, another chair, deeply padded, capacious and upholstered in pale blue leather.

The man who sat in this chair, and to whom the sergeant or the corporal would give the note, was blond, close-cropped and looked incongruously young to have two silver stars on each epaulette of his pale-blue uniform.

On either side of the eight officers who watched the screen, men and women wearing earphones, talked into mikes suspended before their mouths on slim limbs of steel

239

growing out from the headsets, watched the needles of a hundred dials on the wall above the control counter at which they sat, or made small, almost fastidious adjustments among the knobs and switches set into the grey formica top of the counter. From this group, too, an occasional note was sent up to the man on the platform with the stars on his shoulders and the four rows of ribbons above his left breast pocket.

On the bomber three thousand and some plus miles southeast, fifty-three thousand feet above the Atlantic, Captain Walter Fringe, flight engineer, looked at his watch and left his little compartment under the flight deck, just forward of the starboard wing. With head ducked low, he made his way along and up the catwalk to the flight deck. He grinned at the lieutenant who sat on the low bucket seat before the bank of radio equipment, reading *Esquire*. 'How's it coming, Charlie?' Captain Fringe asked him.

'Loud and clear,' the lieutenant said. 'I'm raising them easy. There was a little interference over the Bahamas. Magnetic, I guess. But it's all clear now.'

Fringe went up the flight deck, towards the cockpit. The second pilot looked up from the massed and glowing dials as Fringe leaned his forearms on the back of the gimballed, pilots' seats.

'Shouldn't you be somewheres looking after the bus?' the second pilot said. 'What are you doing up here with the aristocracy?'

'You fly it, boy,' Fringe said. He had a face that smiled easily and becomingly. 'Or at least you sit back and let automatic fly it for you. *Pilots*,' he added scornfully. 'One day the brass is going to wake up and discover that we need pilots like we need Custer and the Seventh Cavalry.' He turned his face to the man in the captain's seat. 'How's it going? Any complaints?'

The captain shook his head. He was older than either

240

Fringe or the second pilot, and he had a square, meaty, good-natured face on to which a Wellingtonian nose had been improbably grafted. Even in the dim, blue light of the cockpit, one could see enough lines around his eyes and enough grey in his short dark hair to know that he was nearing the time when it would be no longer permissible for him to be in charge of a B.52.

'Everything's fine,' he told Fringe. 'Number five was losing thrust a little while back—over Antigua—but it picked up.'

'Yeah, I know,' Fringe said. 'I saw it but it wasn't anything to worry you about. It's like clearing your throat. Maybe a little too much or a little too little in the mixture.'

He left them then and went back across the flight deck and down and through the catwalks to his compartment.

At 9.17 p.m. precisely, he reached up and depressed one of the many switches on the instrument panels that enclosed him on three sides; then he scrambled out and across to a buttress ribbing the port fuselage five feet away from his compartment; he took a small clamp wrench from the pocket on the left leg of his flying suit above the knee and closed it round a valve set into the fuselage behind the buttress. While he was doing this, the major who was the navigator looked up from his little fold-out work table ten feet farther along towards the nose, waved at him absently with a slide rule and smiled, his face bleached by the hard glare from the little bulb in the Anglepoise lamp over his chart. Fringe waved back, gave two more turns to the valve he was opening and returned to his area.

At 9.20 p.m. he took from his pocket a slim instrument with four grooves incised about the point, unhurriedly removed four screws from a square of the panelling and lifted it free. From among the tangle of wiring inside, he removed two from their terminals, using a screwdriver about the size of a nail-file, pulling the freed ends out carefully and letting them dangle clear so they would not cross and short.

On a big dial above the section of panelling he had removed, a needle began to creep backwards, anti-clockwise. Fringe strapped the snout of an oxygen mask over his nose and looked at his watch again. Already in the few seconds since he had opened the valve in the fuselage and disconnected the lead to the other valve on the front wheel landing gear through which the thin air was sucked into the pumps, his eardrums had begun to register the drop in pressure. The emergency signal which should have blared at every post in the plane remained silent, temporarily as useless as the other lead he had disconnected.

By 9.20 and fifty seconds p.m., the huge bomber dipping and rising at six hundred miles per hour into the gold-pointed immensity of black, was a shell without oxygen, suddenly and appallingly cold, filled with a mist of frozen, condensed water particles.

At 9.21 p.m., Captain Fringe left his compartment, carrying the small oxygen cylinder through which he was being fed slung by a strap over his left shoulder. Bent over and almost running, he reached the flight deck in under ten seconds. The signals lieutenant had fallen out of his seat, and was lying with a faraway, uncaring expression on his purple face, his hand resting on the *Esquire* he had pulled to the deck with him.

The second pilot was slumped forward, his forehead wedged between the panel and the fuselage. The captain had fallen back in his seat, his face purple, too, except for the big, curved nose which was pinched, gaunt and dead white.

Moving very fast, without fluster or clumsiness, Fringe reached down beside the captain's seat, straightened holding an oxygen mask attached by a thick ribbed tube to a socket in the deck, and clapped it over the other's unconscious face.

He held it there, frowning anxiously, until the man slowly opened dull, bewildered eyes. He continued holding it while the other breathed deeply and steadily and the eyes gradually became alert and knowing again. As Fringe raised his eyebrows questioningly, he nodded briefly, like a man who has just run a race to the end of his strength, and pointed to the mask Fringe was holding to his face. Fringe nodded in turn and passed the strap attached to one side of the mask around the back of the man's head and fastened it on the other side. Again Fringe raised his eyebrows in query above the grotesque muzzle that covered his nose, the front of his cheeks and his mouth, and the man in the captain's seat nodded once more—strongly, almost impatiently, as he bent forward and surveyed the dense mosaic of instruments on the panel before him. He jerked his gloved thumb back over his shoulder and Fringe inclined his head in acknowledgment and turned and went back along the flight deck to where the lieutenant lay under the complex assemblage of his equipment.

A distant, metallic but very clear voice was saying through a small grill, 'Come in Able Victor Dora. This is Voodoo. Able Victor Dora are you receiving me? This is Voodoo . . . Come in Able Victor Dora . . .' until Fringe stepped over the body on the deck and flicked all the switches on the system to OFF. Immediately, a long, steadily pulsating whine started from another grill, high up on the fuselage beside the man in the captain's seat. It continued until he reached under the crowded panel, groping purposefully. Then the whine as abruptly stopped.

In the bunker under the Ohio field, one of the crawling dots on the huge screen suddenly winked out; one of the officers said 'Jesus! *No!*' and did quick, delicately desperate things with the knobs on the sloping control board before him; he shouted over his shoulder to the blond, close cropped, disturbingly youthful man with the twin silver stars on each shoulder, 'We've lost track, sir! I can't pick 'em up'; but the man who had sat in the big chair watching the operations on the floor of the bunker was already speaking urgently into a red telephone on the desk; along the communications panel, a pert, brown-haired girl with master-sergeant chevrons on the sleeves of her dress kept saying, 'Come in Able Victor Dora . . . This is Voodoo . . . Come in Able Victor Dora . . . You have lost contact . . .'

Three thousand and several hundred miles to the south-east, the man in the captain's seat had switched from automatic to manual and was bringing the bomber down and down to the sea in tight, fast spirals. Fringe was huddled in a ball of agony on the flight deck behind him. And both men were shuddering uncontrollably with a cold that had no register the imagination could contain: a freezing hell beyond the most extreme comparisons of the most vivid fancy. Heat had gone from the bomber along with the pressurised air and they both knew that they were very close to death.

At forty thousand feet, the man in the captain's seat pushed hard on the half wheel around which his fingers had locked and slid the horizontal control column almost flush with the panel. Neither man could hear the muted howl of the six jets for his own screaming as the vacuum they rode, plunged on a steep slant towards the higher pressures above the ocean.

And then, at twelve thousand feet, it was suddenly warm and the air was thick and rich, and the man in the captain's seat pulled back on the half wheel as the giant craft shook itself furiously into level off.

At five thousand feet and still going down, Fringe took off his mask. Blood was running from his nostrils and more blood welled out of his right ear, coursed along the corner of his jaw and dripped on to the collar of his flying suit. The man in the captain's seat was bleeding from the nose too, and from both ears, and as the circulation came back to his fingers, he began to cry helplessly, like a burnt child.

Fringe struggled to his feet and supported himself by resting his hand on the back of the seat in which the second pilot was still slumped over, his forehead wedged into the corner between the fuselage and the panel.

He said, 'I knew it was going to be rough, but not that rough. For a minute there I thought we weren't going to make it.'

The man in the captain's seat was wiping the blood and tears from his face with a wad of tissue. He looked across at the second pilot and then at Fringe.

'Yes. He's dead,' Fringe told him. 'They're all dead. They didn't last long after . . . Well, you know . . . They didn't feel anything . . . Think of the way you were until I put the mask on you.'

'No,' the man in the captain's seat said flatly. 'They couldn't have known what was happening. Not for more than a few seconds anyway. I guess we have that to feel good about.' He switched on to automatic and rose, stepping on to the flight deck. 'O.K., Walter, drive while I get a fix. We should be about a hundred miles south-east of Barbados. When I know for sure, I'll bring us down to five hundred and we'll make it for Candywine that way. Just keep praying that the brass don't have anything special that they think it's maybe better we don't know. Something that can get us back on screen under our radar jam.' He looked down at the dead boy, whose face had now paled and who seemed to be sleeping, and rubbed his square, heavy chin and shook his head. 'I wish there had been some other way,' he said sombrely to Fringe. 'I wish it hadn't had to happen like this.'

Fringe said, 'There wasn't any other way. This was the only way we could be sure. You know that.'

Chapter Twenty-three

Reception committee

Peter Blackmore had few illusions about the way he had lived.

Except for the meticulous, almost puritanical, care of the estate he had inherited, most of his activities had been trivial. He had read widely without attempting scholarship; travelled much without really exploring his impressions; made a lot of love without ever, until he had met Jassy Vane, committing himself very deeply.

Only gambling had ever seemed like taking him out of the comfortable shell of ego he had begun to grow around himself in the days when he was the only child of rich, indulgent, unfailingly courteous parents who had never been able to find the time to treat him as anything more than just another interesting friend.

In gambling, he had discovered an intoxication, an apparent loss of self, so keen and so satisfying that in the end he had given it up, as another man might have sworn off liquor.

For about two years, between twenty and twenty-two, he had risked his considerable fortune in the casinos and clubs of half a dozen countries and at twenty or so private gaming-tables in those countries where he could be sure of his opponents. Several times he had seriously reduced it; twice he had much increased it; he had played his last game with it more or less intact.

But he had known then that if he continued, he would

become an addict, and he had stopped. Some obscure moral prompting, perhaps, that what he was risking did not really belong to him but to the land on which it was made had brought about his decision. And along with this, a sense of fastidiousness: a feeling that those who might win it from him did not deserve it.

Now, as he stood at the big roulette table in the main *salle* of the converted fort on Candywine, he could feel the old need stir within him once more: like that of the alcoholic who has not taken a drink for twenty years but who knows he will be an alcoholic so long as there remains, somewhere, one drink to be taken.

It was the fourth week since Candywine's opening. The looking-glass walls of the main *salle* duplicated a psychedelia of rinsed or metallic hair; mini skirts; Bermuda shorts; plaid tuxedos; costume jewellery; pale, nocturnal faces and reddened, sun-broiled faces hanging over the tables or moving from one table to another wearing an air of instinctive, peaceful purpose, like mingled species of wild game trekking to a salt lick. Waitresses in black mesh leotards and shiny yellow corselets that ended just under the nipples moved among the crowd with trays of free drinks. Most of the waitresses were black or brown and Jamaican, because a locally recruited work force was what the promotion publicity had promised. Six men in dark, tropical suits and with bleak, impassive eyes that missed nothing looked at what the croupiers and dealers were doing. Neither they nor the men in charge of the tables had been recruited locally.

It was just after one-fifteen in the morning and Peter Blackmore had been waiting for Anyo since midnight. Waiting and playing the wheel in his imagination. He had started with plaques worth one thousand dollars and was now five thousand ahead. This was not the sort of money that was riding, in reality, on this big central table. Here, five hundred down or up in a night was excitement enough for most. Beyond the door of padded, pink leather, at the end of the *salle* by the third crap table, in smaller chambers where conversation was as limited and functional as that in a war room, gain or loss took on an almost qualitative change. The men and women who gambled there had the same relationship to those who crowded the main *salle* as does royalty in a fairy tale to the swineherds and goose girls.

Anyo appeared, suddenly, on the other side of the table, sidling fastidiously between a blue-haired woman with skin that looked as though it had been starched and carefully ironed, and a heavy, loudly jovial Texan whose fleshy, handsome nose was hatched with the broken veins of drink and who had been winning steadily all the time that Peter Blackmore had watched the play.

Anyo was wearing slim black slacks and a black Nehru jacket with short sleeves and a design in silver threads around the collar. Like about a third of those in the room he wore dark glasses as big as a wrap around windshield. He held a little pile of plaques in his left hand.

Peter Blackmore watched him with an amusement that was close to affection. For all his conscientious attempt to merge, to fit, the little Chinese looked as uncomfortable in this environment as a vegetarian in a slaughter house. He carried himself stiffly, as though he found the odour not merely disagreeable but immoral. He waited while the croupier called and spun three more coups. On the fourth call, he bent forward and put five plaques on red three, hesitated, then placed the remainder on black ten.

The ivory ball skittered counter-clockwise around the outer rim until the spinning wheel began to slow, dragging it down to the slots. It jumped twice, seemed to settle, tried to jump again and fell back. Peter Blackmore's imaginary winnings went up another six hundred, and he grinned faintly as he saw a small heap of plaques being pushed in front of Anyo by the croupier with the long, wooden scraper. Anyo had played with five dollar plaques and with what he had put on black, he must have won close to one hundred and fifty. As Peter Blackmore turned away from the table, Anyo was picking up the plastic counters gingerly and holding them against his chest as though apprehensive of staining his shirt.

'That's nice, fella,' the big, happy Texan was saying. 'That's the way the wheel's been runnin 'all night. You don't want to pull out now. Let some of those do some more work for you.'

Peter Blackmore grinned again, and strolled over to the second crap table and watched while a taut blonde with big patches of sweat in the armpits of her pyjama suit crooned to the dice she shook in her cupped hands and blew on them before she flung them with a wrist-turning motion up the table and barked, 'Son of a *bitch!*' as they bounced back on the felt and came to rest showing ones.

He left the *salle* then and crossed the lobby in which the one-armed bandits stood thickly and strategically planted like trees in a park, and made his way from the fort.

Outside the water held within the hook of the bay was flat and silky, with a great stripe of moonlight laid across it. Under the brilliant arc-lights, the marina at the top of the hook was like a stage set with yachts, power craft and the four big excursion launches which the casino ran on a two hourly time-table from Montego Bay, on a five hourly schedule back to it. The air was soft and warm, smelling of frangipani, oleander and freshly watered grass. There was a band playing on a dais at the end of the open dance floor outside the L-shaped hotel block, but only three couples were dancing and the big open-fronted bar was nearly empty. Lights shone from the bungalows built between the transplanted trees all round the curve of the hook. From each bungalow, a flagstoned pathway led down to the glimmering beach, and another, broader pathway intersected these, also following the curve of the bay to where a cluster of larger bungalows with double patios had access from their front lawns on to the sand. Indirect soft lights in the trees and half buried at the pathways' edges picked out the ribbons of grey stone.

Peter Blackmore followed the main pathway to where each bungalow had its own strip of beach. He passed one in which all the lights were on, but the doors shut. Another with the sliding patio doors open and from inside which a man shouted, 'Your ol' man's so dumb he'd be sellin' pencils from a cup *now* if it wasn't for what I give him,' and a woman's voice, quieter, like ripping canvas, replied, 'Not so dumb that he *had* to marry your mother. He wasn't as dumb as *that*.' Peter Blackmore turned down the pathway leading to the third bungalow.

It was lit up inside but locked, with the curtains drawn across the glass. He took a key from the pocket of his slacks and unlocked the sliding doors enclosing the back patio, opened one of them sufficiently for him to enter and closed it as he stepped inside, thumbing down the night catch.

Inside there was a lot of silent air-conditioning, Danish style furniture, and wall-to-wall carpeting in material made to look and feel like woven straw. There were two big central rooms, one for eating and beyond that, through an archway and down three wide steps, a white and gold place to sit in and look at the private beach fringing the lawn, the sea and the tops of the St. James hills rising above the horizon on the main island, eight miles to the south. Now, the doors between the room and the view were closed and curtained.

Jassy Vane was stretched out on a long couch in the living-room, asleep. In a deep arm-chair on the opposite side of the room, Helen McKay was turning the pages of *Harper's Bazaar*—or had been until Peter Blackmore came from the dining-area. On the floor beside her chair there was a small suitcase of brown leather with brass reinforcing at each corner.

Peter Blackmore said, 'The transfer starts at ten past three.' He looked at his watch as he said this and she at hers. 'What d'you have?'

'One forty-seven,' Helen McKay told him, and he pulled out the knob on the top of his Rolex and adjusted the minute hand fractionally. He chuckled.

'What's the joke?'

'Anyo. When he passed me the time just now, he won. He must have collected a bundle from what he put on black. When I left him some goon from Texas was about to make him a long lost buddy and persuade him to shoot for the moon.'

Helen McKay smiled faintly.

'He can always pass his winnings over to his chief and claim he quoted Chairman Mao at the wheel.' She pointed at Jassy Vane. 'You better wake her.'

Peter Blackmore crossed the room, bent over the couch and rested the palm of his hand on the cheek of the sleeping woman. After a minute, her eyes opened and she smiled up at him and patted his forearm.

'How much time do we have left?' she asked.

'About an hour and twenty minutes,' he told her and she swung her legs quickly over the edge of the couch and stood. She was wearing a black, cotton sweat shirt and black stretch pants caught under her arches by elastic.

'Mayhew play it close to the chest, don't they,' she said and yawned, stretching. 'All right. I'll go and wash the sleep out and wake Rusty.'

She crossed the room and went out through the doorless opening behind Helen McKay's chair and into the corridor. They heard her voice in the corridor call, 'Rusty . . . Rusty . . . Wake up, dad. We're ready to roll,' then a door close farther along.

'Put this on the table for me, will you please, Peter,' Helen McKay said, and got up, pointing at the suitcase beside her chair.

She went over and sat on the edge of the couch on which Jassy Vane had been sleeping and hauled the low, long coffee table before it close enough to touch her knees. Peter Blackmore brought the suitcase over and carefully laid it flat on the table with the handle facing her. 'My handbag's by the chair,' she said, 'sorry,' and he went back for it. From the handbag she took a small key and turned it in the locks under the two heavy brass clasps and then pressed a stud under the leather along the left-hand side. The clasps flew up and she raised the lid; the inside of the suitcase was lined with bluish steel and contained a transmitting set and a receiver with an earphone the size of a peanut on a thin cord.

Helen McKay put the receiver into her ear and raised a slim, collapsible aerial that pulled out to the length of her arm.

She said, 'Transistors . . . When the Navy recruited me at the beginning of the war, you'd have had to have a truck to carry something with this range,' and grinned embarrassedly at Peter Blackmore as if she had carelessly revealed a guilty indiscretion in her past.

He smiled at her.

'Just get on to that husband of yours,' he said, 'and give him the news. You can also ask him, from me, to tell those crazy Russians to have the trawler exactly where they said it was going to be. As far as I can see, Rusty and I are going to have about half an hour to find it before it starts getting light and everybody else including the United States Navy can get a good look at us.'

Helen McKay was still sending when Jassy Vane came back to the room. She had tied a dark red, silk scarf tightly round her head, with the ends tucked in at the back. The stocky, middle-aged Virginian pilot with the youthfully red hair and the very red face who had flown them over Candy-wine that day back in April followed her.

They waited while Helen McKay listened, tapped at the key again, listened and then tapped briefly what could only have been three or four letters or perhaps a combination of numbers and letters. She removed the earphone and began to wind the cord round her hand.

'We go ahead with it,' she said not looking at them. 'Robin says all hell has broken loose. The plane was on an Eastern Caribbean course, going south, when it went off track. The Americans have been alerting everybody except Castro, but without telling anybody exactly what they're being alerted on. They're pretending it's a transport over-due and we're saying, My goodness what a pity we'll let you know if we see anything.' She sniffed. 'We haven't asked them why if it's only a transport they haven't got on to the com-mercial airlines and on to shipping . . .'

The man who was called Rusty said, 'What I don't see is how those motherin' hijackers expect to get away with it . . . I've come in on all this late, and I don't draw my money to ask questions, but how the hell do they think they'll get through the interception on Florida?'

'Early last year,' Helen McKay told him, 'an American sergeant lifted a Hercules transport from a base in England. He was homesick and couldn't wait for compassionate leave. That's the official story, anyway. He was all over southern England for a long time including a run through the London perimeter warning system where he didn't show on radar.

The Americans have something special and secret installed on all their big stuff now. Anybody who can get within forty miles of London without the Brits being able to count the fillings in his teeth *must* have something special.'

'Yeah,' Rusty said, and scratched his jaw thoughtfully, 'Yeah, I remember readin' about it now. I didn' know that about not showin' on the radar, though. He crashed, didn' he? Near Ireland?'

'English Channel. Again, that's the story . . . They seem to have persuaded him to break radio silence and talk to his wife. Then somebody else talked to him. And then he talked to nobody. They didn't even find any wreckage. Maybe somebody persuaded him to do something that meant there wasn't going to be any wreckage.'

'Like pressing a destruct button?' Rusty asked.

'Maybe. With a man as unstable as that, anything's possible. All we know is he didn't come back.'

Jassy Vane was looking at her watch. Her big dark eyes were dulled and angry. When she lit a cigarette, her movements were too sudden.

She said, 'What's keeping Vestucci? Anyo must have left for the field by now.'

She went to the closed doors and put her head against the drawn curtain as if trying to listen for something outside.

'Easy,' Peter Blackmore told her. He was perched on one of the stools before the trendy little corner bar of bamboo and red cedar, but he was not drinking. 'We've got to take this slow and easy. Vestucci knows what he's doing. If he sends us up to the airstrip too soon after the Mayhew team, they'll hear us coming for sure. And we don't want to have to deal with them on any but our own terms. It has got to be as quick and as dirty on them as we can make it . . . All the same, though,' he added, 'I wish Vestucci wasn't shaving it quite so close,' and he too looked at his watch. 'Have a drink while you're waiting. I'll say this for Vestucci: he stocks only the best.' He heaved himself off the stool and went behind the bar. 'Helen?' Helen McKay nodded and said, 'Scotch . . . On the rocks.' 'Rusty?' Peter Blackmore asked, and the red-haired Virginian pilot shook his head; he was sprawled, on the end of his spine in one of the deep arm-chairs with his eyes closed. 'Not for me, dad,' he told Peter Blackmore, 'I'm drivin' later, remember?'

Peter Blackmore measured three fingers of Chivas Regal over ice cubes and added three fingers of water. Helen McKay came across to the bar, took the drink over to the couch where Jassy Vane had flung herself stiffly with her head laid on the arm-rest. As he was pouring another drink, neat, Helen McKay came back and sat on the stool Peter Blackmore had occupied.

'That's enough,' she murmured. 'I don't really want a drink, but maybe we ought to keep her company.'

'Yes,' Peter Blackmore replied, on the same murmured level, 'she needs company.'

He poured himself a stiff, neat drink, sipped at it, and smiled at her with only his lips: his heavy, carefully nurtured face was rigid, like a war mask, and his eyes were very bright.

Helen McKay said, 'It isn't herself this time. She's worried about you. I hope this is her last operation . . . I shouldn't say this—but I hope it's your last operation too.'

'You mean I'm being fired.'

'You know what I mean. I hope the next time we want you that you're not available . . . That you're too busy or happy or that Jassy's having your baby. Something like that.'

'You're getting old and sentimental,' Peter Blackmore told her. This time his whole face smiled.

'We all get old,' she told him, 'and sentimentality is the only thing that helps.'

II

Two weeks earlier, in a brothel on a side street off the Windward Road at the head of Kingston Harbour, Anyo had told Jassy Vane, 'The transfer is to take place thirteen days from now. I have not been told the hour. They won't tell me that until the night in question.'

'That could make it awkward, couldn't it,' she had said. 'What about the sub? That doesn't give it much time to get in.'

'I know. It will mean frequent transmission on my part, and that can be dangerous. But Mayhew is being very careful. They are worried. There have been too many accidents.'

'They were unavoidable. You know that . . . All,' she had added bitterly, 'except Patterson. That scared fool Harriman didn't *need* to have him killed . . . All right, Anyo, how many on the team Mayhew's sending you?'

'Four. They will come in during the two or three days before the transfer.'

'Only four. But what about the bomber's crew? I mean, Mayhew can't have a whole bloody plane load of defectors. You might get a couple of gutsy characters who could cause trouble. Four men, five if we include you, wouldn't be a safe margin.'

'I understand there will be no trouble from the crew. There are two defectors; they have told me that much, but not, of course, their crew positions, nor how they intend to deal with the others.'

'But we can assume they will be dead.'

'Yes. I think we can assume that.'

'O.K., Anyo.' She had got up, then, from the edge of the small bed in the small pungent room to which she had taken him after he had picked her up in the bar outside. 'We'll contact you—after you get to Candywine.' She had chuckled, and when he looked up in surprise from where he sat in the small hard chair, she had added gravely, 'You owe me five pounds.'

'Five pounds? I don't understand.'

'That's what we're charging for a short time nowadays. In this class of house. The girls out there would never forgive me if they thought I was cutting the rates.'

Mr. Anyo had looked shocked.

Two days after Jassy Vane had talked to Anyo, Peter Blackmore said to Mr. Vestucci, 'We'll need six, but they've got to be hand-picked. We can't afford to take any chances with the sort of material that Mayhew is likely to put in.'

'You'll get good boys,' Mr. Vestucci had said quietly. 'Chances are what I can't afford to take on this, Mr. Broome. Believe me, you'll get good boys.'

'You should have listened to Rilke,' Peter Blackmore had said. 'He didn't know what it was he didn't like about Mayhew but his instincts were sound. What a lot of trouble you'd have saved us all if you had listened to him. Somebody else would have had to worry about Mayhew.'

'Suppose things don't go right?' Mr. Vestucci had asked him. 'Suppose you've made a mistake trying to handle it this way, Mr. Broome? What happens then?'

'The biggest pile of shit you've ever had dropped on your head,' Peter Blackmore had told him. 'I don't know exactly, Vestucci. If things go wrong it's going to be such an international stink that you and I will be forgotten. We'll be dead, but we'll hardly notice it. If things go right then you get to keep your casino, and whatever goes with it. Is that fair?'

'Yeah,' Mr. Vestucci had grunted, 'that's how I figured it. That's why I'm putting in my boys, Mr. Broome. Any other

way and I might as well start running . . . And at my age a
man can't run very far.'

III

When Mr. Vestucci tapped at the door of the bungalow it was
nearly half past two.

Jassy Vane got to her feet and reached the door almost
before the noise from a fingernail on glass had ceased. She
pulled one edge of the curtain aside slightly, looked out and
flicked up the night catch. As Mr. Vestucci slid open the
door to enter he was silhouetted against a backdrop of moon-
spattered sea and a fragrant warm saltiness came and went in
the heavy, air-conditioned air of the room.

'You took your own sweet time,' Jassy Vane said sourly.
'We were just wondering if the little matter had slipped your
mind or something.'

'Everything set, Vestucci?' Peter Blackmore asked.

'Yes, Mr. Broome,' Vestucci said, but addressing himself
to Jassy Vane. 'My boys are waiting up on the road. I have
had a little experience in these things, believe me. It can be
as bad to be too early as to be too late. Exact timing is everything.'

The red-haired Virginian pilot had risen and was standing
by the door, his hands in the pockets of his khaki slacks, as
though he were waiting his turn in a short queue.

Helen McKay said, to Jassy Vane, 'I'll see you,' and
looked at her watch, 'in a little over an hour.' To Peter
Blackmore she added, almost shyly, 'Take care of yourself.'

'Tell him,' Peter Blackmore said lightly, gesturing to
Rusty by the door. 'Tell him I'm valuable and that he mustn't
fold, bend or mutilate . . . Come on, Vestucci.'

Mr. Vestucci opened the door again and stood aside while
Jassy Vane followed by Rusty and Peter Blackmore went out

on to the patio. When Mr. Vestucci had closed the door behind him, Helen McKay locked it again by the night catch and stood for a minute as if listening intently. Then she went to the bar and poured herself an uncompromising drink of Mr. Vestucci's Chivas Regal, diluted it with one cube of ice from the bucket and carried it over to where the suitcase holding the transmitter was open on the coffee table.

Chapter Twenty-four

The graveyard shift

The asphalted road to the airstrip followed the first contour of rising ground behind the complex of offices, casino, hotel and bungalows. Under the fat umbrella of an almond tree on the edge of the road beyond the last of the bungalows, two of the Candywine jeeps were parked. Deeply and brightly cushioned, canopied like picnic carts in an Edwardian musical, they were used to carry visitors between the strip and the development, or down to the golf course two miles away and back; anybody who felt he couldn't make the three hundred yards from the last bungalow to the casino on foot could order one also, at any hour of the day.

Five men sat, packed rather tightly, in one of the candy-striped jeeps; under the shadow of the tree, even with the big moon, it wasn't possible to make much of their features; the stubby, sleek outlines of the automatic rifles they held were shadowed also. Another man stood by the driving-side of the second jeep. Like the others he was dressed in a dark, close-fitting shirt and dark slacks. He had a rifle too, slung over his shoulder. In the past two days, Peter Blackmore had seen him, another foreign body toasting on the beach, another foreign face above the tables in the casino, without knowing who he might be.

Mr. Vestucci said to Peter Blackmore, 'This is Freddy. I've told him he and the boys do what you say, when you say it, just like you say it. He knows,' and turned and walked back along the narrow road. They watched the glimmer of his white head suddenly blotted out as he turned down one of the flagstoned paths under the trees.

Close up, Freddy did not look at all like anyone called by a name so wholesome and four-square. He was perhaps twenty-five; perhaps younger: he did not have the sort of face from which an easy guess could be made.

'Hi,' he said to Peter Blackmore. 'You ready to move?'

Peter Blackmore nodded and went round the front of the jeep and climbed into the seat beside the wheel. Jassy Vane and Rusty got in behind. Freddy unslung his rifle and took one of the big, portable, distress lamps used by yachtsmen off the driver's seat. He handed these to Peter Blackmore, slid in under the wheel and switched on.

'No lights,' Peter Blackmore said as the other engine fired and caught behind them. 'You were told about that?'

'Yeah,' Freddy grunted. 'Mr. Vestucci tol' us.' He glanced at Peter Blackmore briefly, his eyes covering the area between neck and waist. 'You ain't carrying some armour? I mean, like you don't have even a knife or anything?'

'No,' Peter Blackmore told him, 'you have enough for what we need. Except for her,' he added and turned his head to nod at Jassy Vane sitting behind Freddy. 'She has something—in case you need any backing up.'

'Yeah,' Freddy grunted again, without inflection. 'Well, that's it then.'

He pressed the accelerator as the jeep began to take the steeper ground leading up to the little ridge that divided Candywine.

When they were fifty yards from the crest of the ridge, Peter Blackmore said, 'Stop here. They might hear the engines if we drive over. Anyway, they'd spot us against the skyline.'

'Yeah,' Freddy agreed. 'Turds on a sheet. That's what we'd be in this frigging moonlight.'

He pulled over on to the shoulder beside the cactus-dotted scrub, and the other jeep eased in close behind.

'Freddy,' Peter Blackmore said, 'you stay beside me. She will follow you—like she will follow you really close, Freddy.' He turned to the Virginian pilot. 'Rusty, you follow the last of Freddy's boyos.'

He gestured into the bush parallel to the road, and followed carrying the distress lamp.

As they threaded their way through the scrub, edging round the reaching arms of cactus, their rubber-soled shoes squishing in the powdery mixture of limestone and drift sand, Freddy grunted again. 'You don't trust me,' he told Peter Blackmore approvingly. 'I like that. I mean, you got yourself my services. Anything but putting the end of this gun in my mouth an' blowing my head off, you just tell me an' I'll do it. But I feel better working for a man who don't trust a man he's never seen.'

'I'm glad you're feeling good,' Peter Blackmore said. 'Now suppose you close your big mouth real tight until we get over to the strip.'

They came over the shallow slope of the ridge, crouching low among the bottle brush shrub, cactus and Spanish bayonet. Below them, quarter of a mile away, the gently shelving ground became a long, strictly ruled gash between the coarse bush and the wide, shiny sea. In the moonlight, they could see a cluster of round blobs around one square blob drawn set on the inner edge of the strip; another square blob showed, aligned with the nearer, across the strip by the sea. There was a steady norther coming in over the water. Even before the round blobs became the shapes of men and the square blob emerged as another of the canopied jeeps, they could hear low voices carried to them on the wind.

Peter Blackmore closed his hand briefly around Freddy's left wrist, reaching where the man's thumb was hooked in the strap of his automatic rifle. Freddy raised his right hand and the uneven shuffle of feet behind them halted.

'Jassy . . . Rusty,' Peter Blackmore said, more softly than was necessary, 'you stay here. Freddy, tell your boys to open up when I shine the lamp on whoever is by the jeep. Only those around the jeep, you understand. I don't want anything going across the strip.'

Freddy turned and went back past Jassy Vane to the five men. Whatever he told them did not carry the few feet that separated him from Peter Blackmore. He came back.

'O.K.,' he said.

From the last of the scrub fringing the runway, the men around the jeep twenty yards away were strongly angled shapes topped by pale balloons on which the dark glint of eyes moved. One man stood a few feet from the rest, looking up and across to where the road ended at the runway's edge.

Freddy breathed into Peter Blackmore's ear, 'They ain't carrying anything . . . Yeah, that guy; he's holding something heavy. Police Special, maybe, or a .44 magnum. But they ain't carrying anything like us.'

Peter Blackmore who was watching the shape that was much smaller and so much neater than the others, turned his head enough to whisper back, 'Why should they? They're not expecting any trouble.'

Freddy's chuckle was so controlled and faint that it seemed to sound in the head, like a voice in a dream.

'Trouble in something like this is not what you *expect*,' he said. 'It's something you allow for—like burning gas if you drive a car . . . Remember that, mister. It may save your life some time.'

They waited for two minutes. At the end of that time, the smallest, neatest figure in the group around the jeep swung his left arm in an arc and looked at the bright smear of watch on his wrist. They heard him say something in a low voice to

263

the others, something unintelligible that swept past them like scraps on the strong warm breeze; he turned away and walked across the tarmac to the sea.

When the small, trim figure was half-way across the strip, Peter Blackmore thumbed the switch of the light and the figures around the jeep suddenly jumped into solid, glaring nearness.

One man seemed to leave the ground, by two or three feet, before he was slammed on to the tarmac like a flung sack; a second clutched at his stomach and folded over like a savagely broken sausage; the third swayed down, shrinking in on himself.

The man who had been watching the road had hurled himself to the edge of the pool of light almost before Peter Blackmore's thumb had curled back from the switch. He had hit the ground rolling. Freddy's bursts followed him, bounding him along the moonwashed tarmac until he stopped flopping.

On the far side of the strip, the small, neat figure had stopped when the firing began. After Freddy had fired his last burst, it remained still for a few seconds; then it turned and began to come back, trudging precisely and purposefully between the immense sky and sea.

II

The bomber came in from the north-west. They could see it against the moon, far out: a prehistoric shape both terrible and beautiful, like a pterodactyl, seeming to hover over the sea. Then the noise of the six jets rolled over them and it was possible to realise that it was hurtling ahead of its own sound.

In the few moments before touchdown, it seemed to Peter Blackmore that it must dig its own grave with its nose under the asphalt at the end of the runway. The great wings swayed with rigid grace and straightened. It tilted back on itself; and then it was suddenly devouring the runway and roaring between the two jeeps with their switched on headlights.

In the lull as it began to turn in the beam of the distress lamp they had put at the other end of the runway, Rusty said softly, with a sort of sad pride, 'That mothah may be all kinds of a no-account traitor, but he can *fly*. Son of a bitch rode that bus in here like it was a broomstick.'

In the driver's seat of the jeep nearest the sea, Freddy revved the idling engine and swung the vehicle round in a tight circle so that the headlights pointed to the bomber whining its way up to them. On the far side of the strip, one of his men did the same with the other jeep.

The bomber stopped, its nose half turned to the sea, away from the converging beams of the headlights. There was a shattering pulsation from its jets and then they died, sighing.

Peter Blackmore could feel the stiffness of Jassy Vane's body as she stood beside him behind the jeep. He touched her hand and whispered, 'It's going to be all right,' and thought that for her it was never going to be quite all right. Not for a long time anyhow. Somewhere during the five years in which she had done this kind of work there must have been the moment when an area of nerve strained beyond repair and healed treacherously, waiting to give way under the pressure that was too protracted or too sudden. For her it had been the four bodies which Freddy's men had hauled across the runway to the edge of the scrub; each body had left a glistening track as it was dragged. She had supervised the search in their clothing, then, but when she came back to where he stood watching the sky for the bomber, he had known what she must have drawn on to do it. Now he said again, 'It's going to be all right.'

'I think we had better go out now,' Anyo said from his other side. 'Just you and I, Mr. Blackmore; they will not be expecting a woman.'

They walked down the tunnels of light that converged on the bomber. Close up, its sleek hugeness was not quite credible. An awesome power still seemed to throb through it, like the authority in a warrior king asleep in his armour. The swept-back wings dug into the sky.

Above their heads, a small square of silvery window was pushed back; a pale, blurred oval showed.

' "Are you the burial party?" ' a voice asked as if quoting.

' "No," ' Anyo replied in the same manner, ' "we are the graveyard shift." '

'Fine.' They could hear the caution go out of the voice above. 'That's it. We'll be right down. We'll have to hurry. There isn't much time.'

III

The interior of the bomber's opened bay was an electronic jungle of wires, fine branches of metal, improbable blossoms of muted light and dial faces.

The four shapes held within the bay were not anything like what the cartoonists drew. They were not fat black darts with fins; they were neutral coloured canisters about twice as long as Peter Blackmore could have stretched his arms and a foot or so wide. When the killing radius of what you dropped was forty miles, such a concept as target centre was irrelevant.

By the white light of the work bulb high above them in the open bay under which they stood, Peter Blackmore could see clearly the face of the man who had answered Anyo. He did not look like a man who had conspired to and committed the murder of comrades because their presence, alive, embarrassed one part of a plan. But then what did the face of unswerving and murderous faith look like? Again, not as it did in the cartoons. And the word *comrade* was now either an inane sentimentality or a slightly indecent fraudulence like a politician's *my friends* addressed to his electorate. Peter Blackmore found himself hoping that this pleasant, leathery man with the big, hooked nose and steady eyes and with the knowledgeable face of a good middle age had done what he had done for gain. A motive so banal would be somehow more reassuring.

The man said, 'He'll have the first one ready for you in a second.'

'Good,' Peter Blackmore said and turned and signalled to the two jeeps waiting on the tarmac.

They came in slowly, parallel, about a yard apart, under the opened bay. Freddy was driving one. Their canopies had been dismantled and there was a man standing in the back of each.

'You ready, Walter?' the man with the big, hooked nose called up to a pair of overalled legs at the top of the bay.

'Yeah,' a tight, twangy voice called back. 'Line 'em up.'

'You,' the man with the hooked nose said to the other driver, 'reverse and come in just where my toes are. And you,' he said to Freddy, 'you'll have to reverse too and come in beside him. Keep the same distance.'

The jeeps were manœuvred until the man nodded and held up his hand.

'O.K., Walter,' he called.

'Coming down.' The taut voice was resonant in the crowded interior.

From above one of the cylinders began to descend held by a pair of thin, jointed steel arms that ended in claws.

'Magnetic hoist,' the man with the hooked nose said, and Peter Blackmore nodded. In this world of intricate power nothing he could say would make any contribution.

267

When the cylinder rested across the back frames of the two jeeps, Peter Blackmore could see the bodies sag and the rear tyres flatten.

'Yeah.' The man with the steady eyes must have observed his look. 'These things weigh a lot more than you'd think. But the jeeps will carry it as far as you have to go. Take it real slow, though.'

Peter Blackmore swung into the seat beside Freddy who nodded to the other driver and eased up gradually on the clutch. The men in the backs bent over, holding the cylinder as the jeeps crawled heavily down the tarmac.

At the eastern end of the runway, the steep, narrow beach ran its sand right up to the asphalt.

Anyo was sitting on the edge of the tarmac, his feet resting on the sand below. Beside him was the small, deep box holding a transmitter receiver, its aerial still up. He did not turn his head as the jeeps were driven up behind. Nor did he turn when Peter Blackmore climbed out and stepped over to where he was sitting.

He was looking across the beach to where, in the coral-floored shallows, fifteen feet away, eight men in shining black frogsuits stood waiting like experienced soldiers on parade, in the varying 'stand easy' positions that experienced soldiers learn. Or perhaps he was looking out across the shallows to where, in the sudden deep water beyond the lip, a long glisten of metal surmounted by a squat rhomboid profile heaved gently under the bright moon.

'Very pretty,' Peter Blackmore said, with consoling mockery, because he had touched, in himself, a little of the loneliness that is most of a spy's life. 'Now there is something you don't see every night... Shall we deliver now, Anyo?'

'Yes,' Anyo said and got to his feet and called in Chinese across the beach. In the shallows, the eight men seemed to fall in, without fuss or confusion, into some complex formation.

Peter Blackmore went back to where the jeeps had halted. 'If you both reverse,' he told Freddy, 'and come round with your backs to the sea, we'll be able to roll it off. We've got some help down there.'

'More gooks?' Freddy asked, pointing over the steering wheel to where Anyo stood like a cut-out in the headlight beams.

'Yes,' Peter Blackmore said. 'How did you know? Vestucci didn't tell you?'

'Shit, no,' Freddy replied. He sounded almost bored. 'I was just asking. If you and Mr. Vestucci want me to pass the big bang on to the gooks, I'll do it if the money is good. Pass the whole frigging bomber if you tell me how you want it done. The way we've screwed this frigging world, the gooks may well as have the bomb same as us. And if the niggers down in Africa want it, I say let's give it to them too.'

'Freddy,' Peter Blackmore said, and he could feel a bleak hilarity seizing him, irresistible as the effect of the third stick of *ganja*, 'you're a great philosopher. But remember Socrates: he talked himself to death.' As suddenly as it had risen, the sad, not quite sane amusement left him. He said harshly, 'Now roll those fucking jeeps back to the beach. Save your big, beautiful thoughts for your friends.'

Four of the men from the shallows helped them push the cylinder off the edges of the jeeps' frames. It thudded on to the hard, coarse sand with a reverberation they could all feel and rolled dourly like a corpse down the sharp decline to the shallows.

The four men in frogsuits jumped off the backs of the little vehicles and flipper-floppered across the sand to where the twelve-foot cylinder lay awash.

269

As Peter Blackmore, Anyo, Freddy and Freddy's men looked on from the edge of the tarmac, the men in the water slid three narrow bands of metal under the cylinder. At each end of each blade there was a large oblong canister. The men in the water waited until the next surge of sea covered the canister and then heaved. The sea receded and the cylinder went with it, the six canisters riding nearly clear of the water. Six of the men guided the cylinder, three to a side, and a seventh pushed from behind. Soon they were all swimming towards the long glisten of metal in the trench just beyond the shallows, the cylinder riding sluggishly between them.

'An' that,' Freddy said, 'is how you steal a frigging bomb. Water wings filled with helium.'

He sounded genuinely grateful that he had lived to see it.

As the swimmers became seal heads on the luminous water, Anyo stepped down to the sand and walked across to where the last of the frog-suited men was surfacing a submerged rubber dinghy, reaching into the shallow water and tossing aside lumps of coral.

He pushed the dinghy until it rode free and held it by one of the loops of rope around the sausage balloon of hull until Anyo waded out to it and climbed in. Then he heaved himself out of the shallows and sat before Anyo and they both began to paddle out after the swimmers.

Peter Blackmore watched Anyo's back as it dipped and straightened to the motion. He hoped that Anyo would have said good-bye had they not been within earshot of someone who might also speak English and who might later remember that Anyo knew he was saying good-bye, and not simply going out to report a situation.

IV

When they were a hundred yards from the bomber, Peter Blackmore said to Freddy, 'O.K., pretend to stall her.'

Freddy switched off, pressed on the accelerator while switching on and off, making a lot of frustrated snarl from the engine before killing it.

The other jeep swung out from behind and stopped beside them.

'You know what to do?' Peter Blackmore asked Freddy.

'Sure,' Freddy said. 'Mr. Vestucci gave us the picture. We're *professionals*, mister. We can't afford mistakes.'

'I'll take the pilot. The one who was with me under the bay. You take the other one when he comes down. But no killing. I don't want them even bruised more than you can help. And as quick as you can. They might try to commit suicide if they begin to smell something wrong.'

'You really think they'd try *that?*'

For the first time, Peter Blackmore heard emotion in Freddy's voice.

'I know they might try,' he said. 'That's what makes them different from you, Freddy boy . . . Come on.'

He and Freddy scrambled from their jeep and into the other. The driver let out the clutch before they were more than half in.

When they pulled up by the bomber, the leathery, middle-aged man with the hooked nose was standing clear of the glow of light under the bay.

He came forward at a trot and said anxiously, 'What's wrong? What's happened? I saw you stop. We don't have much time . . .'

'Your bloody bomb,' Peter Blackmore told him urgently, 'was too heavy for the jeeps. One of them's packed up.'

'Can't you get another? The time, man! The time! We've got to be out of here in under an hour. You know that. You've got the course orders.'

'Where do I get another jeep just like that?'

'Then you ought to have had a reserve. Or had us park nearer to where we unloaded ... What the hell sort of operators are you this end?' His voice was brittle with anger, but even. He sounded like a man who had ordered his way out of many crises. 'Walter,' he called, turning his back on Peter Blackmore and walking briskly to where the rectangle of light from the open bay was splashed on the tarmac, 'you better come down. These jokers have fouled up. We have trouble, boy.'

Peter Blackmore and Freddy followed him. As they came up beside him, a pair of ankle-hugging flying boots and two overalled legs swung down out of the bomb bay. And at that moment, Peter Blackmore hit the man with the big, hooked, nose, the pleasant face and the nice, steady eyes.

He hit him just under the rib cage with his left elbow driven by the palm of his right hand closed around his tightly clenched left fist. And as the man spun half round and down, he hit him again on the left side of his neck with the side of his right hand.

Freddy said, 'I like that, mister. That looked good, but this will do it just as quick.' He opened his right hand and showed Peter Blackmore a fat tube of brown cartridge paper in his palm. 'Quarters,' he said. 'You dip 'em in lead an' pack them real tight an' you've got yourself real stopping power. It don't matter where you hit a man so long as you make sure you hit him first. After the first time you can select if you have to.'

The man who had come dropping out of the bay was lying face down at his feet.

'I didn't have to do any selecting with him,' Freddy ex-

plained, looking down. 'Back of the head. *Medulla oblongata.*
It's like a shock effect.'

Peter Blackmore was calling into the moonshot dark,
'Jassy . . . Rusty . . .' and the driver of the other jeep was
still behind the wheel, lounging over it like a casually interested follower of the game watching the coming boys work
out in a gym.

Jassy Vane and Rusty came running out of the darkness
into the lit patch under the bay. Peter Blackmore nodded
at the bodies on the tarmac and Jassy Vane dropped to her
knees beside the one with the hooked nose. She slid the straps
of her long, flat handbag off her shoulder, pulled open the
zip along the top of the face and searched inside. Squinting
into the glare of the worklamp up in the bomb bay, she held
up a hypodermic syringe and depressed the plunger. Drops
jetted and sparkled within the light. She pushed the elastic
cuff on the sleeve of the man's left overall as far up his arm
as the crook of his elbow. Carefully and gently, she kneaded
a vein on the inside of his forearm until it stood out against
the flesh. Then she slid the needle into it.

Peter Blackmore went to the foot of the aluminium ladder
which the two men had lowered from the hatchway in the
fuselage behind the flight deck. It was difficult to credit
until he looked at his watch, that they came down not quite
twenty-three minutes before.

He climbed half-way up the ladder and shouted, 'Are you
all right, Rusty?'

'Right enough.' The slow voice came to him muffled and
echoing. 'I'll be righter in about fifteen, twenty minutes . . .
If you can wait that long.'

Peter Blackmore came back down the vertical ladder with
its rungs full of economical holes. He was very tired, suddenly, trembling in the legs as though he had run, in fear,
for a great distance.

'O.K.,' he said to Freddy, 'they should be coming in for the second bomb about now. Drive down and see. When you spot them, give them plenty of light and plenty of noise. But make sure you and your goons don't hit anybody. It has got to look like a takeover bid from out where they are. Enough to scare them back. Nothing else . . . You understand?'

'Sure,' Freddy said. 'We'll lean on them a little. We'll have to really throw it at them, because them frigging gooks looked smart an' they'll know if we don't fake it good. But nobody's going to get hurt. You've got to understand, mister: we can't afford to do a job that isn't professional.'

Chapter Twenty-five

Special delivery

Rusty said, 'I know I can take this mothah up—but when I start puttin' her down, Pete boy, that's when you all stick a cork up your ass.'

'You've said that,' Peter Blackmore told him. 'Twice. What's the matter? Are you as scared as I am?'

Rusty laughed, through his teeth.

'More,' he said. 'A whole greasy sight more, Pete. I know what I can do wrong. I ain't never handled more'n one jet at a time, and that was in Korea . . . Exceptin' when one of the pilots asks me up for a sit in when I'm going up to the States, I don't know how somethin' this size even *feels*.'

They were at the western end of the runway; the noise of the idling jets seemed to rush past outside like strong water where all the force runs beneath a placid surface.

On the deck behind the seats, the men who had brought the great bomber in forty minutes before were lying, padded round with parachute packs and laced into life-jackets. In the bluish glow, their faces had the emptied, gone away look that comes from half-a-gramme of sodium amytal taken intravenously.

Half-way down the runway, the lights from the two jeeps drained the asphalt grey, and the beam of the distress lamp at the end looked very near.

The panel before them was like a galaxy in which con-stellations fought for room, and Peter Blackmore found himself wondering if fifteen minutes cockpit drill was enough even for Rusty.

Then the plane seemed to gather itself on tiptoe and he was looking down on the sea before he had properly registered the huge hand that had pressed him back into his seat. When he licked his lips his tongue too felt dry. Rusty's face looked as it would in ten years.

'That was very nice,' Peter Blackmore said. 'Can we go back and do it again?'

Rusty was nursing the half-wheel on the massive control column as though it were a baby that had swallowed a hand grenade. As the plane levelled out of the climb, he lifted his right hand off the wheel, dug inside his shirt and extracted a long, narrow folio covered in oilskin. He shook it open across his knees and Cuba, Haiti, the Dominican Republic, Puerto Rico and Jamaica appeared successively on a map that was mostly sea.

He said, 'I've got a lot of flying to do . . . Now *this* is the altimeter.' He rested his right forefinger on a dial that glowed obscurely in the clustered panel. 'If you see the needle go below or above seven, you shout . . . And this is air speed . . . I want to keep at three-fifty . . . Three-fifty . . . You got that, Pete boy? If you see it going three-fifty and some, or even a smidge under, you holler, you hear? Now above your mothah-fuckin' head there's six switches . . . One, two, three, four, five, six . . . In that order . . . If I tell you to hit two or five or anything, you hit it fast . . . You got that?'

'Yes,' Peter Blackmore said.

'Great,' Rusty said. 'Now I got me two co-pilots . . . You an' God.'

II

Seven thousand feet under the port window, the south coast

of Haiti was a jumble of great flanks and spines, curiously bleached under the moon, fringed by a bright ribbon of white where the sea gnawed at the land.

A few minutes before the dark slope of Cap had loomed out of the shining sea. Then they were passing over the few lights of Coteaux, and had raised Aquin on the left as they swept across the deep bight between Cayes and Côtes de Fer. Inland, the peaks of the Massif de la Hotte rose higher than they flew.

Peter Blackmore said suddenly, 'There! Is that it? Is that Jacqmel?'

Ahead of them, seeming not to move but magnifying itself rapidly and imperceptibly, a faint, greeny-white aurora of electric light was spread on the sky.

Rusty leaned forward slightly, peering through the perspex, squinting against the glow from the massed dials.

'Yeah,' he said. 'That's Jacqmel ... See that big fat spur like a bear's ass, coming straight down to the water? Just east of the lights? We're on the nose.'

They were abreast of the little town almost as he spoke, and then it and the jagged edge of mountains had dropped suddenly away as he swung the plane dead south and down, on a long, shallow dive, towards the empty Caribbean.

'Three minutes,' Rusty whispered. 'Three minutes at three-fifty. That's what we got, Pete boy, an' then it's the ol' eagle eye. Start lookin', Pete. They're down there someplace.'

He sounded like a man talking in his sleep, and his face was drained of colour, shiny and rigid, as he pulled them level a thousand feet above a sea that had changed from dimpled grey satin to a corrugated blackness full of steely flashes.

The great plane soared down its invisible lane into the night for five minutes before Peter Blackmore turned his head reluctantly from the perspex through which he had been avidly scanning the emptiness below.

'We missed them that time,' he said. 'You'll have to take us back. If they're there we missed them.'

Rusty had already begun to take them up and round on a tight, banking turn as Peter Blackmore began to speak.

'They're there,' he said, and pushed the column forward. 'They got to be there. If they aren't, then we're nowhere.'

They went back up the run, with the black wall of mountain behind the coast they had left five minutes before growing rapidly into the sky, and then Peter Blackmore shouted 'There! There, Rusty! Out on your wing,' pointing across Rusty to where the long beam of a searchlight reached into the sky until the stark gash seemed to dissolve like golden mist among the stars.

On their second pass over the trawler as it lay wallowing easily in the gentle lift and fall of the swell, Rusty said, 'I'm puttin' her in now, Pete. You ready?'

'As I'll ever be.'

'That's the spirit, boy. Shoes off?'

'Yes.'

'Passengers O.K.?'

'Yes. We tucked them in pretty tight.'

'Then hang on . . . An' if I don't see you again, it was nice knowing you.'

'You're not a bad old boy yourself,' Peter Blackmore told him, and pressed himself back into the padded seat and pulled the strap running tightly across his chest a little farther through the buckle on the floor.

They went out and up from where the trawler lay, in a wide circle, until Peter Blackmore could no longer distinguish the hull. Then Rusty pushed the stick forward and they were coming back, and down, down, down, with the blurred outline of the hull suddenly leaping into focus again and the water losing its steely flashes and tilting up to them faster than Peter Blackmore had imagined it would come.

He heard Rusty yell *Now!* and he had only time enough to sweep all the fuel switches to OFF as Rusty showed him before he was flung into the strap across his chest and the nose of the plane was straight above him as the fuselage shook and rang under a tremendous hammer. Then the floor seemed to rise with shocking force into the base of his spine, jolting his head back, and to drop away before slamming into him again. Water exploded across the perspex before him and he could feel the plane trying to lurch clear and the sea pulling it back, and then they were down in an unnatural stillness, with the fuselage around them swaying slightly like the distended carcase of a big, drowned animal.

He was reaching down for the body of the man with the hooked nose before he realised that he had left his seat. Where the hatch had been there was an empty space framing a purple sky and stars, so he must have pulled down the handle and slammed it out. But he could not remember doing that either. The man he pushed into Rusty's hands seemed ridiculously light, or rather no weight at all, and he had gathered the other inert body to him before Rusty fell sideways out of the hatch dragging his burden.

Then he and Rusty were side by side in the warm, heaving water, striking out one-armed, half on their backs, trailing the drugged men they had to keep alive, and looking back to where the hatch from which they had flung themselves had already disappeared. As they watched, the tail swung suddenly up, like the flag on a taxi-cab meter, and then, as abruptly, it was no longer there. Where it had hung between them and the stars there was only space.

At their backs as they swam, they could feel a heavy, assured throbbing, reverberating through the water, and looking over his shoulder Peter Blackmore could see, flattened and foreshortened by distance, the long wedge of a searchlight's beam playing on the water.

It was then that he knew how very frightened he had been.

III

'Eat,' Saratov said scoldingly. 'Go on. Eat more.' He leaned across the table and heaped the big serving-spoon with *solyanka* from the dish and emptied the contents on to Peter Blackmore's plate.

'I've had enough,' Peter Blackmore said.

'Nonsense. You are more than two metres tall and must weigh close to one hundred kilos. You were in the water nearly three-quarters of an hour before we picked you up. Even in these latitudes that is exposure. Go on. Eat.' He put the spoon back into the dish, took a long, slim bottle by the neck and, leaning across the table again, filled the half-empty tumbler at Peter Blackmore's right with thick, very red wine. He watched, indulgently, with understanding, as Peter Blackmore shovelled the food down and drained the wine as though they were the last meat and drink left in the world.

'You see,' Saratov said. 'Your fine big body knows what it needs even if you don't. And your brain. You *do* have a brain, you know. A good one, although you scarcely use it . . . I am joking . . . You are a good man . . . A very good man . . . There used to be some like you once . . . I would have liked to have had you in my squadron . . . No,' he added reflectively, regretfully, 'you are too heavy. We could never have been sure of finding a remount for what you got killed under you . . . Sometimes we used to go into action on ponies that should only have carried children . . .' Behind the burnished, too small spectacles, the green eyes shrewdly appraised the way in which Peter Blackmore used an end of dark, damp-looking rye bread to clean his plate. 'Take some of the *kascha*,' he said. 'And more wine. In my mother's nation we put a tart of *kascha* and a bottle of wine at the bridegroom's side of the bed on the wedding night . . .'

They were in the wardroom of the Russian trawler on to which Peter Blackmore, Rusty and the two men they held under their jaws clear of the sea had all been lifted as they drifted to the east on the slow, meandering Caribbean Current. There was a great deal of chintz around and the bookcase must have cost ten acres of Honduranian mahogany forest; but there were more titles in English behind the glass than there were on the shelves of any Mid-Western or Midlands small town public library. The air-conditioning was at that correct level efficiency where it was too cold for shirtsleeves and not cold enough for a sweater. Pale speckles of light flitted on the white ceiling, reflected from the bright, morning sea outside, as they followed the long silky swells west towards Jamaica.

There was a curt knock at the door and it opened immediately. A tall, middle-aged man with thin, fair hair and a snub nose entered. Like Saratov he wore a white, short-sleeved shirt and white drill trousers, very wide in the turned up cuffs. Although not fat, he had the padded plumpness sometimes seen on senior officers in the Navy, any Navy, and which comes when one reaches the rank where the daily and tedious shipboard calisthenics can be avoided. He looked at Peter Blackmore with angry, small blue eyes and then turned to Saratov and spoke for some time in Russian. Saratov listened, nodding for emphasis twice, and replied in three sentences. The man looked again at Peter Blackmore and left, managing to convey ostentatious disapproval even in the way he closed the door.

'I don't seem to have made a friend,' Peter Blackmore

said. 'I can't think why. As far as I know we haven't met before.'

Saratov was smirking with almost feline contentment. When he twisted the end of his moustache, he looked like a pewter-pointed tom washing its face.

'It is not you,' he said happily. 'It is me. My Navy feels very badly about all this. A lot of people are feeling badly, but the Navy has been particularly ungracious. If you knew the trouble I had getting this trawler put at my disposal. They are all asking each other why they did not uncover Mayhew first. That was the captain, by the way. You are wearing his shirt and trousers.'

'I'll bet he hasn't spent his life catching fish.'

'Well, not exactly fish,' Saratov admitted. 'But he has been very successful in whatever he fished for. You should be flattered, Peter. The Navy do not assign that man to unimportant occasions. If he treats me with the courtesy due to a brother officer in another service, I shall co-operate.'

'Don't hug yourself any harder, Saratov,' Peter Blackmore said, 'or you might break a rib.'

Saratov beamed his appreciation, and poured himself more coffee from the electric pot that looked Scandinavian and was shaped like the missile for the latest in anti-aircraft weaponry.

'He says that your people have raised us. We are to transfer you at midnight, to your coastguard, five miles off Morant Point lighthouse—wherever that is.'

'Ask the captain,' Peter Blackmore said. 'He's probably sleeping with the lighthouse keeper's wife.'

Saratov grinned again.

'I shall be sorry to see you leave so soon,' he said. Then, 'You would not consider working for me, would you? Nothing that would involve doing anything against your country's interests, even indirectly. I promise you that.

But there are things in which you could help. In Latin America and perhaps in Europe. Nothing like what you have just done, but small things that may prevent some fool putting us in a position where we have to use hydrogen bombs and intercontinental missiles against each other as though they were pistols.'

'Saratov,' Peter Blackmore said irritably, 'are you clean out of your crazy Russian skull? Why don't you ask me whether I'll sell love to sailors on a waterfront some place? Work for you . . . Is that why you asked Rusty to eat separately? In case I said yes?'

Saratov nodded.

'Yes,' he said. 'Do not look so indignant, Peter. I did not think you would. But you might have. There might have been that little something in you from which you would have agreed . . . I do not know what to call it . . . A streak of perversion? The need for illicit excitement? Perhaps just what we all have to leave in our childhood . . . A secret life. A world of your own lived under the noses of the unsuspecting grown-ups . . . I am not a psychologist. I do not know the terms for these things . . . But you would be surprised how many people I have recruited because they wanted a private world in which to live. A world they could fashion by pretending . . . I am glad you have said no, but it would have been irresponsible not to ask you.' He paused, and when Peter Blackmore did not reply, added briskly, 'So that is settled then. I like it better this way . . . You ought to sleep now.'

'Yes,' Peter Blackmore said. He felt as though big, petulant men had been hitting him clumsily, for a long time, with socks full of sand. His mind was falling slowly down a hole that grew darker and darker. He lurched to his feet and rubbed his face and his eyes. 'Those two men that we're lending you,' he said. 'The major and the captain . . . They may be bastards, Saratov, and you're welcome to what you can get out of them—but no rough stuff, you understand? I want your word on that.'

Saratov shook his head impatiently.

'Of course,' he said. 'What do you think I am? I want information out of those men when they wake, not a case for the public prosecutor. Most of what they will have to tell will be useless to me, but there will be a few small things . . . I won't get those things by what you call rough stuff.'

'And no double-cross after you've finished with them. They're on loan. Keeping them is not part of the deal.'

Saratov rose, and smiled briefly, and came round the table and put his hand on Peter Blackmore's shoulder.

'Peter, my dear boy,' he said, 'you are tired. Come, I will show you where you can sleep.' He led the way to the door and turned with his hand on the knob. 'What on earth,' he asked, 'would I do with them? They would be an embarrassment to me. Give me five days—a week—and then I will pass them over to the Americans, discreetly wrapped in plain brown paper.' Behind the lenses. the steady eyes lightened with a glint of pure malice. 'You realise, Peter,' he observed happily, 'that somebody on the other side may go mad when I hand them over, trying to work out how I got them.'

Epilogue

'It may be a hell of a good joke for Saratov,' McKay said sourly, 'but it has been damned uncomfortable for me. The Americans have been most unhappy.'

'You knew they would be,' Peter Blackmore told him, 'when you sold this crazy scheme to the P.M.'

'One of them,' McKay continued, 'even went so far as to suggest that we may have connived . . . I must say the P.M. put on a magnificent performance then. I suppose instant indignation comes easily when you're a politician. Like instant integrity . . . Anyway he carried on quite a bit about small countries trying to develop peacefully caught in the web of big power strategies. He was very nasty about Candywine being used by Mayhew, and quoted the Palomares incident and asked for assurances that they'd look after their bombs better in the future. He began to enjoy the act so much that I was afraid he might overdo it.'

It was the Saturday before Christmas; Robin and Helen McKay had driven over the Junction Road from Kingston to the house on the hill overlooking the sea at Coniston, arriving after dinner. Jassy Vane was already there when they arrived. Now she sat dressed in a long, voluminous housecoat of soft towelling, with her bare feet tucked under her, saying nothing and seeming to listen with an effort she made no attempt to camouflage. Below them, as they sat on the broad side veranda, they could see the tops of sugar cane, silvery-grey in the moonlight, and the black, silent bulk of the factory which would be hot and clamorous twenty-four hours a day when cutting began in a month.

'It's not all over,' Helen McKay said. 'Nothing ever is in this business. But it's all over as far as we're concerned. C.I.A. and K.G.B. are still trying to flush Mayhew operatives out of the systems. We're not supposed to know that. We're not even supposed to know there was anything called Mayhew. But Saratov has been very good about giving us what he thinks won't do his people any harm, and Wisdom at Special Branch says that he hears heads are still rolling over at that place in Virginia.'

McKay said, 'We need a better American contact. It's ridiculous that we have to keep on getting so much information through London. The trouble is that Americans are so damned expensive . . . They're still worrying the business about the bomber to death, of course. C.I.A. are accusing the K.G.B. of claim jumping the Chinese, and the K.G.B. are protesting coyly, hoping C.I.A. won't believe them, and trying to decide who Saratov and the G.R.U. could have got to do it. The way things are they're not too displeased they can't find the damned thing. They could never have kept it out of the news if they *had*. Besides, they've got enough on their hands. They won't get half the Mayhew people, naturally. If Mayhew was set up anything like I am sure it was set up then most of them will have simply submerged. In fact, I'll guarantee that some of the busiest investigations now, in both countries, are being done by operatives from Mayhew, covering up.'

Peter Blackmore said, 'Just like that, eh? All neat and tidy, until the next time round.'

But the men on the runway that night were not neat and tidy, he thought, nor those poor bastards we saw in the bomber; and what was left against the side of the ship at Ciudad Bolivar wasn't tidy at all. And David Patterson. And that poor, lost devil, Harriman.

'But of course, Peter,' McKay was saying with patient

emphasis, as if mildly surprised. 'Until the next time. That's the most we can hope for, isn't it? That there is a next time round.'

When they were preparing for bed in the big, high-ceilinged guest room with the four-poster and the old-fashioned window seat, Helen McKay said, 'Well, you can write Jassy out of the organization. We won't be able to use her any more.'

'Oh, I don't know,' McKay said; he sat on the edge of the bed and looked at her doubtfully. 'We won't use her for anything for a while. She's tired. I don't mean physically. But she's used up. It happens to everybody. Particularly to the naturals like her. She'll want to come in again.'

'I doubt it. She's pregnant.'

'What?'

'You know, what happens to a girl sometimes when she . . .'

'All right, all right,' McKay snarled fondly. 'You know how I loathe sarcasm. Are you sure?'

'Sure sure. She just told me.'

She came over and sat beside him and took his hand and slipped her fingers between his. The bed was so high that her stockinged feet swung clear of the floor. They smiled at each other with the preposterous, head-ducking shyness of adolescents.

'She's the best operative I've ever had in the field,' McKay said. 'Where the hell am I going to get somebody else like her? You know how difficult it is to find women who are any damn' good. This is deliberate carelessness. A woman of her experience couldn't have got herself knocked up.'

He grinned at her hopefully.

'You fraud,' she said. 'You don't have to worry. She's pregnant, all right. The lucky bitch.'